Praise for
JOAN JOHNSTON

"IRRESISTIBLE."
Romantic Times

"ONE OF THE FINEST WESTERN ROMANCE
NOVELISTS ... LIKE LAVYRLE SPENCER,
MS. JOHNSTON WRITES OF INTENSE
EMOTIONS AND TENDER PASSIONS THAT
SEEM SO REAL THAT THE READERS WILL
FEEL EACH ONE OF THEM."
Rave Reviews

"JOHNSTON WARMS YOUR HEART
AND TICKLES YOUR FANCY."
New York Daily News

"JOHNSTON DOES CONTEMPORARY
WESTERNS TO PERFECTION."
Publishers Weekly

"JOAN JOHNSTON
UNFORGETTABLE
CHARACTERS
FINE THE
TOU

"KEEP 'EM ____ING, JOAN!"
Heartland Critiques

Other Avon Books by
Joan Johnston

I PROMISE

JOAN JOHNSTON

Heartbeat

AVON BOOKS ◆ NEW YORK

AVON BOOKS
A division of
The Hearst Corporation
1350 Avenue of the Americas
New York, New York 10019

Copyright © 1997 by Joan Mertens Johnston, Inc.
Published by arrangement with the author
Visit our website at **http://AvonBooks.com**
Library of Congress Catalog Card Number: 97-93009
ISBN: 0-380-78241-3

First Avon Books Printing: September 1997

AVON TRADEMARK REG. U.S. PAT. OFF. AND IN OTHER COUNTRIES, MARCA REGISTRADA, HECHO EN U.S.A.

Printed in the U.S.A.

WCD 10 9 8 7 6 5 4 3 2 1

A special thanks to all my readers
who are crossing over from
the historical and category genres
to try my mainstream contemporary novels.
To all of you, and to those of you
who are picking up one of my books
for the first time . . .
enjoy.

Acknowledgments

I want to thank those who gave of their time and expertise to help make *Heartbeat* more authentic, including Texas Ranger Sergeant Rocky Wardlow (it sounds like I made him up, but that's really his name), who told me what I needed to know about this elite force of lawmen; Aileen Staller, Clinical Coordinator for Neurosurgery at Memorial Regional Hospital, Hollywood, Florida, who helped me figure out the best way to murder someone in a hospital without getting caught; Jon Thogmartin, Associate Medical Examiner of Broward County, who explained how I could discover murder had been committed after all; Jerilyn O'Neil, Community Relations Director, Memorial Healthcare System, who put me in touch with all the right people; my friend and fellow attorney Michael Spain, at Fulbright & Jaworski in San Antonio, who was kind enough to point me toward his colleague, Louise Joy in Austin, an expert on Texas medical law; and Louise Joy, for sharing some of that knowledge with me.

A special thanks to my friend Billie Blake Bailey, of San Antonio, and to the Jay and Bethany Staples wedding party, who contributed invaluable "Texas tidbits."

I am indebted to James Farmer, a friend in need, who reconfigured my 286 when it crashed and put in a new drive. I have a sentimental attachment to the old girl. She's helped me write a lot of wonderful books.

The character of the Texas Ranger is well known by friend and foe . . . chivalrous, bold and impetuous in action, he is yet wary and calculating, always impatient of restraint, and sometimes unscrupulous and unmerciful. He is ununiformed, and undrilled, and performs his active duties thoroughly, but with little regard to order or system. He is an excellent rider and a dead shot. His arms are a rifle, Colt's revolving pistol, and a knife.

Luther Giddings
Sketches of the Campaigns in
Northern Mexico by an Officer
of the First Ohio Volunteers, 1853

Heartbeat

❧ *Prologue* ❧

Jack had already looked through the folder once. He forced himself to open it again. Inside were autopsy photos of eight-year-old Laurel Morgan, who had died at San Antonio General Hospital. *Was murdered at San Antonio General,* he corrected. He turned the photograph facedown and picked up an aged newspaper clipping of an obituary.

DAWSON, Trevor Michael. Died on Tuesday, April 1 at Dallas Memorial Hospital. Trevor was born prematurely and died when his heart failed after seventeen hours of life. Memorial services will be held at 2 P.M. Thursday at Parkland Baptist Church. Trevor is survived by his father and mother, Mr. and Mrs. Michael Dawson.

Trevor Michael Dawson had barely had a chance to live before he died. *Before someone murdered him,* Jack amended.

He discarded the clipping and picked up the

hospital records for Frances Petrocelli. Two-year-old Frances had been poisoned by cleaning products from under her mother's sink. She had been in a coma when her heart failed. *With a little help from someone at Houston Regional Medical Center.*

Jack let the clipping fall onto the stack of papers on the coffee table and leaned back in the rocker his father had made for his mother once upon a time. He pressed his palms against weary eyes.

I don't want to get involved in this, he thought.

Jack was in the third day of a thirty-day administrative leave—sick leave, really. Only Jack wasn't ill, just sick at heart. Somebody else would take the case if he didn't. Somebody else could spend his nights dreaming of blank stares and stolen lives.

The face of a little girl with brown bangs and pigtails appeared before Jack. She wasn't one of the victims in the folder in front of him. She was the reason he was on leave.

Jack felt his body begin to tremble. He closed his eyes and gritted his teeth, but she was still there with her frightened brown eyes, her clutching hands, the splash of blood on her dress.

Jack lurched from the rocker and headed for the kitchen. He didn't stop there but pushed on through the back door. He was headed down the porch steps in the dark when something heavy landed on his shoulders. He started to struggle and realized what had happened when four sets of claws embedded in his back.

"Damn you, cat!" he growled. Jack sat down on the steps and hunched over to make it easier for the cat to get off of him. He felt the sting ease as the claws released his flesh, and the cat dropped heavily onto the wooden porch.

He turned to look at the monster that had been the only legacy his mother had left him. He'd thought it amusing the first time the cat dropped out of a tree onto his back.

"That isn't funny anymore," he announced to the cat.

The feline gave Jack a baleful stare, turned its back on him and, with its tail held high, stalked away.

The attack had accomplished at least one thing. It had taken Jack's mind off the disaster that had started him wondering whether he wanted to continue being a lawman.

He dropped his head in his hands and sighed. He had to make up his mind whether or not he wanted to hunt down a serial killer. And while he was sitting here thinking, the primary suspect in the case was working at San Antonio General, maybe targeting his next victim.

Jack rose from the porch and headed inside. He found the phone under a stack of clothes in the living room and dialed a number. His heart began to beat like a butterfly caught in a glass jar, frantically, anxiously.

"Sorry to bother you so late," he said. "I've decided to take the case."

❧ *Chapter 1* ❧

Maggie was running late for her 8 A.M. meeting with the managing partner of Wainwright & Cobb. She had a good excuse for her tardiness, but Maggie knew better than to use it. Explaining, "I was helping out a friend—an associate traveling today on behalf of the firm—by dropping off her daughter at day care," was only going to increase the old man's ire. Porter Cobb expected to get what he wanted when he wanted it. No excuses.

As she headed up the elevator to the top floor of the Milam Building in downtown San Antonio, Maggie's lips curved in a smile. She reached up to touch her cheek where three-year-old Amy had exuberantly kissed her goodbye, leaving a slobbery wet spot. Amy had clung to Maggie for a brief moment before the day care attendant reached out to take her. Even though the child wasn't hers, Maggie hadn't wanted to let her go.

Lisa Hollander's daughter had dark eyes as shiny as seed pods, a smile that lit up like a tin roof on a sunny day, and a cheerful personality to match. Maggie's heart ached for what she was missing. How lovely to have a daughter like Amy. If only . . .

Maggie forced her mind away from the past. She'd had her chance for a family. Now she did what was necessary to get through each day. To give her life purpose she had dedicated herself to becoming the best—most empathetic, considerate, and kind, as well as legally competent—lawyer Wainwright & Cobb had ever had. Considering the bloodthirsty, cutthroat business she was in, that had been quite a challenge. It wasn't always easy balancing what was ethically or morally right with what was legally allowed.

"Hello, Trudy," Maggie said as she stepped off the elevator and passed the firm receptionist on the way to her office. "How's the old man?"

"On a rampage," Trudy whispered. "I've got orders to send you directly to his office when you arrive."

"Call and tell Uncle Porter I'm on my way." Maggie grinned and added, "The moment after I stop by my office to check my e-mail and see if MEDCO has left any messages."

Trudy shook her head in disbelief at Maggie's audacity, then picked up the phone and did as she was told.

Maggie knew that Trudy and the rest of the secretaries, associates, and partners at Wainwright & Cobb believed she had Porter Cobb wrapped around her little finger. It was true her late husband's uncle tolerated a great deal of deviation from the norm where she was concerned. But Maggie knew their tenuous family relationship was not as much responsible for the respect Uncle Porter accorded her as her value to the firm as a rainmaker.

It was through her prior contacts that MEDCO, a huge conglomerate that operated at least a dozen hospitals in Texas, had become a client. Together with Lisa Hollander, Maggie did all of MEDCO's corporate work and was counsel to the various hospitals in the system.

Recently, as Lisa Hollander had become a more experienced attorney, Maggie's protegée had begun traveling to MEDCO's hospitals to put out small legal fires. Lisa had flown out early that morning to attend a deposition at Dallas Memorial Hospital. Since Lisa's husband, Roman—Chief of Staff at San Antonio General—had an early surgery scheduled, Maggie had taken Amy to day care to help them out.

As she entered her office on the southeast corner of the building, Maggie winced at the bright sunlight reflected through the picture window. She loved having a view of downtown San Antonio, but the sun was uncooperative in the morning. She let down the black Levelor blinds, shutting out the brilliant glare in favor of soft overhead lighting.

The computer where Maggie received her e-mail was in a small, private office adjoining the larger, interior-decorated-for-maximum-authority office where she greeted clients. She actually spent a great deal more of her time in the smaller office than in the larger one. It didn't have to be neat because no one saw it. And because no one else was allowed in it— even to clean—she kept some things there that had special meaning for her, but which she didn't want to have to explain to curious colleagues.

A drawing of a train in crayon. A picture of Cinderella and Prince Charming cut from a children's book and autographed "To Maggie from Woody, your own Prince Charming." A photograph of herself and her late husband taken shortly before Woody's death. The April page from a 1987 calendar.

Maggie called up her e-mail and found the information she'd requested from MEDCO. She started reading, then stopped. "Damn." MEDCO hadn't answered all her questions. She e-mailed a message to the CEO of MEDCO pointing out the missing information and requesting he get back to her *by noon* or the pleading wasn't going to get filed today—the last day before the statute of limitations voided the lawsuit.

That accomplished, Maggie figured she'd tried Uncle Porter's patience as far as she dared, and that she'd better answer his summons. She was almost out the door when she saw the red light blinking on the answering machine on her desk.

Maggie hesitated. She had promised Lisa she'd be available if the day care center needed her for any reason and had left the number for her personal line. What if the center had called to say Amy had gotten sick? Or hurt?

Maggie hurried across the carpet, sank into the comfortable leather chair behind her desk, and punched the "New Messages" button on her fax/answering machine.

"You haven't been returning my calls, Margaret," an imperious female voice announced.

Every muscle in Maggie's body tensed. Her former mother-in-law, Victoria Wainwright, seldom had anything good to say to her or about her.

"There's little more than a week left before the Cancer Society Gala," the message continued. "I need to know whether you've confirmed the number of attendees with the caterer and whether you managed to arrange for Tony Sherwin to conduct the orchestra. If you don't call me, I'm going to have to come downtown and find you."

Maggie edged back from the anger she felt hearing Victoria's condescending speech. Getting angry meant Victoria had won. Maggie took several deep breaths, willing her pulse to slow. She couldn't control what Victoria said to her, but she had absolute control over her reaction.

Water off a duck's back, she told herself. *Relax. Focus on the solution, not the problem.*

As chair for the gala Victoria had "volunteered" Maggie for a great deal of the work. Maggie hadn't minded, since she believed in giving back to the community, but dealing with Victoria had turned out to be a nightmare. She had told Victoria she would make sure matters were handled, and she was scheduled to report to the gala committee at a meeting this evening. She had done everything that had been asked of her so far. Victoria should have trusted her.

But Maggie had learned from experience that it was easier to kowtow to Victoria's demands than to defy her. *It solved the problem.* And kept her stress level down. Uncle Porter would have to wait another minute while she answered his sister's call.

As she crossed her legs she realized she had a run in her stocking where Amy's tiny fingernail had caught when Maggie was playing keepaway with Amy's Tickle Me Elmo. She tried pulling the stocking up higher, but her skirt was too short to conceal the run. She opened the cabinet behind her desk, where she kept a spare pair of nylons, but realized when she found the empty packaging that she'd used them yesterday.

Maggie slipped out of her heels, pulled the nylons off, and put them on backward. At least that way she'd look good going into Uncle Porter's office, even if the run showed when she turned her back on him and left. She settled back into her chair, rubbing at the twin knots of tension on the back of her neck as she dialed Victoria's number.

Maggie sagged in relief when the answering machine picked up. "Victoria, I've confirmed with the caterer, and Tony Sherwin is happy to conduct. If you have any other questions, I'll be glad to answer them at the meeting tonight."

Two seconds later she was on her way to Porter Cobb's office. She made herself slow down so she wouldn't arrive out of breath.

"He's waiting for you," Cobb's secretary said.

Maggie smiled broadly, as though she hadn't heard the hint of disapproval in the secretary's voice. "Good," she said as she opened the door, stepped inside, and closed it behind her.

Porter Cobb was sitting behind a massive desk puffing on a cigar, even though the law didn't allow it. Maggie had learned that when Uncle Porter wanted something, the law didn't much get in his way. He was wearing a vested suit in a dark gray wool blend with a crisply starched white button-down shirt. A conservative striped tie was knotted precisely beneath the sagging wattles on his throat that revealed he was older than his rigid bearing suggested.

"You're late," Cobb said.

"I'm here now," Maggie replied, refusing to

apologize or excuse herself. She eschewed the two magnificent chairs in front of his desk, knowing they were purposely low to the ground so that Uncle Porter sat like a king on a dais before whoever came calling. Instead, she settled on the maroon leather couch near the window, laying her arm along the back and crossing her legs in as casual a pose as she could manage.

He puffed on his cigar, ignoring her.

Maggie resisted the urge to speak. This was all part of the power game, and she'd learned to play it well. She tucked a loose strand of hair Amy had pulled back into her French twist, waiting patiently for Uncle Porter to bring up whatever subject had necessitated their meeting. Maggie appeared to be glancing casually out the window, but she was actually watching him from the corner of her eye.

"It's been almost ten years," Uncle Porter said.

Maggie's heart suddenly pounded in her chest, and her gaze shot to Uncle Porter's grim face. "You didn't need to call me in here to remind me. I'm hardly likely to forget."

"I've heard something about you that troubles me, Margaret."

Maggie refused to rise to the bait. She'd been talking with other law firms outside Texas, looking for a place where she could start over without the influential stigma of being the former daughter-in-law of Texas financier and philanthropist Richard Woodson

Wainwright. And without the memories of what had happened between her and Woody ten years ago being constantly thrown in her face by Woody's mother.

Obviously someone had contacted Uncle Porter, and he wanted her to confirm the rumor that she was ready to bolt from the firm.

"I will only remind you that a certain debt has not been paid," Cobb said.

Maggie's nostrils flared as she sucked air. She met Cobb's implacable gaze and said, "If it's the money that concerns you—"

"It's not the money," Cobb interrupted. "I wouldn't want to think you'd move the one remaining connection my sister has to her only son somewhere else."

Maggie's pose of disinterest evaporated as she scrambled to her feet. She felt the heat in her cheeks as the blood rushed to her head. "Victoria doesn't even know—Victoria wouldn't care—Victoria would rather see me gone."

Porter Cobb took a puff of his cigar before announcing, "I would not."

Maggie clenched her fists to keep from extending them in supplication. Begging wouldn't work. Once Uncle Porter saw her crawling, he'd come in for the kill. *Act assured. Act confident. Don't let him know he has you scared.* "You can't keep me here," Maggie said.

Cobb raised a single salt-and-pepper eyebrow. "Can't I? I hold all the aces, Margaret. You might as well throw in your hand."

Maggie wanted to keep on fighting, but Uncle Porter had hinted at a weapon he hadn't drawn yet but was willing to use: If she tried to leave Texas, she wouldn't leave with everything. He'd keep the most important thing, and there'd be nothing she could do about it.

"You don't play fair," she pointed out.

"Does that mean you'll be staying?"

He knew the answer without asking. It was more game playing, where she verbally conceded defeat, thereby making him the victor. She owed him so much; but he made sure she never forgot it. It felt like a black box was closing around her, and Maggie fought to keep open a window of light. Was she going to stay where Porter Cobb's powerful, long-reaching arms could control her life? Maggie gave the most defiant answer she could.

"For the moment."

Maggie had gone to bed at eleven, after an enervating meeting chaired by Victoria regarding the gala. The call from the gatekeeper at 200 Patterson announcing she had a visitor woke her up. "Who is it?" she asked, glancing at the clock. It was 11:33.

"Lisa Hollander."

"Let her in," Maggie said, wondering why Lisa hadn't just called. She must be exhausted from her trip to Dallas. But that was just like Lisa, to thank her right away and in person for helping with Amy—even though it could have waited until morning.

Maggie had slipped on a comfortable terry cloth robe but was barefoot when she greeted Lisa at the door to her elegant tenth-floor condominium. "Come in. You didn't have to—" Maggie cut herself off when she saw the look in Lisa's large brown eyes. "What's wrong?"

Lisa crossed past her and headed toward the kitchen where they'd sat at the table working on numerous legal cases together. Maggie followed her, confused and alarmed by Lisa's strange behavior. She was dressed in a tailored, dark green suit that Maggie presumed was what she'd worn for the trip to Dallas. Which meant either she hadn't been home yet, or she hadn't stayed home long enough to change.

"Do you mind if I get myself something to drink?" Lisa said, heading for the refrigerator.

"Not at all. In fact, get me a Coke while you're at it."

From past visits Lisa knew where to find glasses, which she filled with ice from the refrigerator dispenser. She split a Coke and handed one of the glasses to Maggie, who had settled herself in a chair at the small round kitchen table.

Lisa sat down across from her, set the untouched glass of Coke on the oak surface, and broke into tears.

Maggie set her glass down and knelt beside Lisa, reaching for her hands and gripping them in her own. "Has Amy or Roman been hurt?"

Lisa shook her head vigorously.

"The deposition went badly?" Maggie guessed.

Lisa shook her head.

"You and Roman had a fight?"

Lisa made a keening sound, and Maggie had her answer. She let go of Lisa's hands, rose, and pulled one of the padded kitchen chairs closer so she could sit beside the distraught young woman. "Do you want to talk about it?"

"Yes. No. I don't know."

"That sounds like a lawyer's answer, all right," Maggie said with a rueful smile. "I've trained you well."

Lisa managed a sobbing laugh and knuckled her eyes dry, smearing her mascara. Maggie stretched for a box of Kleenex from the breakfast bar that separated the cooking area from the dining area and placed it in front of Lisa, who cleaned the mascara from her hands, then dabbed at her eyes. "I didn't mean to sound so confused." She looked at Maggie and said, "But I am."

"What can I do to help?"

"I don't know," Lisa wailed. "I don't know what to do!" She grabbed another Kleenex and dabbed at the tears streaming freely from her eyes.

Maggie was at a loss. She had been Lisa's mentor for the past three years and done everything she could to help her succeed professionally. In the process, they had become friends. She had been to the Hollander house several times. She liked Roman Hollander, and from everything she'd seen, he was besotted with his wife. As Lisa's boss she wasn't sure she wanted to get involved with Lisa's personal problems—especially any difficulties she was having with her husband.

But it was obvious Lisa needed someone to talk to, and Maggie didn't have the heart to send her away. "I'm here to listen, Lisa. And to help, if you think I can."

"Roman wants me to quit my job," she blurted.

"What brought this on?" Maggie said.

"You know how busy I've been the past few months, and now I've started traveling. Roman's schedule at the hospital is so crowded he doesn't have much free time, and lately, when he's been free, I haven't. My plane was late leaving Dallas, and instead of getting home at seven P.M., I got home at ten-thirty. Roman was sitting at the kitchen table waiting for me, and I've never seen him so upset. Apparently Amy cried for me for almost an hour before she finally fell asleep."

Maggie felt her insides clutch as she imagined the wounded look in Amy's dark eyes as she cried for a mother who didn't come. One look at Lisa's face revealed the agonizing guilt she felt. It wasn't easy for women who chose to work to balance children and a profession.

Maggie had thought Lisa was doing a pretty good job. But maybe not.

"I'm so sorry, Lisa. It's not your fault the plane was late."

"I chose to go, so the blame's mine! At least that's what Roman said."

"Neanderthal thinking," Maggie muttered under her breath. To Lisa she said, "I wasn't aware Roman had problems with you having a career."

"He's never complained before," Lisa said. "But I never had so much responsibility before. And things are even more hectic right now because the nanny's gone for a couple of weeks. Roman says he can support us on what he makes, and that I'm foolish to work instead of staying home with Amy."

"He might have a point," Maggie said quietly.

Lisa rose abruptly and paced the kitchen. "I can't quit. I won't quit. I refuse to quit!"

Maggie eyes narrowed as she observed Lisa's obvious agitation. Lisa had always seemed to enjoy her work, but Maggie had never noticed that she was obsessed with it. Lisa seemed just as happy being home with her husband and daughter. Why was she so insistent on working? Why not quit her job and make Roman happy and enjoy these years with Amy? "I'd hate to lose you," Maggie began, "but—"

Lisa stopped and stared at Maggie with tormented eyes. "I think Roman might be having an affair with his nurse."

Maggie's jaw gaped. "What?"

Lisa dropped into the chair beside Maggie. "Things haven't been the same between us since I started working on the MEDCO case in Dallas three months ago. I was so busy at first, I guess I didn't notice what was happening. But lately I've watched him avoid my eyes, and at night in bed . . ." Lisa swallowed hard and said, "He doesn't reach for me anymore."

Maggie was way out of her depth. She hadn't the foggiest notion what to advise Lisa under the circumstances. "Are you sure something's going on? Could you be imagining it?"

Lisa's fingers knotted in her lap. "I couldn't find Roman anywhere on Monday. I called the hospital, I called the house, I even called the day care center thinking he might have gone to pick up Amy. When I called the hospital a second time, one of the nurses said if I could find Isabel Rojas, I'd find the doctor because they'd left the hospital together."

"That doesn't mean they're having a sexual affair," Maggie protested. "You know how things often aren't what they seem."

"Isabel Rojas is Roman's surgical nurse. He knew her long before he even met me. He told me before we married that he'd had an affair with her once but that it was over. What if it wasn't over? What if these past four years we've been married he's been carrying on with her behind my back?"

Maggie snorted. "That's ridiculous! I've seen how Roman looks at you. He loves you."

It was clear Lisa wanted to believe her. But she said, "He doesn't say he loves me. Not in words. And he hasn't been near me . . ." Lisa clenched her teeth, but it did little to still her quivering chin.

Maggie put her arms around Lisa and pulled the other woman close. "What you need now is a good night's sleep."

"I can't go home, Maggie."

"I think you should, Lisa. Roman must be very worried right now. He's a reasonable man. When you talk all this over in a calm, rational—"

Lisa pulled away. "My mind is made up. There's nothing to discuss. I'm not quitting, and that's final!"

Maggie squeezed Lisa's hand reassuringly. "All right. Nobody says you have to quit. I'm sure you and Roman can work something out. Maybe he can cut back on his hours, or you can cut back on yours."

Lisa leaned back and said, "I don't want to disappoint you, Maggie. Not after all the help you've given me."

"The only thing that would disappoint me is if you and Roman weren't able to resolve your differences and live happily ever after."

"Life isn't a fairy tale," Lisa said soberly.

"How well I know that," Maggie murmured. Cinderella and Prince Charming hadn't made it.

"I guess I'd better leave," Lisa said, rising on obviously shaky legs.

"You shouldn't be driving in your condition. I'll give you a ride home and pick you up tomorrow morning."

"I couldn't impose like that!" Lisa said.

"Call Roman and tell him you're on your way home while I put on some clothes." Maggie disappeared into the bedroom where she threw on some Levi's, a T-shirt, and boots and pulled her hair up into a ponytail. When she returned to the living room, Lisa was talking to Roman on the phone. Maggie didn't intentionally eavesdrop, but she heard enough to realize the Hollanders were already well on the way to reconciling their differences.

"I'm sorry, too," Lisa said. "Maggie is bringing me home, so you don't have to worry about me driving. I . . . I feel the same way. I'll see you soon."

When Lisa hung up the phone, Maggie cleared her throat. "I couldn't help overhearing."

The beatific smile on Lisa's face made Maggie's throat clog with emotion. How wonderful to be in love—even with all the heartaches and pain that inevitably came along with such powerful feelings.

You had love once and squandered it. You had everything and threw it away.

Maggie swallowed painfully and said, "Let's get you home. We've got a long day ahead of us tomorrow."

"Thanks for everything, Maggie. You're a true friend."

Maggie treasured the compliment. Friendship paled when compared to the love between a man and a woman, or a mother and her child, but considering Maggie's past, it was likely to be all she would ever have. "Thanks, Lisa," Maggie said. "That means a lot to me."

Until she could find a way to break free of the hold Porter Cobb had on her life, she was suspended in a waking nightmare. Appearances, she had learned, could hide a great deal. No one else suspected her of keeping secrets. No one else knew the truth about her.

The sad thing was, Maggie still believed in fairy tales. She still dreamed of happily ever after. Unfortunately, her Prince Charming had come and gone . . . and taken her heart along with him.

❦ *Chapter 2* ❧

In his opinion, she didn't look like a lawyer. Especially not one who negotiated life-and-death disputes. Nothing about her was the least bit staid-looking or reserved or serious.

The female standing at home plate, baseball bat in hand, wore butt-baring cut-off Levi's, a pink T-shirt ripped out at the neck that hit her about midriff, and battered Nikes with droopy white workout socks. One look at her long, slender legs, flat stomach, and small but completely-adequate-for-him bosom, and Jack Kittrick realized it might be easier than he'd thought to forget his troubles for an afternoon.

Of course, none of the Wainwright & Cobb lawyers had worn suits to the firm's spring picnic at Brackenridge Park, in the heart of San Antonio. A few were dressed like him, in Western hats and shirts, Levi's, and cowboy boots, but most of them looked like the conservative top five percent of a top ten law-school graduates they were.

Jack ignored the trickle of sweat crawling down his back. No shade protected the ballfield, but the view was too intriguing to abandon. He lifted his hat and shoved back a handful of dark, damp hair before resettling the new Resistol he'd bought to replace his Stetson low on his forehead, noting absently that his hair had grown too long to meet regulations. Again.

Because he had found himself thinking too much about things he couldn't change, Jack had come to Brackenridge Park this afternoon to seek distraction at the zoo and the Japanese Sunken Gardens. In the parking lot, he'd overheard someone say the Wainwright & Cobb picnic was being held near the ballfield. Since the primary suspect in the case he'd just agreed to work on was married to a Wainwright & Cobb attorney, he hadn't been able to resist meandering in that direction.

Without seeming to observe, Jack let his gaze roam. He could track a wood tick on solid rock. It should be easy to find a murderer at a picnic. Even though he only intended to observe the suspect, he felt the rush of adrenaline, the brace of tension across his shoulders, and the knot of anxiety in his stomach that came with every new investigation.

He saw a lot of men in khaki shorts, golf shirts, and loafers without socks, or in the case of those playing baseball, brand-new canvas tennis shoes without socks. The women, wives and lawyers alike, had merely substituted sandals for loafers. Which made the lady in the batter's box stick out like a sore pink thumb.

Jack had been curious enough to ask about her and was disappointed with what he learned. Not only was Ms. Margaret Wainwright one of the firm's top attorneys, she was also the widowed daughter-in-law of the late San Antonio blueblood and Texas tycoon Richard Woodson Wainwright. That put her way out of his league.

Still, Jack had trouble squaring the renegade in pink with the philanthropic efforts, charitable causes, and sophisticated society parties usually associated with the Wainwright name. He imagined the rest of the afternoon alone with her in a cool, dark room with a big, soft bed and liked what he saw.

Ms. Wainwright—everyone called her Maggie—wore her wheat-blond hair in a ponytail, which flipped from side to side as she wiggled her fanny and lifted the baseball bat higher, waiting for the next pitch. Her chin was tipped up, her mouth was curved in an unselfconscious grin, and her wide-set blue eyes sparkled.

Jack knew he ought to leave the ballfield, since his discreet inquiries had also revealed that the man he had come to find was probably on the golf course. He waited another moment to see whether Maggie hit like a girl. He hoped she didn't.

The pitch was high, and she hit it foul. It was moving so fast when it reached the spot where he was standing along the third base line that if he hadn't put up a hand to snare it, the ball would have smashed his nose flat. The crowd in the stands gasped in alarm, then shouted and clapped in amazed relief as the ball smacked the flesh of his palm.

That answered his question. The lady could hit like a major leaguer. He shook his hand to ease the sting in his palm, then held up the ball and waved it at her. She shrugged an apology and shot him that open, friendly smile of hers. Jack came real close to smiling back. He met her gaze, felt the instant, sparking connection, and quickly broke it.

He wasn't there to meet some high-class legal eagle who probably wouldn't share the time of day with him if she knew what he did for a living. He squared his jaw and threw the ball to the pitcher, then watched as Maggie crouched down, wiggled her fanny, and settled in for the next throw.

He should have left right then, but there was something mesmerizing about Maggie Wainwright—the smile and the wiggle and the glance—that kept him where he was. Jack knew better than to let himself get distracted when he was working, but technically, he wasn't on the job yet. And where was the harm in a little baseball on a pleasant Saturday afternoon? Besides, now that he knew Maggie could hit, he wanted to see if she could run.

Jack heard what sounded like a gunshot, and a kid's sharp cry of fear, and felt his blood run cold. He pivoted, eyes narrowed and intently focused, to locate the child in the stands. He saw the remnants of a red balloon in the grass and watched as a tearful little boy holding the empty string was lifted into his father's arms.

Jack let out the breath he'd been holding. His heart was racing and his hands were trembling. It was too damned soon to be working again, he thought, as he rubbed his sweaty palms on the thighs of his jeans. He just wasn't ready. He'd told the captain he needed more time off, but Harley had said, "Best thing to do when you get bucked off, son, is get right back on."

Jack wasn't so sure. Not when popped balloons sounded like gunshots. A second later, he felt a sharp blow on the back of his head—like a mule's kick—before his knees crumpled, and he felt himself toppling face-first into the third-base-line powder.

"The ball hit him right in the head!"

"Somebody call 911!"

"Go find Dr. Hollander!"

Through the haze, Jack wished he'd been knocked cold. It was far worse to be semiconscious and know what a ruckus he was causing. He'd survived a lot of hard wear in his youth, from getting stomped by a bull in a college rodeo to having buckshot picked out of his hide back home in Hondo, when he'd misjudged old lady Stewart's determination to stop "that thievin' varmint stealin' my watermelons!"

At thirty-eight, Jack was older and wiser. He didn't ride bulls, and he didn't steal watermelons. And these days, if somebody shot at him, he pulled a Colt .45 from his holster—because the SIG-Sauer he'd been issued was usually in the glove box of his pickup—and shot right back.

It was going to be a downright humbling experience explaining to his boss, Captain Harley Buckelew, that he couldn't start investigating that serial killer on Monday because he'd been clobbered by a female with a baseball bat, especially when she hadn't gotten within twenty yards of him.

Jack wondered exactly how bad the damage was. At the moment, he didn't feel any pain. *Must be in shock,* he concluded. The headache, and Jack was guessing it'd be a doozy, couldn't be far off.

The crowd from the stands swarmed his inert body like maggots on a carcass of stolen beef. Somebody turned him over just as someone else warned, "Don't move him!" Jack curled his toes in his cowboy boots to reassure himself he wasn't paralyzed. He wasn't.

He scowled as somebody kicked his Resistol out of the way so they could kneel beside him. *Sonofabitch! That's my best hat. Pick it up!* Jack thought he'd spoken aloud, but realized when nobody reacted that he must not have gotten the words out.

"Who is he? Anybody recognize him?"

"Does he work for the firm?"

"Does anybody know this man?"

Jack heard a lot of "uh-uhs" and "nopes." Naturally they didn't recognize him. He wasn't a Wainwright & Cobb attorney. He sure as hell hadn't planned to get caught snooping. Working undercover meant being unobtrusive. Jack was pretty sure that getting knocked flat on a baseball diamond wasn't what Captain Buckelew had meant when he'd said, "Keep a low profile."

Jack had figured he'd take a quick look at the doctor who was supposedly killing his own patients—kids who'd suffered accidents or injury and gone to Dr. Roman Hollander to get better—and get the hell out of there. If he'd headed for the golf course to find Hollander ten minutes ago, like he should have, he wouldn't be in this fix.

Jack squinted up at the blur of concerned faces hovered over him. So much for being unobtrusive.

"I'm okay," he said. It came out "Mmmk."

"What'd he say?"

"Couldn't tell. Hey, cowboy, how many fingers?"

Jack saw a bunch. He figured he was seeing double and guessed, "Two."

"Concussion," a voice said flatly.

Wrong guess, Jack thought.

"What's your name?" the fellow with the fingers asked, beginning a search through Jack's pockets for identification.

Jack clamped a death grip on the fellow's wrist.

"Hey! What's your problem?"

The problem was, if this Good Samaritan kept looking long enough, he was going to find the five-pointed star that Texas Rangers had carried ever since they were formed as a unit in the days when Texas was a Republic. If that happened, Captain Buckelew was going to have Jack's guts for garters.

"Jack Kittrick," Jack forced out.

"He says he's Jack Kittrick," the fellow announced to the gathered crowd. "Anybody recognize the name?"

Jack heard a surprised female voice say, "I do."

"Who is he, Maggie?"

"He's the new insurance investigator for San Antonio General," she said in a husky Texas drawl.

"What's he doing here?" the Samaritan asked.

"I don't know," Maggie said, kneeling beside him.

Jack tried to turn his head to get a closer look at Maggie Wainwright, but closed his eyes and groaned when a searing pain shot up the back of his neck and exploded in his head.

"He might have come to see me," Maggie said. "I have a meeting scheduled with him at the hospital Monday morning to discuss some malpractice cases."

Jack's brain wasn't working quite right at

the moment, but he thought he'd just heard Maggie Wainwright say that his meeting on Monday at the hospital was with her. *Maggie* was counsel for San Antonio General?

Jack's head was starting to pound, but he knew better than to relax. It appeared his cover was safe for the moment, but until he was on his feet and out of here, his situation was precarious. Jack felt soft fingers smooth the sweaty hair from his forehead. He opened his eyes and found himself staring into Maggie Wainwright's worried blue eyes. All four of them.

Pretty color, Jack thought. *Not purple enough for bluebonnets. More like cornflowers.*

"I'm so sorry, Mr. Kittrick. Please lie still." Maggie put a firm hand on his shoulder to keep him flat, even though he hadn't made a move since he'd been decked by the ball. "The doctor will be here soon to take a look at you."

"He'll probably sue," Jack heard someone mutter.

"Assumption of the risk," somebody else said. "What do you expect, standing on the third base line like that? It wasn't as if he didn't have fair warning the situation was dangerous."

Lawyers, Jack thought disgustedly. Standing there making a case against him in court, when what he really needed was some fast medical attention—like whatever drug would knock him out until the headache was gone.

"How are you feeling?" Maggie asked.

"That's a silly question, I suppose," she said with a throaty laugh that made him think of tousled sheets. "Your head must be pounding. Something similar happened to me once, and it felt like someone was cracking ice with a hammer inside my head."

Jack liked the crooning sound of Maggie's voice. She sounded in control, but he could feel her hands shaking when they touched his shoulder and brushed at his hair, even though it had to be pretty much off his forehead by now. Her fingertips were cool. He just wished his head didn't hurt so damned much, so he could enjoy all the attention she was giving him.

He closed his eyes, hoping to focus them, then opened them again. Two Maggie Wainwrights still hovered over him. Some kind of shampoo smell in her hair—strawberries?— which was brushing against his cheek as she peered into his eyes, and female sweat—the kind he smelled on a woman after some energetic sex—was making him nauseated.

Which was when he knew he was in bad shape. He loved the scents a woman used to attract a man. This was the first time he could remember being flat on his back with a desirable female leaning over him that he hadn't indulged himself by touching all the places on a woman there were to touch.

A guttural sound, as much disgust as pain, rumbled out of him.

Maggie laid two fingertips on the pulse

at his throat, which immediately sped up, causing his head to throb. Jack gritted his teeth and willed his pulse to slow. It never had a chance, because Maggie touched him again, this time brushing at his sideburns. Which he'd better get trimmed before he saw Captain Buckelew again.

"Make room," someone said. "The doc's here."

Jack tried to sit up. He didn't like doctors—never had and never would. His body felt uncoordinated, slow to react, not to mention the objections his head was making to any sort of movement.

Maggie laid a palm in the center of his chest and pressed him back down. "Shh. Take it easy. Dr. Hollander specializes in head injuries. He'll be able to tell us how seriously you're hurt."

Jack suddenly found himself looking into the face of Dr. Roman Hollander, the murder suspect he'd come to investigate.

Jack believed in first impressions. For instance, he'd known right away he wanted Maggie Wainwright in his bed. To his surprise, when he laid eyes on Roman Hollander, Jack didn't get the feeling he was looking at a killer. Wearing a hunter green Polo shirt and khaki shorts, Roman Hollander looked more like a professional golfer than the distinguished physician he was. Jack didn't know too many killers who wore designer clothes.

He reminded himself that Ted Bundy had

looked like a nice college boy. Maybe Hollander didn't look evil because the murders he had supposedly committed had been intended as acts of mercy. If the children in question had lived, each of them would have faced a long and perhaps unproductive rehabilitative process.

Jack couldn't help flinching when the doctor's hands touched his face.

"I'm just going to take a look in your eyes," Hollander explained as he moved a small flashlight across Jack's range of vision. Jack wondered where the doctor had gotten the flashlight and decided Hollander probably carried one with him the way Jack carried a small but lethal jackknife.

The pads of the doctor's fingertips felt smooth on Jack's face, but there was nothing effeminate about his touch. Jack kept silent, watching Hollander, trying to pretend he wasn't still seeing two of everything, trying not to look as helpless as he felt in front of Maggie Wainwright.

Hollander refused to be rushed. He reminded Jack of a horse handler he'd seen working with a stud that had been abused by a previous owner. Hollander's movements were slow, careful, and compassionate.

The doctor had silver-gray hair that receded at the temples and wore wire-rimmed glasses that revealed irises nearly as black as his pupils. Rattlesnakes had eyes like that. But there was nothing cold or heartless about the way the doctor was treating him.

"It looks like he's got a mild concussion," Hollander said to Maggie, as though Jack wasn't lying right there, perfectly capable of hearing and responding.

"The safest course would be to admit him to the hospital for observation overnight," Hollander said. "Tell the paramedics to inform the admitting nurse that he's my patient."

"Thank you, Roman," Jack heard Maggie say. "You're a godsend."

Nobody had asked Jack whether he wanted to go to the hospital. Nobody had asked him whether he wanted a suspected murderer as his attending physician. There was only one word that described the situation he was in. And he was in it deep.

The captain was going to kill him.

Jack sat up abruptly to keep anybody from stopping him, and because he figured he might as well get the pain over with all at once. Everything went dark for a second, then cleared.

"I'm out of here," he announced.

Maggie exchanged a glance with Hollander and said, "You can't just leave. You've got a concussion. You need to be in a hospital."

Hollander's grip on Jack's shoulder belied the softness of his touch. The man was stronger than he looked.

"Is there anybody at home who can keep an eye on you overnight?" Hollander asked.

"I live alone," Jack said.

The doctor shook his head. "In that case, I'll have to insist—"

Jack shoved the doctor's arm away and struggled to his feet, surprised at how shaky he felt. He grabbed for his hat on the way up and bit his lip to keep from yelling at the pain as he settled the Resistol gingerly on his head. An arm slid around his waist to support him, and he looked down to find Maggie Wainwright hip to hip with him.

"Please. I'll worry unless I know for sure someone is keeping an eye on you," she said.

"You're welcome to join me." Jack put enough innuendo in the invitation to ensure she'd refuse it. Not that he wouldn't have liked having her come home with him, but he was in no condition to make a move on a pretty woman. All he wanted was to be prone in a dark room until the pounding in his head stopped.

Maggie looked startled, but stared him straight in the eye. "If that's the only option you're going to give me, I may have to take you up on it."

Jack couldn't believe she'd called his bluff. But then, a shrewd negotiator like her probably figured he'd give in and go to the hospital rather than force a perfect stranger to sit at his bedside. *Tough luck, baby*, Jack thought.

"I'm not going to the hospital," he said curtly. "And that's final."

"Then I guess you're going to have company for the evening," she said, refusing to let go of him.

The crowd parted for a tall, square-shouldered, thick-chested man wearing Western attire. He took up a lot of space when he walked, like he expected the deference he got. As he approached, Jack cringed at the glare of sunshine off whatever silver ornament decorated the man's bolo tie.

"I'd advise against going anywhere with a stranger, Margaret," the man said.

"He isn't a stranger, Uncle Porter," Maggie replied. "And he needs my help."

"No, I don't," Jack gritted out.

"See here, young man, my name is Porter Cobb—" the man began.

Jack recognized the name of the managing partner of the firm, but cut him off. "I don't care who you are. I'm not going to the hospital." Jack realized that if he didn't get out of here pretty soon, he was going to pass out and the discussion would be over. "Excuse me, folks. I've got to go."

He tried disentangling Maggie's arm from around his waist, but she held on tight.

"Paramedics are here!" someone shouted.

Porter Cobb fixed Jack with a penetrating, hazel-eyed stare. "I believe an overnight stay in the hospital would do you good, young man."

It was not a request or a suggestion, but an

order Cobb expected to be obeyed. Jack ignored him. He looked at Maggie and said, "It isn't necessary for you—"

"Where's your car?" Maggie hissed in his ear. "Let me help you to it, and we can argue later."

That made a lot of sense to Jack. Maggie started walking him through the crowd, which parted before them.

"What's he doing on his feet?"

"Is he all right?"

"Where's he going? The paramedics are in the other direction."

Jack focused on putting one foot in front of the other. "I left my pickup near the zoo entrance," he said to Maggie.

"If I help you, can you make it to your car?" she asked, looking up at him, a worried V appearing at the top of her nose, between her eyebrows.

"Sure," Jack said. "But in case I don't, my house is a one-story white frame with green shutters on Princess Pass, right behind Trinity Baptist Church." Jack felt darkness closing in. He gave Maggie his address and tag number and told her where he'd parked his pickup. He met her gaze and said, "Just don't let them take me to the hospital."

"What have you got against hospitals?" she asked.

"People die there." Jack stumbled two steps further. "No damned hospital," he muttered.

Then he passed out.

❧ *Chapter 3* ❧

Maggie went down with Jack as he crumpled. *This is crazy*, she thought as they landed in a jumbled heap on the cool grass. *This guy belongs in the hospital.*

But he had asked her, begged her with those expressive steel-gray eyes of his, not to take him there.

In the seconds it took Maggie to make up her mind what to do, Jack's eyelids flickered and he moaned. Thank God. Lord knew she despised hospitals as much as he seemed to, but she would have taken him there. And might still, if he didn't show more signs of life.

"Jack," she said urgently from her perch atop his body. "Jack Kittrick."

"What happened?" he mumbled, his eyes still closed.

"You fainted."

"No hospital," he rasped. He grabbed at her arm, missed, grazed her breast, and ended up with a fisted handful of her bra and T-shirt.

Maggie froze. It was ludicrous to think she

could have a physical, sexual reaction to Kittrick's touch under the circumstances. He obviously had no idea what he was doing. But Maggie couldn't help taking notice of the first male hand to touch—all right, clutch—at her breasts in nearly ten years.

The problem was, she couldn't even reach up and free herself from Kittrick's grasp, because one arm was caught beneath his body at the waist, and she had used the other to keep his head from hitting the ground. She tried inching herself off of him, but his hand only closed tighter, pulling her stretchy lace bra up so far on one side that her left breast dropped out from the bottom and landed on his chest.

Maggie stared at the spot where her naked breast made contact with Jack's starched cotton shirt. Her breathing became erratic, and she felt warm all over. *The breeze must have died down,* she thought. A zephyr immediately ruffled a few strands of hair that had escaped her ponytail, and she grimaced. *All right. He's the reason I feel so warm. So what? I'm lying right on top of him. Men have always been more hot-blooded than women.*

But she was catching up fast.

Maggie took a quick glance around to see if anyone was watching this comedy of errors. They had taken a short cut across the grass to the zoo parking lot, so she supposed that to anyone passing by on the distant walkways,

she and Kittrick looked like two lovers dally-
ing in the shade of the live oak.

No one was going to come running to help
her, that was for sure. She was going to have
to get herself out of this predicament. Kittrick's hat had fallen off when he collapsed,
and she eased her hand out from under his
head. The thick, raven-black hair at his nape
was silky to the touch. She hadn't had her
hands in a man's hair, either, for ten years. Not
since the last morning she and Woody—

Maggie cut herself off. It was never a good
idea to indulge in memories. Those pathways
became dark and tangled much too quickly.

Once her hand was free, Maggie reached up
to try and pry Kittrick's fingers loose from her
T-shirt and bra.

"I won't go there," he said.

She was lying sprawled across the man in a
way that made her aware of the size of him,
of the contrast of his hardness and her softness. It felt way too good. "Jack," she said.
"You're tearing my clothes off. Let go."

"No hospital," he repeated, tightening his
grasp.

Her other breast fell free and plopped onto
his chest. He made a surprised sound in his
throat.

Maggie felt the bubble of hysterical laughter
building and tried to quash it. But the irony,
the total ridiculousness of the situation, tickled
her funny bone, and a cascade of laughter escaped.

Kittrick's eyes popped open, and their gazes met.

Jack's gray eyes appeared unfocused at first, but Maggie had to concentrate to keep from gasping at the sheer magnetism he exuded. She felt the feral danger of a man willing to fight for what he wanted—*Homo sapiens* at its most primal level and, some would say, its best. Maggie wasn't inclined to agree. She preferred a thinking man who calculated his moves, rather than a savage acting on instinct. Of course, she wouldn't object if her thinking man had a body like Jack Kittrick's.

Jack's size probably helped the overall impression of strength. He was easily six-three and had the kind of rangy body she saw on the cowboys who showed up in town each spring for Fiesta San Antonio, the celebration of the Battle of San Jacinto held at *La Villita* along the River Walk—long-legged, limber, not much more than sinew and bone.

Over the past few minutes she had gotten pretty well acquainted with Jack's broad shoulders, narrow hips, and rock-hard thighs. A woman would have to be downright picky to complain. Not that she was interested. Or cared one way or the other.

It took her a moment to realize Jack was trying to lift his head. And another moment to realize why.

She pressed herself flatter against his chest, to conceal her nipples from view. "Yes, I'm lying practically naked on top of you," she said, "and yes, it's your fault."

Jack's head fell back, and he groaned.

"Mr. Kittrick."

"What?"

"Let go."

His hand relaxed, and she pulled the T-shirt through his fingers. Which was when she realized she still had one hand caught beneath his waist and needed both hands to get back into her bra.

"Can you lift up?" she said.

His eyes opened, and one black eyebrow rose.

"My arm's caught underneath you."

He grunted and arched his back, which caused her hips to slide between his legs as she pulled her arm free. The situation had gone from awkward to impossible. Maggie pushed herself upright and realized Kittrick was *not* politely averting his eyes.

"Enjoying the view?" she demanded.

"Sure am," he replied. "All four of them look just fine to me."

A laugh escaped before she could stop it, but really, this wasn't funny. Though she was embarrassed, Maggie refused to play the flustered virgin. She stared right back into Kittrick's eyes as she reached up under the T-shirt, straightened out her elastic lace bra, and leaned over to let the weight of her breasts slip back into place.

"It's a real shame," he said.

"What?" she snapped, her nerves getting the better of her.

"That I have this godawful headache. Otherwise—"

"Otherwise we would never be in this ridiculous situation in the first place," Maggie interrupted. "I felt an obligation to you at the ballfield, Mr. Kittrick, and I'm trying to uphold it. I'll get you home, like I promised, but cut the crap."

"Crap?" he said, as though he couldn't believe such a vulgar word had come from her genteel Southern mouth.

"You heard me." For a moment Maggie's dirt-poor East Texas roots had showed. Then she was once again the professional.

"Are we clear on what is going to happen from here on out?" she said.

"Yes, ma'am, Ms. Wainwright," he said. "Just get me home. We can worry about the rest of it later."

"Rest of what?" she asked irritably.

"This thing between us."

"There is no *thing—nothing—*" she emphasized, in case he had missed the point, "between us, Mr. Kittrick."

He reached out to brush her flesh along the rip at the top of her T-shirt, and her body quivered like a plucked bowstring.

Maggie stared at him with stricken eyes. She had been so successful keeping her sexual feelings at bay over the years, she was unprepared for how quickly Jack Kittrick was able to make her respond. Maggie hissed out a breath and conceded this just wasn't her day.

This morning, when Victoria had phoned to remind her not to show up at the firm picnic looking like she came from poor white trash, something inside Maggie had snapped. She had ruined her most comfortable Levi's to make the butt-baring cut-offs, and she was going to miss the hacked-up T-shirt, which had been washed enough times to make it truly comfortable. Enough was enough.

"Get up!" she said, grabbing Jack's hand and yanking hard. "Let's get this over with."

He came up slow, but really, it wasn't fair how supple he looked, how graceful and powerful, coming off the ground.

"Here's your hat," she said, snagging it from the ground and thrusting it brim down against Jack's chest. "See if you can keep it on your head until we get you home."

"Yes, ma'am," he said.

Maggie stalked off, then realized he wasn't following her. She turned with her fists on her hips and said, her voice as perturbed as she felt, "Do you need help? What's the problem?"

"I was just admiring the view."

Maggie said something Victoria wouldn't have approved of.

Jack winced as he eased his hat down onto his head, but whether from the profanity or the pain, she wasn't sure.

"I think I can walk on my own if we take it slow and easy," he said.

Maggie realized she was staring at him, at all of him, and imagining something that she hadn't even allowed to cross her mind in years. Herself in bed with a man. In bed with Jack Kittrick.

She turned her back on him, because she was afraid he would see too much in her eyes, and said, "Come on. Let's get this over with."

Maggie could feel him behind her the whole way to the parking lot, moving with long, easy strides. Another man might have tried making conversation. He was quiet. Probably his head hurt too much for him to talk, but she could feel his eyes on her. She was aware of him in a way she hadn't been aware of a man in a long, long time.

Jack led her to a black Chevy pickup with two empty rifle racks in the back window. It wasn't a designer truck, and from the looks of the pickup bed, it had seen some hard use.

"You drive," he said, handing her his key ring. It held two keys—one for the truck and one for something else. He wasn't attached to much, Maggie decided. Probably a loner.

She had to step up to get into the driver's seat, and to her surprise, she felt Jack give her a little lift at the elbow. It was the sort of courtesy men didn't offer in these liberated days. "Thanks," she said.

"You're welcome, ma'am." He tipped his hat by touching the brim, the way cowboys did in the movies. She found the old-fashioned gesture charming. She warned herself that Kittrick probably knew the effect he was having on her, and that a smart woman would keep her mouth shut and her eyes open until she was shed of him.

"I was prepared to sacrifice my gears," he said after she was out of the park and headed down East Mulberry toward the Monte Vista neighborhood, "but I see you've had some experience with a standard shift."

"I drove a truck on my grandmother's farm in East Texas," she said. "Old Ellie Mae had a few years on her, and she could get persnickety at times, but she taught me how to drive."

"I didn't figure you for a farm girl, Ms. Wainwright. Especially not one who gets sentimental over a truck."

"I was speaking of my grandmother," she said, straight-faced.

His jaw dropped.

She laughed. "Gotcha."

His lips curved, and he chuckled. "I take it your grandmother and the truck were equally durable."

"Gram lived a good, long life. I miss her." Maggie refused to acknowledge the rush of nostalgia she felt for the days when it had been just her and Gram on the farm at Ash Hollow. She hadn't understood what being poor meant then. She had loved running barefoot all day in the soft red dirt that bordered the piney woods. It wasn't until much later that she realized nobody ran barefoot unless they couldn't afford shoes.

"My grandparents were gone before I got old enough to really know them," Jack said.

"Too bad," Maggie said. "I wouldn't have missed being raised by Gram for anything."

"What happened to your parents?"

Maggie hesitated, then said, "They died." It wasn't really a lie. They might very well be dead by now. According to Gram, her father had run off when he found out her mother was pregnant, and her mother had been a bare nine months behind him. Maggie-girl was a gift, Gram had always said, a precious treasure her mother had left for Gram to discover. Gram had taught her to believe all children were treasures. But she had not. . . . A chill ran down Maggie's spine.

"How did we get on such a maudlin subject?" she asked brusquely.

"You were avoiding the attraction between us," Jack said.

Maggie turned to stare at him and nearly rear-ended a car that had stopped abruptly at a yellow light. "You don't give up, do you?"

"Not when I see something I want," Jack said. "I was disappointed when I found out you're a Wainwright, but the more I get to know you, Maggie, the more certain I am you're not one of them."

"One of them?"

"You know, stuffy rich folks, full of themselves, hoity-toity."

She laughed. "Hoity-toity? I don't think I've

seen that word outside a book. What does it mean?"

"My mother used it to describe people who act like they're better than other people."

"And I'm not 'hoity-toity?' "

He grinned. "Nope."

"I don't date," Maggie said flatly.

"I'm not much for dating myself. I think we're beyond that anyway, don't you?"

"Once I drop you off, we aren't going to be seeing each other except across a conference table," Maggie said firmly.

"Dr. Hollander said I shouldn't be alone. I have a concussion, remember? I could go into a coma and need medical attention."

Maggie made a disgusted sound. She knew Kittrick was manipulating her, that if he had thought he was really in any kind of danger he would have gone to the hospital on his own. But maybe not. She'd seen guys like Jack before, grown men who'd rather die than cross the threshold of a hospital as a patient.

"Don't you have someone who could stay with you besides me?" she asked. "A neighbor? A friend? A co-worker?"

He shook his head. "I don't know my neighbors, and I travel so much in my work I don't have time for friends. You're the one I'm going to be working with. How about you?"

"Surely there's some woman—"

"I'm not involved with anyone right now."

"Oh."

"You're all I've got, Maggie."

"You don't *have* me, Mr. Kittrick," she protested.

"Call me Jack," he said with a smile. "I figure after spending the night together, you and me are going to be pretty good friends."

Maggie concentrated on the page in front of her, but the words kept blurring. She heard something, a strange sound, and froze. *Somebody . . . or something . . . was at the back door of Jack's house.* Her heart beat a heavy tattoo. Slowly, silently, she uncurled her legs from the padded wooden rocking chair and set her sock-covered feet flat on the hardwood floor so she could run if she had to.

She headed to the kitchen, flipped on the back porch light, and peered out one of the glass panes in the top half of the back door. She saw a wooden handicapped ramp beside the stairs and a half-empty bowl of cat or dog food. So Jack had a pet. Or at least, an animal he fed. Maggie wondered if the animal was what she'd just heard.

Maggie listened, but except for the hum of the refrigerator, she heard nothing. Jack's small, wood-frame house was a far cry from the high-rise condominium she had lived in for the past three years, where she could always hear someone beyond the walls and floor and ceiling. Here everything was so *quiet*.

So maybe there wasn't a man-eating dog at the back door. That's what she got for reading

Stephen King in a shadowy room in the middle of the night.

Maggie rubbed her eyes and wandered back into the living room. As she settled into the rocker again, she glanced at the Cinderella watch Woody had bought her as a present their first Christmas together, when they were both still in college. She had been the poor but beautiful dreamer, Cinderella, and he had been the handsome prince who would take her away from her difficult life to live in his castle.

It hadn't turned out quite that way. When she and Woody had eloped during their last semester of college, his parents had cut off their son without a penny. Maggie hadn't cared. She didn't miss what she'd never had.

Woody had been determined to strike it rich on his own, to prove to his parents he could manage without their money. Maggie had been equally determined to become the best, the most well-known and well-respected lawyer in the state. But they could only afford for one of them to go to law school.

It had seemed more important that Woody make a living for them than for her to fulfill some childish dream of being so successful that her long-lost parents would be sorry they had abandoned her and come looking for her. Besides, her need—her lifelong secret wish—to prove she was someone worth knowing wasn't fair to Gram, who had been the best mother any child could have.

Maggie's resentment over being left behind

as Woody's career took off had built so gradually, had sneaked up on her so stealthily, that Maggie wasn't even aware of it. Until one day it exploded . . . with devastating consequences.

Oh God, Maggie. You fool. You fool. You should have been grateful for what you had!

Maggie closed her eyes. A moment later she opened them again and was back in the present. It was a trick she had learned to stave off the dark memories that always lay in wait, ready to consume her.

Maggie traced Cinderella's gloved hands. 1:58 A.M. Time to wake Jack again, as she had at intervals over the past twelve hours. She rose from the rocking chair in his living room and padded carefully in her stockinged feet along the slippery, polished hardwood floor to his bedroom. She was wearing one of Jack's chambray shirts over her T-shirt and shorts to keep off the evening chill, since she hadn't wanted to leave Jack alone long enough to go home and get what she needed to spend the night.

She had cleared a path for herself from his living room to his bedroom through the clutter of single male paraphernalia. You could supposedly tell a lot about a person by what they surrounded themselves with, but so far all Maggie saw was a mass of contradictions.

The saddle leather couch would have been an easy guess, but she had been surprised by the home-made wooden rocker. She had been drawn to it from the first moment she laid eyes on it.

"My father made it," he said. But he didn't offer any more information, just made sure she knew where the kitchen and bathroom were and retired to his bedroom.

His place was neater than she'd expected, but plenty dusty. Jack obviously read books, but just as obviously got distracted easily, because he had a lot of them scattered around the living room, all of which seemed to have places marked. By now she could find her way around his place in the dark, but he'd insisted she leave the hall light on so she wouldn't run into something.

Maggie eased Jack's bedroom door open and let the light from the hall spill inside. The bedroom had been a surprise, too, since it was filled with more hand-made oak furniture like the rocker. Maggie wondered if Jack always slept as restlessly as he had for the past twelve hours. He had stripped down to a pair of gray sweatpants, and tangled up half naked in the plain white sheet, one pillow tucked under his head and the other at his feet, he looked both imposing and approachable.

As Maggie watched, she realized the noise she had heard before, the one that had scared her, had been Jack, muttering in his sleep. She crossed to the bed and carefully sat down beside him.

"Shh. It's all right, Jack. You're home. Nobody's going to take you to the hospital." She didn't resist the urge to brush the damp black curls from his forehead or to soothe the racing pulse at his throat with her thumb. "Everything's going to be all right," she crooned.

"Don't shoot," he said.

At first, Maggie thought she'd misunderstood him. Nobody at the picnic had threatened to shoot Jack or anybody else.

"I'll put down my gun. Just don't shoot," Jack muttered.

When he cried out in agony, Maggie jerked her hand away and leapt to her feet, staring at Jack as though she'd just discovered she'd been caressing Stephen King's man-eating dog.

When he began muttering again, she leaned down and heard him whisper, "Jesus. She killed the kid. I made her kill the kid."

Alarmed, Maggie shook him hard. "Jack! Wake up! Wake up!"

Jack sat bolt upright, chest heaving, eyes wild. "What the hell are you doing in here?"

"You were having a nightmare," Maggie said.

"I wish the hell it were!"

Her eyes went wide with horror.

He saw the look on her face and snarled, "Get the hell out of here! Get out! Leave me alone!"

Maggie backed away, then turned and ran.

❧ *Chapter 4* ❧

Jack stayed where he was until he could get the trembling under control. When he tried to stand, his knees threatened to buckle, and he slumped back down on the edge of the bed.

"Maggie!" he yelled at the top of his lungs. Too late he realized his headache wasn't gone yet. He heard the ringer clang as the phone hit the floor in the living room, along with several books. "Don't leave," he called out. "I can explain."

"Don't bother," she shouted back at him.

Jack lurched off the bed, moving faster than his head would allow. "Maggie, I'm going to pass out and hit my head on the floor if you make me run after you."

She reappeared in his bedroom doorway, without his chambray shirt and wearing her shoes, bringing him up short. "If you're well enough to start yelling at me, you're well enough to take care of yourself. I promise to forget all this ever happened when I see you on Monday."

"How are you getting home?" he asked, figuring she'd forgotten she had no car of her own.

"I called a cab," she said. "I'll wait for it outside."

That meant she didn't have anyone—another man or a girlfriend or a relative—she felt comfortable rousing in the middle of the night, Jack thought as he followed her to the front door. She was alone. Like him.

That didn't necessarily make her vulnerable, Jack realized. In fact, so far she'd handled everything he'd thrown at her like a trooper. Which made sense, he supposed, if there wasn't anyone around for her to lean on. Jack was ready and willing to offer a comforting shoulder, if only he could get her to use it. "I promise not to yell at you again," he said. "Please stay."

She hesitated with her hand on the front doorknob, her back to him. "You'll be fine," she said. "It's better if I go."

He padded on bare feet the short distance that separated them and put his hands on her hips from behind. He slid them up her body to her waist, then under her T-shirt. His thumbs caressed the center of her spine, while his fingertips eased up her bare midriff, settling along the elastic edge of her bra. If he moved his hands an inch or so higher, he would be cupping her breasts in his palms.

Sexual tension arced between them. The intensity of the feeling surprised him, and he wondered if she felt it, too. "Maggie," he whispered. He brushed his lips against her nape to one side of her ponytail. "Maggie."

It was a plea. And a promise.

She made a keening sound in her throat, a yearning sound, a desolate sound, and manacled his wrists with her hands. "No, Jack. I can't."

"Can't?" He kissed his way across her shoulder, then up her throat to the shell of her ear. He caught the lobe in his teeth and nibbled gently. He could feel her trembling. He squeezed his eyes closed, fighting the headache that throbbed at the base of his skull. *Not now. Not now*, he pleaded.

She let go of his wrists to cover his hands as they closed over her breasts. "Jack."

Jack heard longing. And regret. He understood one, but not the other. Maggie would have nothing to be sorry for. He would make sure of that. He turned her slowly in his arms and captured her body between his own and the door, settling himself in the cradle of her thighs, reaching behind her bare upper thighs and inching her legs apart. He was hard, and her soft flesh yielded to his.

"You feel good, Maggie," he murmured against her throat.

She smelled of strawberries and woman, and he wanted to taste them both. He wanted to stake his claim, to put himself inside her hard and deep.

And they hadn't even kissed yet.

Jack thought about what her lips would taste like, how soft and supple they would be, how wet and hot her mouth would be once he was inside it. He kissed the left side of her lips, then the right, to let her know what he intended, to let her know what was coming.

"No."

It wasn't a murmur or a sigh or a groan. Any of those Jack would have taken for reluctance, but they wouldn't have slowed him down. Maggie had said no with serious conviction. Jack lifted his head and looked into her face.

In the shadows created by the old-fashioned standing lamp beside the rocker, Jack saw panic in her eyes—and the remnants of desire. Her jaw was rigid, as though her teeth were clenched, and the trembling he had thought was the result of sexual excitement, he now saw was something else entirely.

"You're not afraid of me, are you, Maggie?"

"Of course not!"

"What is it, then?" he asked, confused, wanting to understand.

"This isn't going to happen," she gritted out. "I refuse to let it happen."

More evidence—verbal this time—that she wanted him, but had no intention of indulging herself.

"No slumming, is that it, Maggie?"

"Who you are has nothing to do with this!" she retorted. "I'm not like Victoria Wainwright. I don't choose my friends for their blue blood or the size of their bank balances. No matter who you are, I have the right to say no, Jack."

"Your body isn't saying no," he accused, staring at her erect nipples beneath the thin cotton T-shirt.

She closed her eyes, bit her lip, then opened her eyes again. The turmoil was gone, and with it, he suspected, a great deal of her susceptibility to his lovemaking. What he saw now was determination—a squared jaw and a militant stance and defiant eyes.

"I didn't say I didn't want you," she explained matter-of-factly. "I would be a fool to try and deny my physical response to you. What I said was that I don't want this to happen. I don't want to get involved with you or any other man."

"Why not?"

"That's none of your business."

Jack stared at her. Maybe he had rushed things a little. All right, maybe he had rushed things a lot. Maybe she needed a little time to get used to the idea of the two of them. He could wait. He knew where to find her. Now that he knew Maggie Wainwright's wealth and social status weren't an issue, he wasn't going to let a little thing like her unwillingness to get involved stand in his way. Hell, he didn't want to get *involved*, either.

"All right, Maggie," he said. "I can slow this down if you want."

"I don't want it slowed down," she said in

a sharp voice. "I want it stopped."

"For now," he said, reluctantly easing his hips away from hers.

"For good!" Her fisted hands pressed against his chest.

He backed up and let her go. "What's got you so spooked?"

"For one thing, I hardly know you," she said. "That wasn't a dream you were having, was it, Jack? It really happened, didn't it?"

Jack felt a stab of unease. "What is it you want to know, Maggie?"

"Nothing. I just want to leave."

"Will you let me explain?"

Her body rigid, her back to the door, she met his gaze. "Can you? I don't know many hospital insurance investigators who carry guns and get shot at, Jack."

She had him there. Jack thought about making up a story but realized he didn't want to. He planned to be spending a great deal of time with Ms. Wainwright, and he didn't see how he could hide the truth from her for very long if she spent as much time as he hoped she would in his bed.

The main object working undercover was to keep the bad guys from finding out who you were while you found out everything you could about them. As far as Jack could see, telling Maggie his secret wasn't going to compromise his situation. The captain might have a fit, but what the hell.

"I'm not an insurance investigator, Maggie. I'm a Texas Ranger."

Most people were impressed when they found out what Jack did for a living. A select few were chosen from the ranks of the Texas Department of Public Safety to become Texas Rangers, and the elite force was small—no more than 106 Rangers to cover the entire state. A certain mystique had grown around the Rangers over the century and more they had been catching outlaws, and Jack was proud to be a part of that history. So Maggie's reaction to his revelation was a disappointment.

Her eyes narrowed, her face got stony, and she asked, "What were you doing at the Wainwright & Cobb picnic, Jack? What is it you're investigating that you have to work undercover?"

She sounded like a lawyer. Which, of course, she was. "Look, Maggie, I don't see why we have to get into that right now."

"Why not? You brought it up. I think I have a right to know whether I'm the object of some sort of investigation. If that's why you dragged me over here tonight—"

"Whoa! Whoa!" he said. "Rein in those horses, counselor. If I'm not mistaken, you volunteered to see me home. Nobody held a gun to your head. And for the record, I don't usually make a habit of inviting suspects home with me." He paused. What had Maggie Wainwright done that she thought might be worth a Texas Ranger investigating?

About the time Jack started searching Maggie's gaze to see what she was hiding, she lowered her lids.

"Secrets, Maggie?" he murmured.

"None that would interest you," she said, staring at her knotted hands.

Jack felt queasy. What had he just done? It was a little late to close the barn doors now. He might as well finish what he'd started. "I'm posing as an insurance investigator so I can ask questions at the hospital about a suspected murderer."

"Who?"

She still wasn't looking at him, which worried Jack. "Roman Hollander," he said.

Her chin shot up, and her eyes opened wide. "Roman?" She gave a startled laugh. "A murderer? You must be joking! I've never known a more gentle, caring man. He's a doctor, for heaven's sake!"

Jack was surprised at her strong reaction. "You're well acquainted with Hollander, I presume."

"I know his wife, Lisa, very well. She works with me at Wainwright & Cobb. We met when she clerked for the law firm I worked for in Houston, and I put in a good word for her when she came looking for a job in San Antonio. I'm her mentor, if such things exist between women professionals. I've been to their house for dinner. I attended their daughter Amy's third birthday party last week."

Maggie shook her head. "Roman, a murderer? I don't believe it. Who is he supposed to have killed?"

"Laurel Morgan, an eight-year-old accident victim with head trauma that he operated on a year ago," Jack said. "Somebody injected an overdose of potassium chloride into the kid's IV, causing her heart to stop. If her parents hadn't made a stink, it would have gone on the books as a case of heart failure following surgery."

She frowned. "Why would Roman save the child on the operating table if he planned to kill her later?"

"I give up. Why?"

Maggie snorted and crossed her arms. "There is no why, because Roman didn't kill that child."

"We think he did," Jack said, leaning his palm on the wall beside her. It had the effect of hemming her in, but he did it because he was starting to get dizzy.

"My turn to ask why," Maggie said, edging past him and crossing to pick up a book from the floor and set it on the coffee table.

Jack turned to face her, leaning back against the door to stay on his feet. "The way the Morgan child died last April—heart failure in the ICU after a serious accident and surgery—doesn't look suspicious until you realize that an insurance investigator for MEDCO, the corporation that owns San Antonio General and a dozen other hospitals in Texas, discovered that at least five other children have died the same way over the past seven years in Houston and Dallas. We're not sure yet how many other victims there might be in hospitals around the state." Jack headed for the sofa as he said, "We're still investigating."

Maggie put the rocker between them and asked, "Roman is a suspect in all those deaths?"

"All of the children who died were his patients," Jack said, easing down onto the sofa. "And we haven't found any other common links."

"Lots of people have access to the ICU."

Jack laid his head carefully against the back of the couch and rubbed at his blurry eyes. "Maybe so. But I'm putting my money on Hollander."

"What's his motive?" Maggie demanded.

"Hollander's written a bunch of journal articles suggesting he considers quality of life more important than mere survival."

Maggie snorted. "I feel the same way. Does that make me capable of murder?"

"Under the right circumstances, anyone's capable of murder."

Maggie stared at him, her eyes stark, her hands gripping the back of the rocker so hard her knuckles turned white.

The lawman in Jack saw guilt, and he fleetingly wondered whether he was making a mistake telling her so much. The man who was attracted to Maggie saw distress and concern. That man kept right on talking.

"All of the children who died would have faced some serious physical or mental handicap if they had survived," he said. "We figure Hollander did his best to fix them up, but when he couldn't, he killed them out of kindness."

"What *evidence* do you have that he did it?" Maggie demanded.

"You sound like Hollander's attorney!" Jack bolted upright, then froze, waiting for the dark to recede and things to come into focus again before he eased himself back down onto the arm of the couch. "Are you going to represent Hollander if I arrest him?"

"I don't do criminal work," she said. "But I'm certain you have the wrong man, Jack."

"Maybe Hollander doesn't want his failures hanging around to remind him he's not God."

"That's preposterous!" Maggie started pacing between Jack's stone fireplace—useful in South Texas maybe two or three weeks a year—and the rocker. "Anybody, even someone off the street, could be giving those kids an overdose of potassium chloride, and you'd never know who it was unless you had a video camera in the ICU."

Jack tried to wrinkle his brow in a frown, realized that was a bad idea and, keeping his head as still as he could, said, "You seem to know a hell of a lot about it."

"I overheard the nurses talking about the perfect way to kill a patient without getting caught," she said, her lips twisting wryly. "Murder 101. Insulin came up, but they all agreed potassium chloride was a better killing agent."

"Explain."

"Potassium chloride—the nurses called it KCl—is readily available around a hospital because every patient on an IV for more than twelve hours needs potassium to replace what they've lost. It's not a controlled substance, so it isn't locked up. A little too much potassium in an IV, and wham—" She slammed her hand on the coffee table. "You're dead of an apparent heart attack, and no one's the wiser."

Jack winced. "That's for damn sure." He rubbed his throbbing temples. "Unless you're looking for an overdose, and sometimes even if you are, it doesn't show up in an autopsy."

"It doesn't?" Maggie asked, settling on the edge of the wooden coffee table far enough away that he couldn't reach out and touch her. "The nurses didn't mention that."

"The way it was explained to me, the heart stops beating so quickly the potassium chloride never reaches the ocular fluid, which is where a forensic pathologist checks for poison," Jack said. "And because red blood cells create potassium when they break down after death, it's hard *not* to find massive amounts of it in your system. When you're embalmed, the evidence of the crime drains away with your blood."

"So how did you discover the Morgan child

died of an overdose?" Maggie asked.

Jack smiled ruefully. "MEDCO was looking for a way they could avoid malpractice liability, so the investigator asked the medical examiner to look for some cause of death other than negligence by the doctor, like foul play. The hospital sent Laurel Morgan's body for an autopsy with all the IVs intact, and the medical examiner discovered enough excess potassium chloride in the tubing to verify an overdose."

"Couldn't a nurse simply have made a mistake? Given an accidental second dose?"

"Of course," Jack said. "But that wouldn't have gotten MEDCO off the malpractice hook. The investigator did a computer search for similar deaths and found five of them, all with the same primary care physician. Assuming Hollander was committing murder rather than malpractice, and assuming MEDCO had no reason to suspect him of such nefarious activities before they hired him, they were home free. Because it's an interjurisdictional matter, MEDCO called on the Texas Rangers to investigate further."

Maggie knew most of MEDCO's business, but this had escaped her because it was a criminal matter, and the firm did no criminal work. She was appalled at what she'd just heard. "You mean Roman became a murder suspect because MEDCO didn't want to pay a malpractice claim against him?"

"That's about the size of it."

She rose and paced away from him. "That's absurd!"

"Somebody's killing kids, Maggie," Jack said seriously. "All the victims were less than ten years old. A couple were only babies."

Maggie sank into Jack's rocker. "Oh, God. It can't be Roman. He has a little girl of his own. He could never—"

"Hollander may turn out to be innocent," Jack interrupted. "But right now he's my number one suspect, and I need the complete co-operation of the nurses and the staff when I'm asking questions about him. That's why I'm posing as an insurance investigator looking for evidence to defend Hollander against the Morgan malpractice suit. If everybody I interrogate thinks they're helping the doctor by giving me information, I'll get more of the truth out of them."

"Are you sure you're looking for the truth?" Maggie said. "It sounds to me like you've already got Roman tried and convicted."

A horn blared in the quiet.

"That's my cab," Maggie said, rising and heading for the door.

Jack stepped in front of her before she could get there but was careful not to touch her. "Are you going to blow my cover?"

"Roman is my friend. He has the right to know he's a suspect."

"All I want to do is ask a few questions, Maggie. If the doctor's innocent, no harm done. If he's not . . ."

"You don't play fair, Jack."

"I'm not playing at all. Someone on staff may be a murderer, Maggie. I intend to find out who it is, so I can stop him. Are you going to help me?"

"I'll have to think about it," Maggie said. She stared into his eyes, the message clear: *Stand aside, Jack.*

He took a step to the left.

"I'll see you Monday," she said as she walked past him, shoulders back, chin high. She pulled the door open, then turned to look at him. "Oh, and Jack . . ."

"What?"

"Don't go to sleep tonight. You might not wake up."

❧ Chapter 5 ❧

Maggie was chagrined that for the second time in two weeks she was running late. This time, she was tardy for SAG's Monday morning Bioethics Committee meeting, where she acted as counsel for the hospital. That was a problem because the chair, Roman Hollander, was never late. The meeting always started on time and latecomers had to catch up as best they could. Maggie had never like playing catch-up.

She bypassed the crowd at the elevator and headed up the stairs to the second-floor conference room. She was wearing a black double-breasted Nieman Marcus knit with gold buttons and a tuxedo-fronted white silk blouse. If she had to confront Jack Kittrick sometime during the day, and she did, she wanted all the armor and ammunition she could muster.

Maggie had spent the rest of the endless night after she left Jack's house trying to decide whether to keep his secret or tell Roman what was going on. She had tossed and turned, plagued by vivid memories of the Texas Ranger's potent kisses. She had spent a groggy day Sunday doing housework and laundry and thinking unaccountably—and constantly—about having sex with Jack Kittrick.

When her alarm had gone off at 6 A.M. this morning, she was still suffering heart palpitations from an incredibly vivid dream, but she was too keyed up to linger in bed. She had climbed into her jogging shorts and shoes for her usual five-mile run, determined to sweat Jack Kittrick out of her system.

Maggie was halfway out the door when she had turned back around, grabbed the kitchen phone, hit the button for a frequently dialed number, and waited for the call to be answered.

"Jack Kittrick is a Texas Ranger," she blurted. "He's looking for somebody killing kids in the ICU with potassium chloride."

She listened impatiently, rubbing at her bloodshot eyes. "Easy for you to say. He wants me to help him with his investigation."

She frowned and shook her head. "I suppose it makes sense to help him. At least that way I'll know everything he knows."

Maggie hung up the phone and headed out the door for her run. But the conversation had left a bad taste in her mouth. She hated the secrets, all the sneaking around. To make matters worse, Jack Kittrick struck her as the kind who always got his man . . . or woman . . .

Maggie had run out of time after she'd showered to dry her hair completely. She'd put it up in a French twist and pulled a few wisps free, but it felt heavy on her head. She had just stepped through the stairwell door onto the second floor of the hospital—a little breathless because she'd decided to haul up her skirt and take the stairs two at a time—when a voice stopped her.

"You're a disgrace."

Maggie had learned to expect the insult every time her mother-in-law—*former* mother-in-law—addressed her, but it didn't make it any easier to take. She pulled down the skirt that was hiked halfway to her hips, turned, and faced her nemesis. "Good morning, Victoria."

Maggie struggled mightily, and frequently failed, to achieve the "old money" look Victoria seemed to manage effortlessly. Of course, Victoria cheated. She really was "old money." Victoria Cobb Wainwright had been rich and privileged from the day she was born.

Despite Maggie's personal feelings about the woman, she couldn't help admiring Victoria's perfect, blond coiffure, short and off her forehead, the pearl studs in her ears, the soft rose Chanel suit bearing a simple pearl and diamond bow-shaped Cartier pin, the dyed leather heels from Italy, and the matching clutch purse caught beneath her elbow. Victoria didn't have a wrinkle anywhere—not even on her face.

"I'm in a hurry, Victoria. The meeting's about to start," Maggie said.

"I know. I've agreed to serve another term on the committee myself."

Maggie managed not to sigh. Victoria sat on the SAG Bioethics Committee as a concerned citizen—and a major contributor to the hospital's expansion fund. The Wainwright Trauma Center, devoted to neurological patients, had been named after her husband, Richard Woodson Wainwright, who had died of a stroke two days after his only son's death.

Sometimes Maggie felt sorry for Victoria, losing both her husband and her son in so short a time, and ashamed that she'd done nothing to help ease her mother-in-law's grief. But the truth was, Maggie had been too devastated to deal with her own grief, much less someone else's. They had been no comfort to each other then. And they were a thorn in each other's sides now.

Victoria glanced at her diamond-studded Piaget and said, "Since the meeting has already started without us, I want a word with you before we go in."

"Make it quick," Maggie said, glancing just as obviously at Cinderella's gloved hands, working to keep the irritation out of her voice.

"Was it really necessary for you to expose yourself that way at the picnic, Margaret?"

"I don't know what you're talking about," Maggie said.

"I am talking about the 'Daisy Dukes,'" Victoria said, her voice dripping with disdain.

"I don't see what's wrong with wearing a pair of cut-offs to a picnic," Maggie protested.

Victoria pressed her lips flat rather than argue, and Maggie was left to accept the censure or continue a dispute she had no chance of winning. The situation was especially galling because she had known the cut-offs were over the edge.

"I also heard you left the picnic with a strange man," Victoria said. "Is that true?"

Maggie knew explanations were useless, but she made them anyway. "I left the picnic with a man, but he wasn't a stranger. Jack Kittrick is an insurance investigator for the hospital. I accidentally hit him in the head with a baseball, and I escorted him home to make sure he arrived there safely."

"I advise you not to do it again," Victoria said. "So long as you bear the Wainwright name, you owe a responsibility to this family."

"I know exactly what I owe this family," Maggie said in clipped tones. Ten years ago, in the throes of unbearable grief, Maggie had made a confession to Victoria that—with the help of her brother—she had used to keep Maggie from abandoning the Wainwright family. It was something neither of them would ever forget, something Victoria could never forgive.

Tension simmered between them, while Maggie braced herself for the next attack. "Is that all, Victoria?"

"Are you attending the Cancer Society Gala on Friday?"

"I have tickets." Because Victoria was hostess for the fundraising event, Uncle Porter had bought a table for ten and given two tickets to Maggie and the rest to associates at the firm.

"Do you have an escort?" Victoria asked.

Maggie knew from experience that Victoria had stringent ideas about what was and was not socially correct at a charity function. One did not arrive at an event like the Cancer Society Gala alone. One came as half of a couple, and one's partner had better be someone socially prominent. If Maggie didn't speak up, she was going to find herself saddled with some scion of a noble Texas house who would bore her to death before they had gotten through the shrimp cocktail.

"I've invited Mr. Kittrick to come with me," she said. Surely the Texas Ranger had a tux. And she already knew he wasn't likely to be out with friends or have a date on Saturday.

Victoria's brows lowered in disapproval, but not enough to wrinkle her forehead. And she didn't come right out and say an insurance investigator wasn't blue-blooded enough to suit her, so Maggie considered her escort approved.

She stared into Victoria's pale blue eyes, wondering what went on behind them. The

woman puzzled Maggie. She should have
wanted Maggie to stay as far away from her
as possible, yet Victoria seemed to thrive on
their confrontations. Could anyone really be as
self-controlled, as self-disciplined as Victoria
was? Maggie had never seen a hair out of
place, never seen her mother-in-law flustered
or frantic—not even during that bitter, wintry
week in Minnesota when first her son, and
then her husband, had died.

Nor had Maggie ever met anyone as coldly
calculating as Victoria. Mother Wainwright
had done her best from the start to separate
"that conniving female" and her only son. Until the day Woody died, the two women had
done battle over him. Maggie had won his
heart. Victoria had claimed his soul.

They could never be friends, and Maggie refused to expend the energy it would take to
deal with Victoria as an enemy. It was easier
to allow herself to be bullied on occasion. She
didn't mind giving Victoria her way to keep
the peace. Especially since moving away from
San Antonio was out of the question—for the
moment.

"Shall we go in?" Victoria said.

"After you," Maggie replied.

Maggie watched Victoria through the door,
but before she could follow, felt a tap on her
shoulder. She turned and found Jack Kittrick
standing right behind her.

Her heart speeded up to a trot. So much for
armor. Her power suit wasn't working worth
a damn. She felt as pliable as Silly Putty, as

gooey inside as a bowl of her grandmother's cornmeal mush and black-eyed peas.

Jack was close enough that she got a whiff of his cologne, a spicy smell that made her think of pine trees and mountains. Texas Rangers didn't wear uniforms, but unless they had on a Western-cut suit—and she was beginning to wonder if Jack owned one—they stuck to buff or dark brown Wranglers, a white shirt, tie, light-colored Western hat, and cowboy boots.

Jack was wearing denim Levi's, and he had skipped the tie and put on a fringed calfskin vest. He wasn't dressed as a Ranger, but he didn't look like any insurance investigator she'd ever met, either. On the other hand, in Texas, where individuality was admired and freedom insisted upon, Western attire was always proper.

"How long have you been standing there?" she asked.

"Long enough to know I'm your date for the gala," he said with a grin that crinkled his eyes at the corners and showed off the creases on either side of his mouth. "Will there be dancing?"

"Victoria insists on an orchestra," she said, "but I don't usually dance."

"Don't know how? Or haven't had the right partner?" Jack asked.

"Of course I know—Maybe it would be better if I tell Victoria your plans changed, and you couldn't make it." Maggie was distressed at the way the teasing laughter in his eyes tied her up in knots, like a homemade grass rope on a cold, wet morning. She stared at him, tongue-tied for maybe the first time in her life.

"Dancing. Saturday. I know a good opportunity to hold you in my arms when I see it."

"Mr. Kittrick—"

"Jack," he said. "We'd better get moving, Maggie. We're late for the meeting."

"You aren't invited, Jack."

"I had a talk with your hospital administrator, Mr. Delgado, and I have the run of the place until my investigation is complete. Shall we?" he said, gesturing toward the conference room door.

Maggie turned her back on him and stalked off, then waited at the door and motioned for him to go in first. As he sauntered past, he shot her a suggestive, lopsided grin that made her insides clench.

Maggie stood frozen beside the doorway. When it came to matters of the heart, she set the rules herself. No dating. No involvement, because involvement led to commitment. She had proved ten years ago that she wasn't capable of committing for the long haul. Three strikes and you were out. Maggie had retired to the dugout, but Kittrick kept dragging her back onto the field, demanding she play.

And God, she wanted to play.

Maybe it was some mid-life crisis thing. She had turned thirty-five last month and been forced to acknowledge her life was nearly half over. Maybe she wanted one last, desperately romantic fling before she hit middle age.

That must be it. She missed the romance. Hell. She missed the sex.

Maggie pursed her lips. What was wrong with that? It meant she was normal. If only she hadn't ended up sprawled on top of Jack on Saturday. If only he hadn't given her that toe-curling, early morning kiss. If only he hadn't pressed his body against hers at the door and let her feel the irrefutable evidence of his desire.

Maggie sighed inwardly. She was going to have to make some sort of decision about Jack Kittrick. But not right now. Right now she had business to attend to.

Maggie hadn't realized how long she'd hesitated at the door. The minutes of the previous meeting had already been read and approved by the time she took her place at the foot of a large, rectangular conference table. She set her black leather briefcase on the polished surface in front of her and opened it to retrieve a yellow legal pad and the silver Tiffany pen that had been her law school graduation gift from Uncle Porter. He had made her dream of becoming a lawyer come true, but his generosity hadn't come without strings. She was paying him back every penny . . . with interest.

Jack took a chair in the corner and winked when he caught her peeking at him. She was appalled at the way her body tightened inside.

She averted her eyes, focusing on the pad in front of her. She doodled a daisy, something she used to do in college when she was day-dreaming about the future. She clutched the pen, took a deep breath, and concentrated on what was being said.

Once odds and ends of business had been dealt with, Roman introduced visitors to the meeting, including Jack.

Then they went to work.

Whenever a serious ethical dispute arose over treatment of a patient, the SAG Bioethics Committee, composed of doctors, nurses, social workers, and interested members of the community like Victoria, listened to the facts given by the doctor, the family, and whatever legal counsel might attend on behalf of the family, and came up with a nonbinding recommendation for action. The committee served as an arbiter of community feeling about medical procedures and hospital policy and helped to keep the hospital functioning within acceptable ethical parameters.

This morning Joe Ray Belton and his mother sat near the head of the conference table, waiting for the committee's recommendation on whether Joe Ray's father, Sam, should be removed from life support.

"Eighty-three-year-old Sam Belton suffered a heart attack at home and was put on life support in the emergency room at the hospital," Roman began, stating the facts of the case. "Unfortunately, Mr. Belton suffered a stroke later that same day and slipped into a coma. Tests revealed the patient has no brain activity, and I recommended life support be discontinued. Mrs. Belton agreed."

It should have been a simple matter to turn off the machines at that point, except Joe Ray Belton had objected.

Normally, this sort of decision never got as far as the bioethics committee. Texas law was pretty definite on the subject of unplugging folks who could be sustained on life support. The wishes of the patient were followed, or if those wishes weren't known, the doctor and the family made the decision at bedside.

Only, sometimes the doctor and the family didn't agree what should be done. Or, as in this case, the doctor and one family member agreed, while another family member didn't. Those cases were presented to the hospital bioethics committee for discussion and a nonbinding disposition that usually helped families come to some agreement.

"I can understand Joe Ray's concern for his father," Roman said. "But I concur with Mrs. Belton in this matter. Machines are keeping Sam Belton's body alive. The rest of him, the thought processes that made him who he was, are already dead. It's time to let him go."

Maggie watched Joe Ray's face as Dr. Hollander put the weight of his medical opinion on the side of Joe Ray's mother in the decision to unplug his father. The forty-seven-year-old plumber's mouth twisted in an agonized grimace. His eyes looked tortured, as though his own life were at stake.

Maggie looked away to avoid his pain.

"Maybe he'll get better," Joe Ray pleaded. "Maybe—"

"I'm very sorry," Dr. Hollander said with authoritative finality. "Your father is legally dead, Mr. Belton. The machines keeping him alive are needed for other patients who can survive only with their help."

Joe Ray made a sound in his throat like a wounded animal. It was obvious he didn't want to let go, and just as obvious he wasn't being given much of a choice.

Maggie's job at the meeting was to make clear what legal options were available to the doctors and the hospital and to avoid legal pitfalls where they threatened. No legal issues were involved here, only the moral and ethical . . . and human ones.

The committee didn't take long to make its recommendation.

"So we're all agreed," Dr. Hollander said. "Life support should be discontinued."

Joe Ray hissed out a long, rattling breath that sounded a lot like a dying man. "All right," he said. "I give up."

"It's all right, Joey," Mrs. Belton said. "He's with God already."

Joe Ray rose slowly, tears visible on his cheeks, and helped his mother from her chair. They left the meeting clinging to one another.

"I'll arrange for Joe Ray to have some time

with his father before we turn off life support," Roman said.

Heads nodded and voices murmured assent for the doctor's compassion.

Maggie shot a sideways glance at Jack. Surely Roman's consideration for Joe Ray Belton had convinced him the doctor was no murderer.

"Since there's nothing else for us to consider today," Roman said, interrupting her musing, "this meeting is adjourned."

As the committee members dispersed, Maggie was surprised to see Jack approach Roman—his prime suspect—directly.

"Doctor, may I have a word with you?"

Maggie eavesdropped without feeling the least bit guilty. She had a stake in making sure Jack didn't arrest the wrong man.

"I'd like to ask you a few questions about the death of Laurel Morgan," Jack said.

Maggie's jaw dropped. She closed her mouth and ogled the Texas Ranger. If Jack was just going to come right out and ask like that, why was it necessary to hide his identity?

Jack identified himself as an insurance investigator for MEDCO and thanked Roman for his examination at the ballfield.

"How's your head?" Roman asked.

"Still attached to my shoulders," Jack answered with a friendly smile. "I need to know everything there is to know about the Morgan case, doctor, if I'm going to save you a big malpractice claim."

Roman smiled. "I'd appreciate whatever you can do, Mr. Kittrick. I did everything I could to save Laurel Morgan. I treated her as carefully, as skillfully, as though she were my own daughter."

As the two men walked out the door engrossed in conversation, Maggie realized why Jack wanted to stay incognito. She couldn't imagine Roman talking so freely with Jack if he'd announced he was a Texas Ranger who wanted to question Roman as the prime suspect in a murder case. Maggie supposed she had a lot to learn about the police business. She intended to ask Jack plenty of questions when he returned to the conference room for the scheduled 10 A.M. meeting between MEDCO's insurance investigator and SAG's attorney.

"Are you sleeping with him?"

Maggie looked up to find Victoria staring after Jack as he walked down the hall with Roman. "That's none of your business."

"Make sure he wears a decent tuxedo on Saturday. I imagine he'll have to rent one, so send him to Anthony's."

Maggie felt the heat rising at her throat. Embarrassment on Jack's behalf? She had wondered herself whether Jack had his own tuxedo, and, to her chagrin, had been thinking about having a tux from Anthony's delivered to him. Had she really become as class-conscious as her mother-in-law? What had become of poor, good-hearted Cinderella?

"I'm sure Jack will be able to come up with something appropriate," Maggie said. "Anything else, Victoria?"

"You're missing a button."

Maggie looked down. All that remained of the accent button on the upper left-hand pocket of her power suit was two black strings. "Thank you for pointing that out," she said.

"Don't mention it," Victoria replied.

Victoria continued looking at her, and Maggie asked, "Is there something else?"

"Be discreet."

Maggie lurched from her chair. "My personal life—"

"I can see why you find Mr. Kittrick attractive, Margaret. There is something coarse and primitive about the man—the possibility of being carted off by a barbarian in civilized clothes?—that is quite appealing."

Was that why she found Jack so attractive? Maggie wondered. Because he would take all the choices out of her hands?

"But really," Victoria continued, "Jack Kittrick is not at all the sort of person you should be associating with."

"I can't believe what I'm hearing," Maggie said. "What difference could it possibly make to you whether I dance, date, or sleep with the man?"

"You're a Wainwright," Victoria said. "Wainwrights have a certain position to uphold in this community."

"I've never done a thing to cause gossip since I came here," Maggie said between clenched teeth, furious that she felt the need to defend herself, but unable to resist doing so. "What makes you think I'm going to start now?"

"I recognize that look, Margaret," Victoria said.

"What look?" Maggie demanded.

"Although one can hardly blame you," Victoria murmured. "He looks at you the same way."

"What way?" Maggie asked, wanting Victoria to name what it was she saw in Jack's eyes.

"Don't be coy," Victoria said. "You know perfectly well 'what way.' Satisfy your craving for the man if you must, Margaret, but beware your sexual prey doesn't turn and gobble you up, along with your reputation."

Sexual prey? Maggie was too stunned by Victoria's use of such a term to make any sort of reply. It had never crossed her mind to wonder what Victoria had done to satisfy her own sexual urges over the ten years she had also been a widow. Maggie had never even considered Victoria as a sexual creature, probably because children—and she and Woody had been the children—never imagined their parents "doing it."

How did Victoria satisfy her baser urges? she wondered. Did Victoria take lovers? Who were her *sexual prey?*

"It is difficult sometimes to make the choice that duty requires," Victoria said. "But that choice must be made."

Maggie gritted her teeth to keep from giving Victoria a pithy, one-word response. Instead she said, "I'll bear that in mind."

"Remember what I said," Victoria cautioned as she headed out the door.

Maggie snorted. Jack Kittrick as *sexual prey*. That wasn't something she was likely to forget.

❧ *Chapter 6* ❧

Victoria drove south, then east across town from the hospital and finally north again to the Menger Hotel, leaving her car to be valet parked at the side entrance on East Crockett. The Menger had been built in the 1860s but had been renovated to preserve its detailed historical lushness while offering the most up-to-date amenities. The hotel was famous for its discreet staff. For over a century, cattlemen, oilmen, and financiers had conducted their affairs—business and personal—without worrying that word would get back to the wrong parties. The Menger served Victoria's needs perfectly.

Enough committee meetings were held at the Menger to make it possible for her to explain her presence there if someone saw her. But there was no need for her to go into the lobby, because she already had a key, and once she left her car, the elevator was no more than five steps through the sliding glass doors.

A young man stood at the window in the

elegant second-floor room which overlooked the Alamo, another precious bit of Texas history that had been preserved, incongruously, in the midst of downtown. The shrine to the heroes of Texas freedom stood across the street from the Cowboy Museum, with its life-size replica of Trigger out front on the sidewalk. Hungry tourists could leave the Alamo and stroll over to Wendy's or Burger King or Pizza Hut, then visit another antiquity—an F. W. Woolworth featuring an unbelievable array of tasteless Texas souvenirs.

"You're late," the young man said as Victoria closed the door behind her.

"I am never late," Victoria replied. "Since I never agree to be anywhere at a specific time."

"You said to come early."

Victoria unfastened her Piaget and set it on the table beside the bed. "Did I?"

The young man already had his shirt and shoes off and Victoria admired the muscles in his shoulders and arms, the triangle of dark curls on his chest, and the well-defined abdominals separated by a line of black down leading into his trousers. "Come here, Tim."

"Tom."

She had reached beneath her skirt to readjust a garter and asked distractedly, "What?"

"My name is Tom."

He crossed to her and stood by the bed, staring at her legs. Victoria had very fine stems for a woman of fifty-three. She hesitated as Tim—no, it was Tom—settled on his knees before her and slid his hands up under her skirt. She set her manicured hands on his strong young shoulders and felt him quiver.

It was only the second time they had been together. She didn't use them often, these young men. She didn't keep them long in her web. But sometimes she needed to feel the warmth, the closeness of another human being. It was appallingly easy to lure them here: a smile that promised everything, the suggestion of influence. Never money. She didn't want to taint what happened between them with money. Besides, it wasn't necessary.

She slipped off her Chanel jacket and carefully laid it across the arm of a nearby chair.

Tom shoved her skirt above her hips and put his face between her legs. She could feel his moist breath against her naked pubis and spread her legs to give him freer access. His tongue was hot and mildly abrasive and the feelings delicious. Her knees quickly turned to jelly.

She took a step back, unzipped her skirt, and slipped it up over her head, laying it neatly beside the jacket, leaving her wearing a lacy black bra, garter belt and stockings, and three-inch high heels.

"Tom," she murmured, brushing his springy black hair away from his forehead. "Let's lie down on the bed. I would like to return the favor."

He looked up at her, his brown eyes dark, the pupils huge, his eyelids heavy. He stood

and picked her up, carried her to the head of
the bed, and laid her down. He undid the belt
on his pleated trousers and shoved them
down along with his briefs, standing before
her with his engorged member pulsing to the
rapid beat of his heart.

She lay on her side, her hand supporting her
head, and lifted one knee, posing provoca-
tively, watching him quake with need, making
him wait for permission to come to her. She
loved the different sizes and shapes men came
in, the difference in the way they tasted. Tom
was larger than most. Saltier, too.

She gestured with a forefinger.

The young man scuttled onto the bed, pushing his face between her legs and shifting his
hips toward her face, offering her the gift he
had brought. Victoria opened her mouth and
let him push inside, hard and tight against the
roof of her mouth. At the same time she felt
his tongue slide into her like liquid fire.

It was a long time before either of them had
another rational thought.

Victoria wasn't sure why she enjoyed this so
much. She was astute enough to reason that it
had something to do with the fact that in her
day, "nice girls" weren't even supposed to
know about such things, let alone indulge in
them, and God forbid *enjoy* them.

She had been a virgin on her wedding night,
as had been expected of her. But that had
merely been a technicality. Victoria had long
before learned the joys of sex without penetra-

tion. It was a way of keeping herself "perfect" for her husband, yet indulging needs she could not deny. Nevertheless, she had intended to be a faithful wife. Until she had caught Richard indulging himself with another woman at his office a mere two weeks after their wedding.

She had made a scene. Really, looking back, it had been a childish thing to do. She knew better. She had been trained from birth to defer to the men in her life. Her father had been a hard taskmaster, and nothing less than perfection would suffice—in dress, in manners, in behavior. Well, she had certainly thrown a perfect tantrum.

She had raced home to her father, expecting him to take her side. He had corrected her with a slap that had stopped her tears. "You're Richard's wife now," he had said in cold, steely tones that had chilled her to the bone. "Your husband's word is law as much as mine ever was. Listen to him and do exactly what he tells you. Don't contradict him or correct him, no matter how wrong you may think he is. Those are the rules, Victoria."

The slap had left her dry-eyed, and the lecture had left her raging inside. If her father's tirade had stopped there, she might have divorced Richard and led an entirely different life. But her father had been so much smarter than she was. He had known all the right things to say.

He had pulled her into his arms close

enough for her to smell the familiar, pungent odor of Cuban cigars embedded in his blended wool suit. He had rocked her and smoothed her hair and said, "Do you want to be loved, Victoria?"

Who did not? "Yes, Father."

"Do you want to know the secret to being loved."

Who did not? "Yes, Father."

"Obedience," he said. "That is the secret. Do as you're told. Follow the rules perfectly, and you will be loved."

He demonstrated the truth of his words by hugging her and kissing her forehead and telling her he knew she was a good girl and a good wife and that she would learn not to feel slighted by Richard's indiscretions. "A man sometimes needs a different kind of woman," he said. "It has nothing to do with you personally. Be as obedient as I know you can be. That is the way to win Richard's love."

She had followed her father's advice. She had become a slave to Richard's every whim. She had set perfect tables and held perfect parties and kept herself looking as perfect as she'd looked the day she married him. She had never caught Richard with another woman.

But somehow, she had never felt loved.

She had substituted what she could get: respect and admiration. Of course, it came mostly from other people besides Richard, but it had filled the emptiness inside her. Even today Victoria kept herself perfect because that earned her the respect and admiration of those around her.

When she was struck with lustful urges, she satisfied them with the young lawyers at Porter's firm, or the young interns at the hospital, where she was on the board of trustees and the bioethics committee and served as a volunteer reader for the Wainwright Pediatrics Wing on alternate Mondays and Wednesdays. The young men knew better than to kiss and tell. She made it clear from the start that Victoria Wainwright had the power to help them—or destroy them.

It wasn't an altogether perfect life, but it was close.

Victoria felt the young man's lips graze her cheek as he said, "I need to get back to the hospital. When can I see you again?"

"You can't."

He frowned, putting old-man wrinkles in his young brow. "Why not?"

"Don't be a child about this, Tom," she said.

The young man flushed to the tips of his ears.

They were always aware of the age difference, even if they never mentioned it, she had learned.

"That's it? You're through with me?" he demanded angrily.

"Yes." She didn't bother to keep the irritation out of her voice or the annoyance from her face. They all knew the rules. When she

called, they came. When she was done playing, the game was over.

The embarrassed flush had receded, leaving
his cheeks as pale as chalk. He looked like he
was about to throw up, and in fact, he took a
step toward the bathroom before he stopped
and swallowed convulsively.

Usually she let them down easier, but she
was feeling peeved at the thought of Margaret
indulging herself this way with Jack Kittrick.
Although why that should bother her, she
couldn't imagine.

Because you want him for yourself.

Victoria sat up, patted her hair into place,
and languidly walked to the window, still
dressed in her black lingerie and high heels.
She ignored Tom, who was gathering up his
clothes and sulkily putting them on, while she
tried to figure out why she should be interested in Kittrick, when he was nearly twice the
age of the men who usually caught her fancy.

It was probably the masculine aura she had
mentioned to Margaret. There was something
raw and elemental about the man, something
unconquerable and unconquered. It would be
interesting to have such a man in bed.

Victoria heard the door snap closed and realized she was alone. The problem was, lately,
she felt alone even when she was with the
young men. The approaching anniversary of
Richard's and Woodson's deaths was causing
the problem, she knew. She fought the same
battle every year, raging against fate for taking

the perfect husband and the perfect son from her.

Margaret was to blame, of course, for both deaths. She was the one who had sent Woodson out onto an icy road that day in early April. And Richard's stroke had occurred on the corporate jet as they were landing in Minneapolis to be with their mortally injured son. She would never let Margaret forget what she had done, or forgive her for it. But hating Margaret did little to ease her through the horror each year.

Thank goodness she had a full life. Thank goodness she had her charities and the hospital and Porter. And the young men, of course. Without them, what would she do?

Jack had missed his 10 A.M. appointment with Maggie. He figured she would understand when he filled her in on what he'd been doing. His interview with Roman had been enlightening—for the five minutes he'd spent with the doctor before Hollander got a STAT call and disappeared behind a pair of swinging doors.

It was the discussion he'd had with Isabel Rojas, Roman's head surgical nurse and, according to the doctor, his "right arm" in surgery, that had gotten Jack excited enough to make him forget all about his meeting with Maggie.

Once Ms. Rojas realized he was trying to help Dr. Hollander, she'd been willing to tell him anything he wanted to know. Across the table from each other in the cafeteria, where they had sat drinking black coffee, he discovered Isabel had grown up just over the American side of the border in El Paso. Her family had been illegal aliens, but she'd been born in the states, thus securing her citizenship. Determined to live the American dream, she had decided to become a nurse.

"It was better than smuggling marijuana over the border." She smiled and said, "The way I'm shaped, I'd have looked like Dolly Parton once I got a few three-finger bags tucked in my bra. The border guards would've searched me just for the fun of it!"

It didn't take Jack long to figure out why Hollander liked her so much. Besides being a competent nurse, Isabel Rojas had a dry wit that kept Jack chuckling almost the whole time they talked about her life growing up. He couldn't understand why some man hadn't snapped her up years ago.

"Why aren't you married?" he asked, an instant before he realized the rudeness of the question.

"I decided to join the Cucumber Club instead," she answered.

"What's that?" Jack asked warily. The name sounded self-explanatory, with lurid possibilities he would just as soon not explore, but he had learned not to make assumptions in his line of work.

"There are only three qualifications for

membership," she said. "You must have loved
or hated a man in the past, love or hate a man
in the present, or think you might love or hate
a man in the future. Our motto is: 'A man is
no better than a vegetable.' "

Jack wasn't sure whether to be appalled or
amused.

Isabel laughed merrily. "The look on your
face is priceless."

"I'm trying to imagine what your meetings
must be like," he said.

"The last time we got together at a restaurant, the waitress asked if we were fran-
chised," Isabel said.

"Are you?" Jack asked incredulously.

"We ought to be," Isabel said with a laugh.
"One of the nurses started the club as a hu-
morous support group for divorced and
dumped women, on the theory it's better to
laugh than to cry."

"Is it love or hate for you?"

"A little of both," Isabel confessed, sobering.

"Would you mind if I ask you some specific
questions about the little girl whose parents
are suing Dr. Hollander for malpractice?" he
asked.

"Shoot."

"What do you remember about Laurel Morgan?"

Isabel didn't have any trouble remembering
the case, but Jack was surprised at what she
recalled first.

"She liked Winnie-the-Pooh," Isabel began.

"Her parents brought her a stuffed Pooh bear, but of course she couldn't have it in the ICU. So Mrs. Wainwright sat beside the little girl for hours reading Pooh story after Pooh story, even though Laurel never regained consciousness after the operation."

Jack's heart was thumping hard. "Maggie did that?"

Isabel shook her head. "No, I meant Victoria Wainwright."

Jack was taken aback. "What was Victoria Wainwright doing in the ICU?"

"The lady goes pretty much where she wants, when she wants," Isabel replied.

"Why is that?" Jack asked.

Isabel laughed. "You haven't looked at many of the signs around here, have you?"

Jack turned and looked where Isabel pointed. "Wainwright Cafeteria."

"Wainwright Trauma Center, Wainwright Pediatric Wing—" she recited.

"I see what you mean," Jack said. "What made Mrs. Wainwright come in and read to this particular little girl? Did she know the family?"

"Victoria Wainwright is a regular volunteer reader in the pediatrics ward," Isabel explained. "Once in a while she'll come up to spend some time with a kid who's stuck in the ICU." Isabel took a sip of coffee and asked, "Is any of what I say going to get back to her?"

Jack shook his head.

"Then I'll be honest and tell you she's arrogant and condescending with the nursing staff. Like her money makes her a better person than the rest of us. The nurses do the best they can to keep their distance when she's around. But to be fair, I've never seen anyone more sympathetic and loving toward children," Isabel conceded.

That behavior didn't fit Jack's first impression of Victoria Wainwright. He couldn't imagine Victoria having the patience to read to a child, much less a child who probably couldn't even hear her. She struck him as the self-centered, selfish type. What made her so attentive to the children? he wondered.

He would have to ask her and see what she said.

"What can you tell me about Laurel's injuries?" Jack said.

"She was hit by a car while riding her bicycle and ended up with a fractured skull. Dr. Hollander did everything he could to save her. He's a brilliant surgeon, but there was just too much damage to her brain."

"She had no chance of survival?" Jack asked.

"If Laurel had survived the swelling in her brain, she probably would have lived, but it's questionable how much of a real recovery she would have made."

"Then it's a blessing she died of heart failure?" Jack said, watching Isabel's face closely.

Without blinking she replied, "It's never

good when a child dies. But sometimes it is a blessing."

Jack drew several conclusions from his conversation with Hollander's surgical nurse. First, Isabel Rojas was a smart, funny woman. Second, she idolized—even loved—Roman Hollander. And third, she shared the doctor's feelings about quality of life.

By the time Jack went looking for Maggie in the conference room shortly before noon, he discovered she was gone. No one at the nearest nursing station had seen her leave, but Jack figured the obvious place to look for her was at the offices of Wainwright & Cobb, a couple of blocks away on Travis. From the front door of the hospital, he could see the Texas flag flying all alone atop the Milam Building on a tall brass pole.

Jack smiled. Texans put Texas first, with God running a close second, and the United States of America a distant third. But after all, from 1836 to 1846, Texas had been an independent nation, a republic with its own president and vice-president and army and navy, something no other state could boast.

Jack discovered Wainwright & Cobb took up the entire top floor of the Milam Building, a yellow-brick and glass structure with hand-carved Corinthian columns in the lobby and cherry-wood railings in the Mexican-tiled stairways. Built in 1927 as the first air-conditioned high-rise in the country, the Gothic structure had aged gracefully, maintaining its dignity and charm.

Jack decided the attractive blond receptionist who greeted him at the entrance to the Wainwright & Cobb offices had been chosen as much for her good looks and fashion sense as for her ability to answer a bank of telephones. She gave Jack a friendly smile and said she'd locate Ms. Wainwright for him.

Ninety seconds later Jack found himself headed down a wall of doors toward the southeast corner office, which belonged to Maggie Wainwright.

The center of the twenty-first floor was taken up with secretarial cubicles, while the lawyers' offices ringed the building. Considering where she was situated, Jack figured Maggie had a great tourist's view of downtown from her windows, including Hemisfair Plaza, with its revolving restaurant at the top of Hemisfair Tower, the Alamodome—the godawful wired-up stadium built for the Spurs that was sometimes described as "a riverboat on a freeway," and the city's famous River Walk.

The River Walk was fifteen feet below the downtown street level but visible from the twenty-first floor as a reflective silvery ribbon lined with colorful red, blue, and yellow dots that Jack knew were umbrellas at outdoor dining tables. Tourists could walk the flagstone that meandered along both sides of the thirty-foot-wide San Antonio River or take red motorized flatboats—which looked like floating toys from where Jack stood—to get to outdoor restaurants, souvenir shops, and hotels.

When Jack reached Maggie's office, he found her sitting behind a stylish, glass-topped desk with marble supports at each end, deep in conversation with a petite woman in a tailored suit. He leaned a shoulder against the door jamb and crossed his booted feet at the ankles, waiting for the two of them to come up for air.

He had time to examine the other woman, whom the receptionist had identified as Lisa Hollander, his primary suspect's wife. She had short sable hair and bangs that emphasized her immense brown eyes. Lisa Hollander's face reminded Jack of the winsome, doe-eyed children painted on cheap black velvet and sold to tourists at border towns like Juárez and Piedras Negras and Nuevo Laredo. There was something infinitely and inexplicably sad about her countenance.

He wasn't sure what gave him away, but Maggie suddenly looked up. She didn't seem altogether pleased to find him there. "Jack. You should have said something. I didn't realize you'd already found your way here."

"I didn't want to interrupt. Go ahead with what you were doing."

Maggie rose, suggesting the meeting with her colleague was at an end.

Jack uncrossed his legs and entered her office, his boots sinking into thick oatmeal carpet. He stopped behind one of the black leather wing chairs intended for clients and glanced at Lisa Hollander, who was eyeing him curiously.

"Jack Kittrick, I'd like you to meet Lisa Hollander," Maggie said.

Lisa extended her hand, and Jack reached out to shake it. "Nice to meet you, Mrs. Hollander."

She smiled, and her face changed completely. Jack decided she should smile more often. The large, liquid eyes exuded warmth as she said, "Call me Lisa, please."

Her voice was raspy, as though she were just getting over a case of laryngitis, and with her soft Texas drawl, unbelievably sexy. Considering the whole package, Jack could see why Hollander, a confirmed bachelor, had suddenly decided to marry four years ago.

"I've heard so much about you from Maggie, Mr. Kittrick, I feel like I already know you," Lisa said. "I hope you're feeling better."

"Make it Jack," Jack said. "Thanks to your husband and some nursing from Maggie, I'm fine."

Lisa shot Maggie a questioning sideways look. "Nursing?"

Even though he'd obviously been a topic of discussion between the two women, it was plain Maggie hadn't told Lisa everything. "Maggie was kind enough to keep me company for a while on Saturday night," Jack said.

"So you're returning the favor by keeping

her company this Saturday night," Lisa quipped.

Jack returned her irresistible smile. "Right," he said.

From the vexed look on Maggie's face, Jack figured she wasn't used to being teased. Too bad. The lady needed to lighten up, and he was just the man to help her do it.

"I'm sorry, Maggie. I couldn't resist teasing you," Lisa said. She turned to Jack and said, "Roman and I will be joining you at Mr. Cobb's table."

The gods sometimes did smile on the wicked, Jack thought. "I'll be looking forward to talking more with you," he said.

"I've got a pleading to write, if you'll both excuse me," Lisa said. "Nice meeting you, Jack."

"You, too, Lisa." Jack made a point of closing the door behind her. "She seems like a nice person."

"She is. And so is Roman. I hope you found that out for yourself this morning."

"I didn't have much chance to speak to the doctor. He got called away on an emergency." Jack crossed to Maggie and settled himself on the edge of her glass desk where the marble supported it.

"There are two perfectly good chairs behind you," she said.

"I can see your eyes better from here."

She rose abruptly but had nowhere to go, since Jack had put himself between her and the door. He stood and took the steps to close the distance between them, so they were toe to toe, breast to breast. "Good morning, Maggie."

She hissed in a breath as he leaned down and brushed his lips against hers once, then again, lips catching, tongue teasing, before he captured her mouth in a searing, bone-melting kiss. As he released her mouth, she made a grating sound in her throat, as though she couldn't bear for him to let her go.

Her kiss was everything Jack had hoped it would be. It felt as if some giant empty place inside him had begun to fill. But he wasn't ready to stop there. He wanted, desperately needed, more.

He studied Maggie's face, wondering whether she had been as moved by the experience as he had. Her eyes were heavy-lidded when she finally opened them and looked up at him.

"Oh, Lord," she whispered.

Jack felt a tight place ease inside him. Yeah. She'd felt it, too.

He brushed his thumb across her still-damp lower lip and said, "That's what I wanted to do when I saw you come out of that stairwell this morning with your hair still damp from the shower and your skirt halfway up your legs."

She cleared her throat, eyeing him warily. "My skirt is down now, Jack. And it's staying down."

His hands were already in her hair taking out the pins, and he lowered his mouth to hers in a gentle caress meant to convince her she was safe with him. The kiss quickly evolved into something more than a meeting of lips. He felt her heat, her passion, her need . . . and the inner struggle she waged, unwilling to surrender completely to him.

She wrenched her face aside, breaking the kiss, panting as though she were running for her life. "I thought you understood this can't happen, Jack."

"It already has, Maggie."

She started to back away, then hesitated. Maggie hadn't struck him as the kind of woman who backed away from anything, and sure enough, she stood her ground.

"All right, Jack. You've had your kisses. You've made your point—you can flip a switch and turn me on. Now, can we get down to business?"

Jack let go of her and settled himself back onto the edge of the tempered glass desk. He was going to have to find out what made her so leery of men. He meant to have her, and he wasn't going to let any obstacles—like her reluctance to get involved—stand in his way.

"All right, Maggie. Let's do business," he said. "I've got some good news for you."

Once he wasn't crowding her, she put some space between them, crossing to the window, giving him the chance to look around.

Besides her desk and the two leather wing

chairs, the only furniture in her office was a glass-topped credenza with a black and gold wooden Egyptian cat sitting on it. A single file was scattered across her glass-topped desk, but everything else was apparently tucked away in the floor-to-ceiling black cabinets behind her desk. All that clear glass and marble, and the complete lack of vibrant color, made the place feel cold and sterile—not at all like the Maggie he was coming to know.

Maggie leaned back against the window ledge, crossed her arms, and said, "All right, Jack. I'm listening. What's your good news?"

"I've got another suspect," he announced.

She raised an inquisitive brow.

"Isabel Rojas, Hollander's surgical nurse."

She made a derisive sound and shook her head. "What makes you think Roman's nurse is a killer?"

"I only said she's a suspect."

"What makes her a suspect?" Maggie asked.

"She's been with Hollander as his nurse for the past seven years. Like him, she worked at the hospitals in Houston and Dallas where the other five suspicious deaths occurred. She had the same opportunity as the doctor to commit the crimes."

"Surgical nurses often transfer along with a doctor. That doesn't make her a suspicious character. What's her motive supposed to be?"

"The same as the doctor's—easing the pain and suffering of the patient."

Maggie shook her head. "It's not enough,

Jack." She crossed back to her glass-topped desk, but it wasn't much to hide behind. He noticed she was careful not to get within arm's reach of him. "People don't commit murder for reasons like that," she said. "They let the patient die a natural death."

"What if the patient isn't going to die on his own?"

"People who dedicate themselves to saving lives aren't purposely going to murder someone, especially not a child, just because that someone might be suffering."

"You're wrong, Maggie. Doctors and nurses do it all the time."

"I suppose you have statistics," Maggie retorted, pacing agitatedly behind her desk.

"Studies have been done."

She stopped and stared at him. "You're kidding, right?"

"When I got assigned to this case, I looked at a lot of literature on the subject. Twenty percent of the critical care nurses in one study admitted they had hastened the death of a terminally ill patient, usually by giving an overdose of painkillers."

Maggie pointed an accusing finger at him. "There's the flaw in your reasoning."

"What?"

"You said they helped 'terminally ill' patients to die. The kids in question weren't going to die. Ergo your study doesn't fit."

Trust a lawyer to find the flaw in his logic. "Maybe not precisely, but—"

"Not at all," Maggie insisted. "You need to find another reason for the murders besides mercy killing. Like a life insurance policy or selfish parents who don't want to care for an invalid or—I've got it," she said excitedly, "the money they'd get suing Hollander for malpractice."

"A conspiracy of parents killing their children for malpractice settlements?" Jack said dubiously.

"It makes as much sense as believing Roman Hollander is killing patients so they won't have to live a difficult life!"

Jack sighed. "Mercy killing made sense when Captain Buckelew suggested it to me."

"You hadn't met Roman then. Can you really believe he's a murderer, now that you've seen him in action at the bioethics committee meeting? Now that you've spoken to him personally?"

"Neither of those meetings has changed my mind about the doctor, Maggie. Besides, I've heard of parents killing their children rather than watching them suffer," Jack said. "Why not a doctor, especially a compassionate one, or his nurse?"

Maggie shoved an agitated hand through her fallen hair.

Jack was distracted when the sunlight caught it, turning wheat to gold. He imagined it spread across his chest or tangled in his hands as he angled her head for his kiss.

She looked up, caught his hungry stare, and rolled her eyes.

He flushed like a teenager caught with his zipper down and realized he'd lost his train of thought. "Where was I?"

"Saying some very disturbing things about Roman and Isabel."

"Oh. Yeah. Closing your eyes to the truth isn't going to make it go away, Maggie. If Roman Hollander or his nurse is playing God, I intend to find out and stop it."

A phone call interrupted them, and Jack fiddled with a toy on Maggie's desk—a bed of headless nails that took any shape he pressed into it—waiting for Maggie to finish.

She put the call on hold and said, "This is going to take a while."

"How about dinner tonight? We can finish our conversation then."

"I have to work late tonight. And every night this week," she added.

"You're avoiding me," Jack said.

"I'm a busy woman," she countered.

"I guess I won't see you again until Saturday."

"I guess not."

Jack backed off. He could read a No Trespassing sign when he saw one. He was tempted to ease himself out of the picture by reneging on the Saturday invitation, but as he watched Maggie's hands fidget, he realized she wasn't as unaware of him, or as unmoved by his presence, as she wanted him to believe.

"What time should I pick you up on Saturday?" he asked.

"Eight o'clock."

He turned and headed for the door. "I'll be there."

"Jack," she said, catching him before he could leave. "It's black tie. You can rent a good tux at Anthony's."

He glanced at her over his shoulder, his lips curled in a bitter smile. "Thanks," he said. "I'll try not to embarrass you."

"I only thought . . . I wanted to help," she said lamely.

He hadn't figured her for a snob, and he didn't like the way she'd made him feel. He wanted to hurt her back and found the words to do it.

"Watch out, Maggie," he said. "You might turn out to be more like Victoria Wainwright than you think."

✒ *Chapter 7* ✑

Jack spent the rest of the week interviewing Dr. Hollander's colleagues at the hospital. On Friday morning, he headed to Austin to make his weekly report to Captain Buckelew at Ranger Headquarters. He could have done it by phone, but ever since Jack was nine, and his own father, also a Texas Ranger, had died in the line of duty, Harley Buckelew had been like a second father to him. The truth was, he enjoyed visiting the old man, which was a damned good thing, because he didn't have much to report.

During the sixty-odd-mile drive from San Antonio north to Austin, Jack went over every detail he'd learned about Hollander and his nurse, Isabel Rojas, in his head. All he managed to do was give himself a headache. He already had a fairly constant ache in his gut, or thereabouts, because Ms. Maggie Wainwright was stuck deep in his craw.

I should still be on leave. I should be up in the Hill Country on the Guadalupe River, fly-fishing for some of those Colorado brown and speckled trout the Fish and Wildlife guys have stocked up there. I should never have let the captain talk me into taking this case.

But Harley Buckelew was not only his captain, but a surrogate father. Jack wanted his captain's respect. Even more, he wanted Harley to be proud of him.

The captain had dropped off the folder of information the first day of Jack's administrative leave and said, "I've got an assignment for you—investigating a possible serial killer."

"I'm not sure I ever want to pin my star back on, and you want me to track down a serial killer?" Jack had asked incredulously.

"I need somebody to go undercover, and since that isn't something we Rangers do a whole lot, you're the man with the most experience. Putting on those lieutenant's bars you just earned and settling in at a desk can wait a while. I need you on this."

"I'm on leave for a reason, Captain. Find somebody else."

"He's killing kids, Jack."

Jack had felt the squeeze inside and knew Harley had him by the short hairs. He'd also heard the waver in Harley's voice that revealed he wasn't as certain of Jack's response as he wanted Jack to think. And the warmth that showed he cared.

"I'll think about it," Jack had said.

Two days later, he'd agreed to go back to

work. Jack wondered now if he'd made the right decision. He didn't seem to have the distance from the case that would allow him to see the situation objectively. Maggie's opinion of Hollander and his nurse mattered, even though it shouldn't have been a factor in his investigation.

As Jack neared Austin on I-35, he saw more results of the previous year's drought. What should have been acres of bluebonnets and Indian paintbrush spreading a blanket of lavender and orange along the roadside had been reduced to patches of blue here and there amid the green. Without enough rain, the wildflowers—compliments of Lady Bird Johnson's Texas beautification program—simply didn't bloom.

Once in Austin, Jack exited the interstate onto Lamar and caught sight of the large brown metal B bolted onto the side of the Headquarters Building, an off-white concrete two-story built like a bunker, so half of it was underground. He pulled into the lot and parked beside a Jeep Cherokee he knew Buckelew had claimed as his ride, even though the captain didn't usually venture into areas where he needed four-wheel drive.

Every time Jack entered Harley's office, he wasn't sure whether to chuckle or groan out loud. The captain collected Texas souvenirs— no matter how much in poor taste—just like a tourist. The Ranger's wall boasted not only a legitimate eight-foot set of horns from a Texas longhorn steer, but the mounted head of a jackalope, a fictional Texas animal consisting of a rabbit head with tiny deer antlers.

Once Jack was settled in front of the captain's desk in a genuine black-and-white cowhide chair with arms and feet made of cow horns, Harley slurped tar-black coffee from a giant mug bearing the motto EVERYTHING IS BIGGER IN TEXAS and said, "What have you found out?"

"Not a hell of a lot more than you told me in the first place," Jack admitted. Maggie's defense of Hollander had jibed with everything he'd discovered about the man over the past week. "Roman Hollander seems like a competent, dedicated doctor. Personally, I don't see him killing kids, even as a favor to them. You'd have a hard time making even a circumstantial case against him because too many other people have access to the ICU, a needle, and potassium chloride."

Maggie's defense of Isabel Rojas had turned out to be equally compelling in light of Jack's investigation. "Hollander's surgical nurse, Isabel Rojas, has been with him almost from the beginning of his career," Jack continued, "and seems as dedicated to the doctor as she is to her job. But she doesn't strike me as the type to run around killing kids, either. Are we even sure yet whether the other five deaths were murders?" Jack asked. "Maybe Laurel Morgan's death was an accident. Maybe some nurse didn't write it down when she gave the kid a dose of potassium, and somebody gave the kid another dose."

Buckelew shook his head. "I wish the Morgan case were an isolated incident, an accident. But we've heard back from the medical examiners in Houston and Dallas we asked to take a look at those five bodies we had exhumed. They'd all been embalmed, just like we figured, but one of the mortuaries left all the IVs and shunts intact, and massive amounts of potassium chloride showed up in the kid's IV tubing.

"Another one of the victims was a preemie with veins too small for an IV. A catheter was inserted in the shinbone to the marrow. By using bone from the uncatheterized shin as a control, the ME was able to document a lethal dose of potassium chloride in the other shin."

"Aw, damn," Jack muttered.

Harley swatted at a fly with a souvenir fly-swatter the size of a paper plate, since even the flies were bigger in Texas. "We can't prove the other three kids were murdered, but it's a good bet they were. We're dealing with someone ruthless enough to snuff kids," Harley said soberly. "If Hollander's nurse has been with him for years, she's also a viable suspect."

Jack settled his booted ankle on the opposite knee. "The problem is, short of putting a video camera in the ICU—"

"All right," Harley said.

"All right what?"

"I'll take care of the paperwork to authorize surveillance video cameras in the ICU. You tell the guys where you want them, and I'll arrange to have them monitored twenty-four hours a day by local police."

"I count six deaths in seven years, Captain. We could end up with a helluva lot of videotape waiting for the murderer to show up."

Harley smacked a fly and shoved it off his desk with the flyswatter. "I guess I haven't told you."

"What?"

"Every one of those kids died between March 31 and April 6."

Jack glanced at the wall where the captain's Texas-shaped yearly planning calendar was tacked up with Alamo stickpins. Each day that passed was stamped with a red boot. Today was March 28, Good Friday. According to Harley's information, if the killer held to the previous pattern, he might strike as soon as Monday—and had a mere seven days in which to claim his seventh victim.

"I don't know whether to hope the doctor or his nurse try something or not," Jack said. "What if we get them on video but can't catch them in time to keep them from killing a kid?"

"We do the best we can, Jack. We can't save them all."

A poignant silence fell between them as they both remembered why Jack had requested an administrative leave.

"You did the best you could, Jack."

"My best wasn't good enough." Jack couldn't look at Harley. His nose stung, and tears were too close to the surface. "I keep thinking that if I'd done something differently . . . kept my distance . . . or kept my gun . . . something . . . that little girl would be alive today."

"Hindsight is always twenty-twenty, Jack. You have to trust yourself to make the right decision at the time."

"That's just it," Jack said. "I don't trust myself anymore. Are you sure you want me on this case?"

"You're the best there is in a hostage situation, Jack. I want you there if it comes down to that."

The silence grew uncomfortable again.

"Is that all you have to report?" Harley asked.

Jack nodded because he couldn't talk past the Texas-size frog in his throat.

"Then let me throw another can of beans on the fire," Harley said, leaning back and threading his fingers over his belly.

"What?" Jack croaked.

"We have another suspect."

"For Christ's sake! Why didn't you say so in the first place?"

"I'm telling you now," Harley said, "if you'll shut up and listen."

Jack pressed his lips flat.

"The MEDCO investigator did a computer check of all common factors and identified another person with a link to all the purported victims in San Antonio, Houston, and Dallas."

"Who is it?" Jack asked impatiently.

"Margaret Wainwright."

Jack's heart jumped from a steady thump to full speed like a jackrabbit taking off from a standing start. "That's bullshit."

" 'Fraid not, son. The situation's delicate enough with Hollander's wife being an associate with Wainwright & Cobb. I can't tell you how sensitive this case becomes if we start investigating one of the Wainwrights for murder."

Jack ground his teeth, thinking what a fool he'd been to tell Maggie Wainwright who he was. It was like announcing to a burglar when you were going to be gone from home so he could come over and help himself. He opened his mouth to confess to the captain what he'd done, but what came out was, "In what way is Maggie Wainwright connected to all of these deaths?"

"She's been counsel for the hospital in each and every case."

Jack heaved a sigh of relief and slumped back into his chair. "Hell, Captain. You had me going there for a minute. Of course she'd show up on the computer as counsel for the hospitals. That's no reason to suspect—"

"She wasn't just counsel, Jack. She was

there. She did her clerkship one summer in Houston for a firm that represented a MEDCO hospital, and she was recruited by a law firm in Dallas to work with a MEDCO hospital. After that she moved to San Antonio to work for Wainwright & Cobb and began representing MEDCO hospitals statewide."

"Are you suggesting *she's* the murderer?"

"She's certainly one of the suspects."

Jack tried to laugh and couldn't manage it. He rose and paced the cowhide that covered the floor. "I've met Maggie Wainwright, and I can tell you she's not a murderer."

"Did you know she had a couple of kids who died?"

Jack stumbled. It felt like all the air had been sucked from his chest. *"What?"*

"MEDCO dug up the information from her health insurance records. She had two live births, but the investigator found out both boys drowned ten years ago, in 1987. Seems one of the boys was DOA, but the other survived on life support for a while. The family removed the kid from the hospital, and the investigator couldn't find a record of what happened to him after that. At least no insurance claims were ever filed."

"Jesus." Jack slumped into the horn and hide chair. "She never said a word."

"I don't expect it's something Ms. Wainwright cares to talk much about," the captain said. "But her background definitely gives her a motive, Jack."

"What motive is that?"

"The same one we've given the doctor and his nurse. Ms. Wainwright, of all people, would know how much a family can suffer in a situation where a child is on life support without much expectation of a full recovery."

Jack set his jaw and shook his head. "She's not the one. It's Hollander or the nurse. Or somebody else we haven't tied to the victims yet."

"I take it you like the lady," Buckelew said.

"You could say that," Jack conceded. He hadn't realized until this moment just how much he liked Maggie Wainwright. Way too much. He knew better than to think they were headed for any kind of long-term relationship. After all, neither of them wanted to get involved. But he liked the look and taste and feel of her. He wasn't done with her by a long shot.

"Are you going to be able to stay objective about Ms. Wainwright, Jack, or should I assign somebody else to this case?"

Maggie a killer? Jack tried to imagine it and couldn't. He sorted through some of the things she'd said, things he hadn't thought much about at the time—like the fact she believed as much in quality of life as Dr. Hollander. *"Does that make me capable of murder?"* What if she and the doctor and his nurse had formed their own mercy-killing society?

Jack's stomach churned, and he swallowed down the bile in his throat. "I'll do my job," he said through tight jaws. "If Maggie Wainwright is killing kids, I'll be the first one in line to make sure she hangs for it."

It was easy enough to say he would stay objective, but Jack was having a hell of a time doing it. As he perused himself in the steamy bathroom mirror, straightening his cummerbund and adjusting the bow tie that had come with the tux he'd rented from Anthony's, he looked like a man on his way to an execution.

He'd been waiting all week for Saturday to come so he could spend the evening with Maggie. He had planned to hold her and kiss her and had certainly imagined making love to her. Right now he felt about as comfortable as a horse thief at a necktie party. What if Maggie was guilty? What if she'd used the information he'd given her about being a Texas Ranger to throw him off her scent?

Jack hadn't always been scrupulous about his bed partners, but he wasn't ready to make love to a murderer. So where did that leave him? He was tempted to confront Maggie with what he knew and see what she had to say for herself. Unfortunately, he wasn't sure that would solve the problem. What if she told him she was innocent? That didn't necessarily make her so.

He was still sorting through everything in his head when he arrived at the guard gate for the address off Broadway Maggie had given him, 200 Patterson. He waited while the guard called to make sure he was welcome, then drove past the black wrought-iron gate through what amounted to a manicured park surrounding the exclusive high-rise condominium.

Jack left the keys in his truck when he got out at the etched glass doors under the portico and belatedly realized—when he saw the smirk on the parking attendant's face—how awkward it might be for Margaret Wainwright to arrive at the Cancer Society Gala in a pickup.

Hell, Maggie knew he drove a truck. If she hadn't wanted him to pick her up in it, she should have said something. Except they hadn't spoken all week. Jack was both nervous and anxious, two things he hadn't felt because of a woman for a long time.

On the way up to her tenth floor apartment in the elevator, he stuck a finger between his bow tie and his throat. The damned thing seemed to have tightened by itself. The doorman downstairs had called up to let her know he was coming, so he knew Maggie was expecting him.

Still, when she opened the door to his knock, she looked surprised. "Jack. Come in. You look wonderful."

Does that surprise her? Jack wondered.

Before he had time to be offended, she said, "I'm almost ready. Would you like a drink? There's liquor on the bar in the living room and beer in the small refrigerator behind it. I'll only be another minute."

She closed the door behind him without touching him and headed down the hall to the bedroom before he could say a word. Not that he could have spoken to save his life.

She had looked exquisite in a form-fitting, full-length black sheath which, he realized only when she turned her back on him, had no back. He could see the dimples at the base of her spine. The saliva pooled in his mouth, and he swallowed hard.

"Jesus," he muttered. That outfit was like the come-hither nicker of an eager mare. Jack told his body "Whoa," but it was hearing "Giddyap."

He hurriedly stepped down into the sunken living room and headed for the wet bar in the corner. Maybe a good, strong drink would help.

Maggie's living room reminded him of the outdoors, with pale green carpet underfoot and a rose silk couch covered with a half dozen pillows that matched the same flowery print as a nearby overstuffed chair. A ficus stood in a Chinese pot in the corner and a profusion of wildflowers filled a basket on the mantel above a white-brick painted fireplace. He leaned over to sniff and only then realized the flowers were fake.

She obviously liked cats, but the ones in her living room weren't any more real than the flowers. She had tossed a pink, pillow-shaped cat on the chair, while a clear crystal one sat on the pine coffee table, and a sleek black ceramic feline reclined at the foot of the fireplace. With the one at her office, that made four fake cats she owned. Not that Jack was counting.

As he got himself a Pearl beer from the small refrigerator behind the bar, Jack couldn't help thinking something was out of kilter in Maggie's apartment. He just couldn't put his finger on what it was.

Before he'd taken more than a gulp or two of the ice-cold Pearl, she was back. "That was quick," he said.

"I just needed to put on my earrings and some lipstick."

The diamond earrings dangled enticingly from her ears, and the lipstick was a bright red that had a lot more to do with GO than STOP. Jack figured if he didn't get her out of there pretty damn quick, they weren't going to leave at all.

When he set his beer on the bar, she said, "We have time to sit for a while. Please go ahead and finish your beer."

Sit beside her? In that dress? Was she crazy? "Will you join me?" he asked, staying right where he was.

"I don't drink."

Jack didn't drink much either, a beer once in a while to be social. An alcoholic mother had convinced him of the dangers of indulging. He looked at the bottles on the bar and noticed none of them were open. "Did you buy all of that for me?"

Two pink spots appeared on her cheeks. "I wasn't sure what you drank."

It was apparent Maggie didn't normally entertain guests in her home, which meant he was a special case. "I appreciate the thought," he said.

"Woody used to insist the bar be kept—" She frowned and looked around the room as though expecting to find something—or someone. When she didn't, she crossed and sank into the flowered chair, picked up the cat pillow, and hugged it close.

Jack suddenly realized what was strange about Maggie's apartment. Despite the fact she'd been married and had two kids, there were no pictures of her husband or her sons in the room. She had apparently cut them out of her life. Like the real cat she so obviously wanted, but hadn't let herself have, along with real flowers and a real ficus. In fact, there wasn't a single living thing in the apartment besides the lady herself.

"What's wrong?" Maggie asked.

"I wondered why you don't have pictures of your husband and kids sitting around."

Her eyes rounded in alarm. "Who told you about my sons?"

"The question is, why didn't you tell me, Maggie?"

She looked around the empty apartment before she met his gaze and said, "I try not to spend much time thinking about them. How did you find out?"

"My captain has a file on you." Which Jack had taken with him, hoping it would tell him more about her. The information had been sketchy at best—except it revealed her sons had drowned on April 2, and her husband had died on April 6.

"Why would the Rangers be interested in me?" she asked.

Jack took a deep breath and said, "Because you're a murder suspect now, along with the doctor and his nurse."

Maggie leapt to her feet, abandoning the cat. "But why? I haven't done anything!"

"You had opportunity, Maggie. You've worked for law firms representing all three hospitals where the suspicious deaths occurred. And you had motive."

"What motive?"

"The same as the doctor and his nurse. Sparing the families of those kids the same kind of suffering you endured when your kids drowned and one of your sons ended up on life support."

Her complexion turned chalky, and she swayed. He crossed quickly to catch her, afraid she was going to faint. He eased her onto the flowered chair and knelt in front of her. "Maggie? Are you all right?"

She nodded, then looked earnestly into his eyes. "I'm not the one who's killing kids, Jack. I won't deny I've suffered because of what happened to my sons. But I would never . . . I could never. . . ."

He wanted to believe her. But how could he, when all the murders had occurred during the same calendar days each year that her family had died? It was too much of a coincidence to ignore. Nevertheless, the rational part of him that argued "She's the killer" was being out-shouted by the impassioned part of him that said he couldn't want her so much if she was capable of such heinous crimes.

"Aw, Maggie," he said in a soft, husky voice. "What am I going to do with you?"

"Hold me, Jack. Please hold me."

It would have taken a stronger man than Jack to refuse her plea. He pulled her onto her feet and into his arms. She clung to him, her nose pressed against his shoulder, and Jack felt the warmth that was missing from the room seep into him.

"Maggie?"

He was asking if he could kiss her, if he could love her . . . if he could trust her. He felt her hesitation, heard the hitching breath she took. The tension in her body revealed the tug-of-war she was waging with herself.

At last she looked up at him, her heart in her eyes, her terribly lonely eyes, and said, "All right, Jack."

❧ *Chapter 8* ❧

There was no question of having a long-term relationship with Jack Kittrick. Maggie would not allow it. Besides she had proved with Woody that she didn't have the inner fortitude it took to make a lifetime commitment. She wasn't about to end up with another death on her conscience. She was willing to take the gamble of letting Jack get close, because she felt certain he was no more inclined to make permanent ties than she was.

It was safe to have an affair with him, because he was not likely to complicate matters by falling in love with her. He seemed to desire the same thing she did—a brief, close encounter with a willing partner. The fact Maggie had not once, in ten years, been tempted to have sex with a man should have given her fair warning. But she rationalized that after ten years, she was due a superficial sexual relationship.

She lifted her face and watched Jack's gray eyes darken as he lowered his mouth to hers.

The kiss was unexpectedly gentle. It wasn't until she parted her lips that he revealed the sexual hunger she had seen in his rigid features. His tongue surged into her mouth, mimicking the sex act and making blood rush to her extremities. She slipped her hands beneath his tux jacket to feel his strength as he pulled her close. His callused fingers made her shiver as they roamed her naked back from her shoulder blades to her nape, and back down the curve of her spine.

She could see the rapid pulse at his throat, knew hers must be beating just as fast. She felt breathless, excited, aroused. And terrified of taking that final step over the brink.

Abruptly she pushed at Jack's chest with the heels of her hands, but she didn't make much headway putting any space between them. He was big and strong and determined, and Maggie realized she might be in serious trouble. "Jack, stop!"

His hands paused at her shoulders, and he took a shuddering breath and let it out. "What's wrong?"

She wished he had separated them, but she remained wedged securely between his thighs. The heat and hardness of him were like a magnet drawing her closer. She tried to ignore the danger she faced if she let things proceed to their natural conclusion, but it was impossible.

"I thought I was ready for this, but I'm not," she said.

Jack sucked gently on her throat beneath her

ear, and she felt her body clench as though he were already inside her. She moaned a protest that sounded more like a passionate response to his lovemaking.

"You react to my kisses like a woman who's ready. What's the problem, Maggie?" he murmured, his breath warm and moist against her flesh.

"Jack, I can't get involved with anyone."

"Fine. We won't get involved."

She made a sound that was half laughter, half a plea for mercy. "I wish I could believe you."

He kissed her again, claiming her mouth with his, coaxing her to give in to the pleasure. For a brief moment she did. It was wonderful. Her blood thrummed. Her skin heated where he touched her. She felt more alive than she'd felt in ten long years. She could leap tall buildings. She could soar over mountains. The future was an open book, and all she had to do was rewrite it to include Jack Kittrick.

Maggie tore herself from Jack's embrace. "No! I won't let this happen."

Jack's eyes narrowed, and his brows lowered. "Won't let what happen? It's just sex, Maggie. We're two consenting adults. Where's the harm?"

"I've never been with any man except my husband," she admitted breathlessly. "I've never done this when I wasn't in love. It feels . . . I don't know . . . wrong."

His eyebrows rose halfway to his hairline.

"Your husband died ten years ago. You mean you haven't once—"

"No, I haven't," she interrupted.

His lips curved in a satisfied smile. "I see."

"What is it you see, Jack?" she said, afraid he saw way too much.

He backed away and picked up his Pearl from the bar where he'd left it. "You need a little time to get to know me. That's fine. To tell the truth, I'd be more comfortable if we prove you're not a serial killer before we hit the sack."

Her jaw gaped. "You mean you were considering making love to me even though you think I might be a murderer?"

Jack shrugged. "I was willing to give you the benefit of the doubt."

"But you're not entirely convinced I'm innocent?"

He hesitated, then shook his head.

"This is insane." Maggie crossed to the bar, opened the bottle of Jack Daniels black label, and poured an inch into a glass. She stood with her back to him, contemplating the liquor. *She had nearly made love to a man who believed her to be a child killer. She still wanted him, was still vulnerable to his kiss, to his touch. He made her feel . . . everything . . . again.*

Maggie wanted not to feel anything. She wanted not to have to make any choices. It was tempting to seek oblivion in a bottle. Sorry to say, it wasn't the prospect of being a murder suspect that bothered her, so much as the fact she didn't seem to be able to let herself enjoy sex with a man she didn't love. It wasn't fair.

Jack came up behind her close enough that she could feel the heat of him, smell the scent of fresh-cut evergreens in his cologne. "If you're taking that drink because of me, don't. I'll leave if you want me gone."

She grasped the edge of the bar and held on for dear life. "I haven't had a drink in over nine years," she said. She turned to face him, her lips curved in a self-deprecating smile, wanting desperately to lean on somebody—on him—but knowing she had to stand on her own two feet. "I suppose I can resist another day. That's how it's done, you know. One day at a time."

He was standing too close, invading her space as a lover would, and he seemed to realize it, because he took a step back. His eyes searched her face, and she wondered what he was looking for.

"You're an alcoholic?"

He said it like he wanted her to deny it. Unfortunately, she couldn't. "Afraid so. When my sons drowned and my husband died all in the same week, I wanted to die myself." She hesitated, debating how much to tell him. *As little as possible,* a voice warned. At last she said, "I couldn't face life without my family, so I lost myself in a bottle. That's where I stayed for nine long months."

"What turned you around?" Jack asked.

She managed a smile. "Uncle Porter gave me a reason to come back from the dead. I've managed to stay sober ever since."

"What happened just now?"

"This isn't the first time I've been tempted to take a drink, Jack," she said. "So far I've managed to resist."

"What happens when you can't?" he asked.

"I hope I never find out."

He played with his beer bottle, but he didn't drink from it again. "My mother was never able to quit for very long."

"You mother's an alcoholic?"

"Was," he corrected. "She started drinking for the same reason you did, I expect—loneliness after my dad was killed in the line of duty. She died about two years ago. The liquor finally ate up her liver."

"I'm sorry."

"So am I," Jack said. "When I was a kid. . . ."

He didn't finish the sentence, but Maggie could fill in the blanks for herself. His mother had most likely embarrassed him in front of his friends, maybe even mistreated him. Drunks were an unreliable bunch. She felt sorry for Jack but knew he wouldn't appreciate an offer of sympathy. "A lot of folks don't make it back to sobriety, Jack," Maggie said. "I have."

"But it's a constant struggle, isn't it?" Jack prodded.

"Of course. Alcoholism doesn't go away."

"Hypothetically, you could fall off the wagon at any time."

He was pushing her, challenging her. "I suppose it's possible," she conceded.

"I just watched you pour yourself a drink, Maggie. It's more than possible." He sounded angry. His jaw was taut, his gray eyes dark as an East Texas thunderstorm.

"What's the problem, Jack?"

"I don't have much use for alcoholics, Maggie. They're doomed individuals."

"What about reformed alcoholics?"

"I don't know any." His features were rigid, his muscles taut. "Isn't it about time we got out of here?"

Maggie picked up her stole from the sofa and slipped it over her bare arms. She stood silently while Jack adjusted the black, satiny fabric around her shoulders. She felt tight inside, sick to her stomach. She understood where his lack of tolerance came from, but there was nothing she could do to change the facts. If Jack wanted her, he was going to have to accept her, flaws and all. At least now they both knew where they stood.

Jack watched Maggie's face as the attendant brought his Chevy pickup to the front of her condominium but didn't see any signs that she was upset he hadn't come in a car. He opened the door for her and helped her up into the truck, then scooted around the hood and got in himself.

He couldn't think of anything to say, and she didn't speak. In silence they headed out onto the MacArthur Freeway toward downtown and Alamo Plaza, where the outdoor gala was being held.

He probably should have kept his mouth shut about his mother's alcoholism, Jack thought. It was none of Maggie Wainwright's business. But he'd been shocked to discover she was an alcoholic. His mother's alcoholism had made his childhood hell—between the fear that she would die and leave him alone, the humiliation when his friends saw her drunk, and the shame that he was ashamed of his own mother. He had sworn on her grave that he'd never put himself in a situation where an alcoholic could hurt him again.

What he ought to do was get as far from Maggie Wainwright as he could as fast as he could. But that wasn't possible, because she was a murder suspect. And because he wanted her more than he could ever remember wanting a woman in his life.

It dawned on him that it shouldn't have mattered one way or the other whether she was an alcoholic, if all he wanted from Maggie Wainwright was sex. In fact, now that he thought about it, he'd made love to a few women over the years who drank to excess. So why did it make such a difference with Maggie?

Jack didn't have time to answer the question, because they had arrived at the Rivercenter, an indoor mall and hotel near the Alamo, where the gala attendees were supposed to park. The Cancer Society Gala was spread out on the paved courtyard directly in front of the Alamo. Tables had been set up, and a small orchestra played in the gazebo on the square.

The weather was beautiful, clear and cool and calm, with a full moon above. Jack took the parking stub from the valet and went around to help Maggie out. He had to hand it to her. She managed the most graceful exit from a truck he'd ever seen by a woman in an evening gown.

He offered his arm, and as they walked the short distance to the Alamo said, "Have I told you how beautiful you look tonight?"

She stumbled, and he slipped his arm around her to keep her upright. She glanced back as though to see what had tripped her, but there was nothing but flat sidewalk. She avoided his eyes as she replied, "Thank you for the compliment. You look very nice, too."

"I usually clean up pretty good."

"I should have trusted you—"

"I rented the tux from Anthony's," he said at the same time.

She flashed him a startled look, then laughed, a silvery sound that made the hairs stand at attention all over his body. Her eyes looked bright and excited, and all he could think of was taking her somewhere dark and private and finishing what they'd started.

"I hope you won't mind sitting with a

bunch of lawyers," she said. "You already know Roman and Lisa. You'll also meet—"

She cut herself off as they reached the greeting line established on the south side of Alamo Plaza. "Good evening, Victoria," Maggie said. "I don't believe you've formally met Jack Kittrick. Jack, this is my mother-in-law, Victoria Wainwright."

"It's nice to meet you, Mr. Kittrick. Margaret's told me so much about you."

There was a great deal of innuendo in Victoria Wainwright's voice. Enough to make Jack uncomfortable and to put a dusky flush on Maggie's cheeks.

"I'm glad you could come this evening," Victoria said. "It's always nice to have attractive people attend these events. It helps increase the newspaper coverage."

Jack couldn't quite believe what he'd heard. He wasn't sure what reply to make, and thankfully he didn't have to come up with one. The curtness of Maggie's voice when she excused them from the line said it all for him.

"I'm sorry," Maggie said, as soon as they were far enough away that Victoria couldn't overhear them. "Among society women like Victoria, charity fundraising is a fiercely competitive sport. It's a game to see who can raise the most money, who garners the most important people, the most coverage of the event in video and print. Victoria lives for it. And she seldom loses."

"What did you tell her about me?" Jack asked.

Maggie stopped abruptly and turned to face him. "Not enough for her to insinuate more."

She met his gaze directly, even though he could see, with help from the decorative red, white, and blue lights hung all around them, that her color was still high. "Victoria would be happy to run my life. I'm happier running it myself. Can we just forget about her and enjoy the evening?"

"That's fine with me," Jack said.

Maggie led them through the milling crowd of socialites dressed in World War II fashions to their numbered table, which had been set up far enough from the gazebo that they could hear themselves talk over the orchestra. Jack was glad to see the table had already filled up with people. He didn't want to be alone with Maggie right now, because he was tempted to throw caution to the wind and suggest they forget about the gala and get a room at the Menger, next door.

When they reached their table, the decision was taken out of his hands as Maggie began introducing him to everyone. She started with Roman and Lisa, probably because he already knew them.

He thought Lisa looked great in a strapless gown that revealed a great deal of cleavage. She had dressed for a man, but her body language announced that the man she had dressed for was her husband. Jack noticed the surprised look she gave the doctor when he slipped his arm protectively around her shoulder.

With his attention focused on Roman and Lisa, Jack missed the next few introductions. It was a change in the tone of Maggie's voice to something warmer, more intimate, that made him look closely at the man she was introducing.

"This is Tomas Sangamo, our newest partner," she said.

Sangamo appeared to be in his mid-thirties, of Latin descent, with black hair and brown eyes that had long black lashes most women would have envied. The guy could have been a model or a movie star. Tomas stood graciously to shake Jack's hand, his grip brief and firm. His gaze was open and friendly without being intrusive, and his voice was a pleasant baritone.

Jack glanced at Maggie, then back at Sangamo, and wondered why they hadn't been lovers. They obviously shared a deep affection. He waited for Maggie to introduce him to Sangamo's date, or his wife, but the man had come alone. Had Sangamo expected to spend the night dancing with Maggie? He could think again.

Jack smiled and slipped a possessive arm around Maggie's waist. "Nice to meet you, Tomas." He wasn't so different from good old Roman, Jack mused as he met Maggie's startled gaze. He kept his eyes on hers as he tightened his hold on her waist, drawing her closer.

From the corner of his eye, Jack saw eyebrows rise and astounded looks exchanged around the table.

They're not used to seeing her claimed by a man in public, he realized. *Or at least, not used to her accepting that sort of advance.*

He waited for Maggie to give him some sign to let her go, but it didn't come. So he held on. It was male instinct that had caused him to stake his claim on her and pleasure that made him keep her hip pressed against his own. She felt delicate and womanly, and Jack started thinking of a dark room and a soft bed again.

Before he could stop her, Maggie settled in the vacant chair next to Tomas. He pulled out the last empty chair, which happened to be next to Roman.

Lisa leaned across Roman and said, "We're having a picnic and Easter egg hunt tomorrow afternoon at our house. You'll have to compete with our daughter, Amy, for eggs, but there'll be plenty of good food. Maggie will be there, and Tomas and Roman's nurse, Isabel Rojas. I hope you can join us."

Jack saw Maggie roll her eyes at Lisa, obviously deploring her matchmaking techniques, but he wasn't about to give up the opportunity to spend more time with Maggie and, of course, observe the doctor and his nurse. "I'd like that," Jack said with a smile.

"We live in Alamo Heights. Maggie can give you directions," Lisa said.

"I guess the ladies have decided to have us spend some time together, doctor," Jack said.

"Call me Roman, please," Hollander said.

Jack noticed the doctor seemed distracted and wondered if Hollander really felt some other man could steal his wife away. Jack took another look at Lisa Hollander and snorted under his breath. Lisa was leaning toward Roman, and she hadn't once taken her gaze off the doctor. The anxiety was all on Roman's side. Unless . . . Jack wondered if Lisa was keeping such a sharp eye on her husband because she expected *his* eyes to roam.

He remembered she had referred to Isabel Rojas as "the doctor's nurse." Shouldn't she be on more familiar terms with the woman after all these years? Were Hollander and his nurse perhaps having an affair? Or were they just plotting mercy killings together? At least if they were here, they weren't at the hospital killing kids.

"Jack?"

Jack turned back to Maggie and only then realized she had put her hand on his to get his attention. A surreptitious glance revealed that he wasn't the only one at the table to notice her touching him. "Did I miss something?"

"I asked if you'd like to dance."

Jack worked to keep the confused frown off his face. Maggie had made a point of telling him she didn't dance, yet here she was, asking him onto the dance floor. She gave a slight, jerky nod, and he realized she must want to tell him something without anyone else over-hearing them.

"I'd be glad to dance with you, Maggie," he said, rising and pulling her chair back as she stood. "Excuse us, please," he said to the rest of the table.

"I think we'll join you," Roman said. "Lisa?"

Lisa shot her husband a brilliant smile. "Thank you, Roman. I'd love to dance."

Two other couples joined them, leaving Tomas and a single woman—one of Maggie's associates—at the table together.

"Jack? Are you there?"

Jack turned his attention to Maggie and realized she was perturbed with him. "What is it you got me out here to say to me, Maggie?"

She didn't answer.

Jack gently lifted her chin and asked, "Maggie? What's going on here?"

"I just wanted to dance."

Jack heard the yearning, the suggestion that she wanted more. Since he was the one who'd backed off at her house, it was up to him to make the next move. Jack ignored the voice that warned *Be careful, Jack*, and said, "I still want you, Maggie."

She looked up at him, her eyes wary. "Warts and all?"

"You've got warts?" Jack exclaimed in mock horror. "Where?"

Maggie laughed, then sobered. "You know what I mean. Can you deal with the fact I'm an alcoholic? Because if you can't—"

Jack cut her off with a quick, hard kiss. "I'll deal with it." He felt her body relax into his. "Does this mean you're ready for a relationship?"

"Not a relationship," Maggie corrected. "An affair."

Jack pulled her close, as he deftly turned her to the music. "Between the two, an affair isn't the choice I'd expect most women to make."

"Maybe they don't know what they want. I do."

"Which is?"

"No complications. No commitment. A brief, mutually pleasing interlude."

Jack looked at her and shook his head. "You only think that's what you want."

"Why do you say that?"

"Because women always end up wanting commitment. It's the nature of the beast."

"Not me, I assure you."

Her eyes slid closed, and she leaned her cheek against his shoulder. "Oh, God," she murmured. "I want you so much."

He could feel her nipples, pointy against his shirtfront, and his body hardened like a rock. "Let's go somewhere we can be alone. Please, Maggie."

"All right, Jack," she whispered.

Jack felt a tap on his shoulder. He turned irritably to brush off whoever had interrupted them and found himself looking into Victoria Wainwright's pale blue eyes.

She smiled and said, "May I cut in?"

✤ *Chapter 9* ✤

Roman pulled his wife close on the ballroom dance floor, moving to the nostalgic forties sound of "Sentimental Journey" being played by the orchestra. The decorations at the Cancer Society Gala matched the music. Red, white, and blue bunting had been hung everywhere in Alamo Plaza, and World War II posters adorned the gazebo.

All of the women, including his wife, had donned 1940s fashions—clingy, silky, slinky gowns—and wore their hair to look like Betty Grable and Rita Hayworth and Barbara Stanwyck. Roman thought Lisa, with her short brown hair swept under in back, looked a lot like Navy nurse Patricia Neal when she was wooed by Commander John Wayne in *Operation Pacific*.

Roman was aware of other men staring at his wife and felt a sick churning in his stomach. He was losing her. Even after their desperate lovemaking the night she'd come home from Dallas, things weren't the same as they'd been three months ago. That was when things had started going wrong between them.

At first, he'd been understanding when Lisa turned her back on him, pleading fatigue, but he'd missed the physical closeness they'd always shared. When she was still turning him down two weeks later, he'd stopped asking, waiting for her to reach for him when she was ready. To fight his frustration, he'd worked longer hours and come home so tired he wondered if he'd have been able to make love to her if she asked. But she never had.

He'd thought the problem had finally resolved itself when they'd made love last week after their argument. Lisa had been every bit as excited and excitable a lover as she had ever been. But they hadn't made love since. Roman had been afraid to ask for fear she'd turn him down and the cycle of rejections would begin again. And Lisa hadn't reached for him, either.

What was going on? What had happened to their perfect marriage? Everything had been so wonderful. What had gone wrong?

It was still hard for Roman to believe how hard and fast he'd fallen for his wife four years ago. How amazing it was that Lisa had loved him back. How intense and uncontrollable his feelings for her still were.

When Lisa nestled her cheek against his shoulder, Roman reached up to caress her nape but eased his hand back down to her waist without touching her. His parents had always been appalled at any sort of intimate gesture in public, and Roman had to catch himself whenever he felt such an urge with his wife. It wasn't much easier for him to make such tender gestures in private. And lately he hadn't made them at all.

He'd rarely been able to tell his wife in words how much he cared for her. Every time he tried to say "I love you," his heart pounded and his throat felt like someone had garrotted him. His feelings were stuck inside, and he couldn't get them out.

But over the years of their marriage he had shown her. He sometimes wondered what she thought of how often and how fiercely he had made love to her. Of course, all that had stopped abruptly three months ago, and the fear of losing her had become a claw tearing at his insides.

"You're all tensed up," she said.

Her warm breath in his ear made it even more difficult to relax. "It's hard sometimes to forget about everything going on at the hospital," he said by way of excuse. "Are you enjoying the dance?"

She murmured agreement deep in her throat, and the sound made his groin tighten. As simply as that, she could make him ache to put himself inside her. But he hesitated to ask her to come home with him now and make love, because he wasn't sure what he'd do or say if she refused him again.

Had she fallen out of love with him? Roman wondered.

Roman had never understood what it was about him that Lisa had found so admirable that she was willing to overlook his age and the tremendous commitment of time he gave to his work to marry him. And these days, between his job and hers and the time they gave to their daughter, Amy, there was little left for the two of them. There wasn't time to nurture their love. No wonder it seemed to be dying.

He had asked Lisa several times to quit her job, but she was adamant about having a career. They'd had harsh words over it last Thursday. "I need my work," she'd said. "It's important to me. You never said anything before. Why are you objecting now?"

It should have been obvious to her; it was to him. "I never see you anymore," he'd said. "I want you to think about quitting your job and staying home."

For a moment her eyes had seemed . . . frightened. "I'm not giving up my job, Roman. I can't. I won't!"

"Why not? What's so damned important about your job?"

She'd given him a panicked look, opened her mouth to speak, then shut it again without a word.

When he reached for her, she'd whirled and run from the house. Thank God she'd gone to see Maggie. Thank God Maggie had convinced her to come home.

Making up had been emotionally wringing

for both of them. He'd apologized for yelling, and she'd apologized for running away. He'd started kissing away her tears and his mouth had ended up on hers. He'd made love to her as though it were the last time he'd ever have her in his arms . . . because he was uncertain what the future held for them.

Tonight he'd felt jealous when Jack Kittrick had conferred his wife with an admiring look. Not that Lisa had ever given him reason to be jealous. He didn't believe their problem had anything to do with another man. But he found himself leaning over to ask, "What do you think of Jack Kittrick?"

"He doesn't strike me as Maggie's type," Lisa replied.

"Why not?"

"In the years I've known her, I haven't seen Maggie with any man who wasn't too old and stodgy for her—or interested in the wrong sex. Jack Kittrick is a real man."

Roman's neck hairs bristled at Lisa's complimentary assessment of the other man, but he forced himself to stay calm. "What does that make me?" he asked.

She looked up and met his gaze, then laid her head back on his shoulder and said, "The man I love."

It should have been enough that she'd said the words. Except she hadn't been looking at him when she'd said them. She never did. It had never bothered him until they had become estranged, and he realized his own shortcomings in the same area.

"Why do you do that?" he asked abruptly. He felt her stiffen in his arms and realized his voice must have been harsher than he'd thought.

"Do what?" she asked.

He forced the fear—and the consequent anger—back down and said, "Why do you always look away when you tell me you love me?"

She looked up at him again, a fleeting glance, before she tucked her head back under his chin. "I don't know."

She had to know. She just wasn't telling him. But he knew better than to pursue the subject. Whenever he pushed, she backed into a protective, noncommunicative shell, like a turtle, and waited safely inside until he no longer threatened her with questions she wasn't willing to answer.

Consciously, Roman knew that if Lisa hadn't truly loved him, she could easily have left him anytime during the past four years and supported herself on what she made as a lawyer. For a brief period he had feared she stayed with him only because Amy needed a father.

Stop torturing yourself. Accept what she says at face value. Lisa loves you, and you love her. Don't

*worry away your happiness. Things will get back
to normal. Just be patient.*

But he could feel Lisa drifting away. Fear
encircled him like a net, and no amount of
struggling freed him from the torment of
knowing he was going to lose his wife unless
he did something to turn things around. He
could cut out a cancerous growth with preci-
sion, but he couldn't heal what he couldn't
see. And Lisa's problem, whatever it was, remained a mystery to him.

He pulled Lisa more tightly into his arms,
and to his relief, she burrowed closer to him,
clinging to him as though she needed him as
much as he needed her.

"Roman," she said against his throat. "Amy
should be asleep by now. Why don't we go
home?"

His mouth went dry at the thought of what
Lisa was suggesting. "Don't you have to stay
and be sociable?"

"You can say you have an emergency at the
hospital."

"What a clever wife I have," he murmured,
wanting to kiss the shell of her ear, imagining
it in his mind, but remaining aloof in public,
as he always did.

"Let's hurry, Roman. I don't think I can wait
much longer to have you inside me."

When she said things like that, the top of
his head nearly came off. Maybe tonight
would be the turning point. He took her hand
and dragged her through the stifling crowd, un-

caring of the stares they were getting, single-minded in his determination to get her where he could lay her down and take what she was offering.

"Roman," she said with a laugh. "Stop. Let me tell Maggie we're leaving."

They had reached their table, but everyone was still on the dance floor except Tomas and one of Lisa's female colleagues.

"Would you please tell Maggie that Roman got a call, and we had to leave?" Lisa said to Tomas.

"I'll be glad to pass on the message," he replied.

A moment later they were headed for the Rivercenter. Roman gave the valet his parking stub and gripped Lisa's hand tighter while he waited for his Mercedes to arrive.

She put her other hand over his and said, "I'm not going anywhere."

"Am I holding you too tight?"

"A little," she said. "But don't let go."

He drove home in a sort of mindless state, aware of her hand on his leg, near his hip. Aware of the weight of her breast against his arm. He knew from experience that she would already be wet and ready for him. His whole heart and mind and soul were focused entirely on her.

Before Lisa, he had been following in his parents' footsteps, devoting himself utterly and totally to being the best doctor he could be. Nothing else had mattered. In one fleeting glance, Lisa had turned his life upside down. He understood now, with the possibility of losing her so real, that without her—without her love—life wasn't worth living.

He skidded to a stop in the red-brick driveway of their Alamo Heights mansion and heard Lisa's throaty chuckle before she said, "Patience, my love. Patience."

He walked behind his wife, aching to put his hand on the small of her back as he ushered her inside the two-story Victorian house but denying himself the pleasure. Even without touching her, Roman felt her warmth all the way to his toes.

Just inside the door, she slid her hand down the front of his tuxedo pants and said, "Hurry back. I'll be waiting for you," then ran up the winding wooden staircase.

Roman stood behind the breakfast bar in the "kitchen hiding his arousal and explained to the teenage babysitter that they'd had a change of plans. She looked outraged, as only a teenager could, until he promised she wouldn't lose anything because of it.

"I'll be paying you for the whole evening."

"All right!" she crowed happily.

Roman wished he didn't have to postpone their assignation to take the babysitter home. What if Lisa changed her mind? Unfortunately, the young woman they'd hired to live in when Amy was born, Connie Sanchez, had gone home to Mexico for a week to be with her mother, who was recovering from a gall bladder operation. Since the situation couldn't be helped, he and Lisa had been making the best of it.

Roman tried to keep the irritation out of his voice as he said good night and dropped the teenager off at her door, ten blocks away. He ran most of the stop signs getting back home but took his time getting up the stairs, taking off his bow tie and jacket long before he got to the bedroom door. He stopped cold when he saw Lisa wasn't in bed waiting for him, or as far as he could see, anywhere in the bedroom. *Not again.*

"Lisa?"

The bathroom door was open, and he stepped close enough to see whether she was in there. She wasn't.

Suddenly he knew where she had to be. He dropped his tie and jacket on the bed and headed for Amy's room. He eased his daughter's bedroom door open and saw Lisa sitting on the bed beside Amy, who was sound asleep. He came up behind Lisa and slipped his hand possessively around her nape and felt her shiver in response. *I want you. I need you.* He thought the words but didn't say them.

"I couldn't resist saying good night to her," Lisa whispered.

"I know." He leaned over to kiss his daughter's brow. With Amy he was able to exhibit so much more affection than he could with his wife. "She feels a little warm," he said.

"She's fine," Lisa answered. "You worry too much."

It was true. But how did one stop? He loved them both so very much. He did not know how he had survived before they came into his life, but he knew he could not live long without them.

Lisa reached for his hand and led him out of Amy's bedroom, tugging him toward their bedroom doorway. She shut the door behind them and turned to him, her dark eyes glowing. "Please, Roman. I need you."

Roman's throat ached. All his fears seemed so foolish. Lisa wanted him. She needed him.

He knew he ought to ask her for some explanation of what had been troubling her, to get it out in the open, so it never came between them again. But he decided it could wait.

Roman reached for his wife and enfolded her in his embrace.

Jack felt flags of heat on his cheeks as Victoria Wainwright looked him up and down. She couldn't miss his erection. From the sardonic curve of her lips, she hadn't.

He turned to Maggie and said, "Would you mind if I danced with Mrs. Wainwright?"

"Of course not," she said. But her straight-backed, chin-upthrust exit from the dance floor told Jack she wasn't too happy about the situation. As far as he was concerned, the interruption couldn't have come at a worse time.

"Shall we?" Victoria said, holding out her arms to him.

Jack didn't see how he could refuse. He was careful to keep her at arm's length, though it was plain she wouldn't have minded dancing a lot closer. He had to admit she was well preserved. The clingy material in a deep plum color she wore didn't reveal any bulges that shouldn't have been there. Mrs. Wainwright was a damned fine-looking woman. But she was too perfect to be real, like a mannequin.

Jack wanted more than anything for the dance to end so he could get back to Maggie . . . until it dawned on him this would be a perfect time to ask Mrs. Wainwright why she spent so much time with the children at the hospital. He figured he'd better ease into the subject and started with something neutral. "The decorations are nice."

She surveyed Alamo Plaza like a queen eyeing her domain. "It was an inspired choice, if I do say so myself, Jack. May I call you Jack?"

Jack would rather not be on any closer terms with the lady but knew better than to say so. "Sure," he answered.

"All those World War II movies being promoted this year with Tom Hanks and Arnold Schwarzenegger have brought the period back into vogue. Women love to dress in figure-enhancing styles like those of the forties, and a war theme has the additional cachet of being patriotic."

She smiled and added, "Kitty Nickerson

will be sick when she finds out my Cancer Society Gala has outearned her Heart Association Ball."

"Does it really matter who makes the most? I thought the object was to raise money for charity," Jack said.

Victoria laughed. "My dear Jack," she said, running a blood-red fingernail across his cheek, "among those of us in Texas society who matter, it matters."

"Like reading to kids in the hospital matters?" Jack said.

A confused expression appeared briefly on Victoria's face, replaced by a shrewd, calculating look. "Why, Jack, I didn't know you were aware of my activities with the children."

Jack shrugged. "It came up in conversation when I was interviewing the nurses about a malpractice claim."

"What did the nurses have to say?" she asked archly.

"That you're devoted to the children."

"Did they?" Victoria said, relaxing slightly, her smile less rigid. "I try to help where I can."

"Why do you do it?"

"What?"

"I heard you spent hours reading to a child who was in a coma—Laurel Morgan. Why would you do that?"

Victoria's eyes narrowed. "The child deserved to hear her favorite stories in her last moments."

Jack tensed. "Her last moments?"

"The prognosis was not good for Laurel. I stayed with her, read to her, because I didn't think she should be alone at such a time."

"Were you there when she died?" Jack asked.

Victoria's gaze shifted to somewhere in the distance. "Poor child. She was alone at the end."

Did Victoria know what he'd been driving at? Did she know that by saying the child was alone, she was exonerating herself from murder? Jack was having a hard time reconciling the sensitive, sympathetic Victoria Wainwright at the hospital with the woman who treated charity fundraising as a competitive sport. It didn't compute. Nevertheless, he was at a dead end. "I think what you do is a good thing," he managed to say.

Victoria smiled approvingly at him. "Now Jack, we have more important matters to discuss."

Jack eyed her warily. "We do?"

"I want to know your intentions."

"Intentions?" Jack was genuinely puzzled by the question.

"Toward my daughter-in-law."

"I don't think that's any of your business, ma'am."

"Victoria, please," she corrected with a forced smile.

"All right, Victoria. What is it you want from me?" Jack said bluntly.

"I want you to stay away from Margaret,"

she said, just as bluntly. "She's not in your class."

"I think you have that backward. Don't you mean I'm not in her class?"

"I meant what I said. Margaret's a babe in the woods where men are concerned. She doesn't recognize a lone wolf when she sees one. I do. Leave her alone."

"Why? What's your interest in this?"

"Margaret is a widow, a Wainwright, and the mother of my one remaining grandchild. She has a reputation in the community to uphold."

Jack was stunned by Victoria's revelation. "Maggie has a living child? I thought both her sons died."

"Brian lived. Didn't she tell you?"

Jack shook his head, unable to speak.

"I'm not surprised," Victoria continued. "She won't even tell me where she keeps the boy. It's no wonder she keeps him hidden, the condition he's in."

"What condition is that?" Jack asked.

"Brian drowned, Mr. Kittrick. He suffered brain damage and spent a year in a coma. What condition do you think he's in?"

"I wouldn't know, ma'am. That's why I asked you."

Victoria's lips pursed. "It sounds to me like Margaret has been keeping secrets from you, Jack."

"Like what?" Jack asked.

Victoria's blue eyes narrowed, and her lips

thinned. "Like the fact she murdered my son and my husband. Like the fact she's responsible for my grandchildren drowning."

A shudder curled down Jack's spine. He let Victoria go as though she'd suddenly opened her mouth to reveal poisonous fangs. His skin felt odd, prickly, and he realized the hair all over his body was standing straight up. "Those are serious accusations," he said.

"Ask her," Victoria said. "See if she denies it. She won't, because she can't."

❧ *Chapter 10* ❧

Jack left Victoria Wainwright standing in the middle of the plaza and went searching for Maggie, expecting to find her at their table. He finally located her on the dance floor—in the arms of Tomas Sangamo.

He hesitated only a moment before he threaded his way through the dancing couples and tapped Sangamo on the back. "I'm cutting in."

Sangamo's wide, toothy smile looked brilliant against his bronze skin. "Of course. But I warn you, Maggie's a terrible dancer." He laughed as Maggie made a face at him.

Jack swung Maggie into his arms, pulling her close. "I think it depends on her partner."

Tomas watched them move together for a moment, saluted Jack with a flick of his finger against his brow, and said, "I concede the issue, *señor*."

Jack tried several times in the next few minutes to ask Maggie to confirm or deny Victoria's accusations, but couldn't find the right words to ask.

"I can see you've got a burr under your saddle," Maggie said at last. "What did she say to you?"

"That you murdered your husband and father-in-law. That you were responsible for your children drowning. And that one of your sons is still alive."

Maggie shivered in his arms.

"Was she telling the truth?" Jack asked.

Maggie stopped moving and stared wordlessly at him. He let her go, even though she looked like she needed desperately to be held.

"I'd like to go home," she said.

"All right. I'll take you."

She stared him in the eye and said, "I won't talk about it, Jack."

"I think I'm entitled to an explanation."

She shook her head. "No, you're not."

"You're a murder suspect, Maggie," he reminded her.

She lifted her chin. "Are you going to arrest me?"

"You know I don't have enough evidence to do that. Yet." He didn't know why he'd added the "yet." Surely there was some explanation for Victoria's accusations. Surely if Maggie were really guilty of all Victoria had accused her of doing, she would be in jail right now.

Jack figured he could probably find out most of what he wanted to know by prompting Victoria, but he wanted to hear what Maggie had to say for herself. He took one look at her defiant stance and realized this wasn't the place to pry it out of her. "Let's go."

"I can get a ride from Tomas," she said.

"I brought you. I'll take you home." The song ended, and they threaded their way through the mass of couples dancing in front of the Alamo.

Maggie picked up her wrap at the table and said good night to Tomas and the other associates sitting there, but before the two of them could make a graceful exit, a trumpet fanfare sounded, a spotlight hit Maggie full in the face, and the strings of red, white, and blue lights above them were extinguished.

Jack stood beside Maggie, out of the spotlight, unsure of what was going on. Another spotlight picked up Victoria Wainwright sitting at a table with the mayor of San Antonio, the governor of Texas, and several other dignitaries and philanthropists.

A microphone screeched, and when it quieted a man said, "Ladies and gentlemen, may I have your attention, please?" Another spotlight picked up the speaker on the steps of the gazebo wearing a World War II marine officer's dress uniform. "Victoria, Margaret, will you join me up here, please?"

Jack suddenly recognized the man in uniform as Porter Cobb. "What's going on?" he asked Maggie.

"I can only guess." She hesitated, and for a moment he thought she might leave with him, after all. But however reluctant a participant she might have been in whatever was about to happen, she apparently didn't dare opt out.

The spotlights followed her and Victoria onto the steps of the gazebo, where they stood on either side of Porter Cobb.

Jack sank into the chair beside Tomas, who said, "I don't think our Maggie is happy with this command performance."

Jack made himself ignore the reference to "*our* Maggie" and asked, "Why did Cobb call her up there?"

Tomas arched a brow. "You don't know? Mrs. Wainwright might have chaired the gala, but Maggie took care of all the details."

"Meaning, I suppose, that Maggie did the work and Victoria is taking the credit?"

Tomas grinned. "Very astute, *señor*."

"So if Victoria wants all the credit, what is Maggie doing up there?" Jack asked, pointing with his chin at the trio on the stairs.

Before Tomas had a chance to make any sort of response, Victoria took Porter's place in front of the microphone and said, "We have a very special guest here tonight, a soldier who fought in World War II. A soldier whose father fought in World War I, and whose great-grandfather fought for the Confederacy. A soldier whose great-great-grandfather fought for Texas freedom at the Alamo! Ladies and gentlemen, Henry Zamora."

A spotlight hit a thin, elderly man in a poorly fitted World War II private's uniform as he stepped out the front door of the Alamo and followed him as he marched over to join

Victoria on the steps of the gazebo. He smiled and waved at the crowd, who went absolutely wild.

The orchestra played a loud, up-tempo version of "The Yellow Rose of Texas" while cowboy "Yee-haws!" and shouts of "Remember the Alamo!" resounded. The string lights snapped back on as confetti rained down on them and red, white, and blue helium-filled balloons floated in the sky over the Alamo. The whole place suddenly resembled a political convention with the next presidential candidate on the platform.

Jack looked around and realized it was one of those utterly Texan moments from which myths and fables arose—totally ridiculous, yet almost glorious at the same time.

"Mrs. Woodson Wainwright will partner this descendant of the Alamo in a dance, which we hope you'll all join," Victoria said.

It was clear to Jack from the brief expression that crossed Maggie's face, that this was the first she'd heard of it. But she smiled graciously at the old man and helped him off the steps and onto the dance floor, spotlighted the entire time.

The orchestra began playing a familiar-sounding forties tune and the dance floor, which was already filled with people, separated visibly into smiling, happy couples. A few began singing the words to "I'll Be Seeing You," and soon everyone had joined in.

Jack stood along the adobe wall that had

served as part of the Alamo fortress, watching Maggie dance with the World War II veteran, knowing he couldn't very well cut in on a Descendant of a Hero of the Alamo. He kept a close eye on Maggie, not at all sure she wouldn't take advantage of the opportunity to sneak away and avoid answering his questions.

He watched her move to the music, admiring her grace. He saw her mouthing the words to the song and smiling at the old man, then looking for Jack . . . and finding him.

Jack knew he'd never hear that tune again without thinking of Maggie. He would always remember her eyes as they looked at that moment. Desolate . . . and yearning.

The instant the dance ended, he was at her side. He edged her through the crowd, but Victoria Wainwright caught them before they got away.

"You can't be leaving so soon," she said to Maggie.

"I'm tired, Victoria," Maggie said.

Jack wondered why Maggie hadn't added, "And furious with you!" but took one look at the tension between the two women and realized it wasn't necessary. Victoria knew exactly how Maggie felt. She just didn't care.

"Get out of my way, Victoria," Maggie said.

"I've stood by for ten years and watched you pretend none of it ever happened," Victoria said. "But I don't intend to let you forget,

Margaret. You killed them all with your self-ishness and your—"

Maggie tried to step by her, but Victoria grabbed her forearm, her blood-red nails tearing into Maggie's flesh and leaving deep gouges. Jack caught Victoria's wrist and tightened his hold to force her to free Maggie. The three of them stood connected in the violent tableau until, with a grunt of pain, Victoria let Maggie go.

Jack instantly released her. "Go wait for me by the gazebo, Maggie."

"I can handle this myself, Jack. Why don't you go—"

"I'm not leaving without you," Jack said.

Victoria clapped. "Quite a lovely scene of devotion." She eyed Jack and warned, "Just don't turn your back on her. You may not live to regret it."

Victoria stalked away and left them standing there, Jack fighting back the reckless urge to strangle the woman, and Maggie trembling with . . . fear? No. It was rage, Jack realized. Very controlled rage.

"Shall we go?" he said.

"You heard Victoria's warning. Are you sure you still want to take me home?"

"I can take care of myself."

Maggie's lips curved. "It's a good thing you didn't say you could handle me."

"I was going to say that next."

"Be glad you didn't," Maggie said, heading for the Rivercenter.

The drive home was as silent as the drive to the gala had been, but the space between them seemed electrically charged. Jack's hackles were still up from the confrontation with Victoria, and his heart was pounding hard in his chest. It took him most of the drive back to Maggie's condominium to figure out why.

"This is far enough," Maggie said, when he pulled up under the portico at 200 Patterson.

Jack scowled at the attendant, who was careful to keep his face blank. "I'll see you to your door," he said. By the time Jack got around the truck, Maggie had already let herself out. He laid his callused fingertips on the small of her back beneath the satin stole, a constant flesh-to-flesh touch that she fled as she moved quickly ahead of him into the elevator.

She unlocked her front door and turned to keep him at bay. "Good night, Jack. I—"

He reached behind her, shoved open the door, and edged her inside. "We have some talking to do."

She walked away from him, gathering the satin stole protectively around her, before she turned to face him. "What is it you want from me?"

"The truth, Maggie."

"About what?"

"About you. About your past. Tonight was the second time I've learned some startling information—unbelievable information—about you from a third party."

"I'm not a murderer, Jack. I'm not a horrible person."

"What happened to your kids, Maggie? What happened to your husband?"

"My sons drowned, Jack," she said in a hard, cold voice. "And Woody died."

"That isn't enough, Maggie. I want to hear all of it. How did they drown? How did he die? The truth. Everything you've been hiding from me, starting with why you never mentioned one of your sons is still alive!"

Her eyes went wide with fright before she turned and ran for the bedroom, abandoning the satin stole, which floated toward the carpet.

Before it could land, he caught her, shoving her back against the wall, pinning her there with his body. He swore under his breath when he realized he was hard and ready, and what he really wanted to do was put himself inside her.

But he couldn't. Not with all the lies of omission that stood between them. He felt so much, too much, all of it feral. His eyes burned into hers, and what he saw made his gut twist.

Hopelessness . . . and raw anguish blurred by tears that spilled as she tried to blink them back. She was rigid as a fence post held taut by barbed wire. When he reached out to brush a tear from her cheek, she bucked against him, inflaming him even more.

"I don't owe you anything, Jack. If you don't let me go *this instant*, I'll—"

Jack backed up, his breathing choppy, his

pulse pounding at his temples, his hands balled into fists to keep him from reaching for her again. "I'll find out the truth, Maggie."

"Nobody knows the truth but me, Jack. It's nobody's business but mine."

"The police in Minnesota—"

"Despite Victoria's accusations, no charges were ever brought against me."

"What happened to the son who didn't die, Maggie? Where is he?"

She looked as though he'd kicked her in the stomach. "I can't tell you that, Jack."

"I need an answer, Maggie."

"Brian's someplace safe," she said. "Someplace where he can be cared for properly."

Safe from whom? Jack wondered. Then he remembered how upset Victoria had been that Maggie wouldn't tell her where her surviving grandson was. *Safe from his grandmother?* Jack thought with horror.

"Do you see him, Maggie? Do you visit your son?"

"Of course I do! What kind of mother do you think I am?"

He forked a hand though his hair, leaving it askew. He didn't want to believe the worst of her, but for an innocent woman, she had an awful lot of secrets. "I don't know what to think of you, Maggie."

Her shoulders squared, and her chin tilted up in defiance. But he saw the defeat in her eyes.

What was it she had lost?

The same thing he had lost, Jack realized. Any hope of a relationship . . . even a superficial sexual one.

"I still want you, Maggie."

She hissed in a breath, and the pulse at the base of her throat speeded up, but her stance didn't soften. "Go home, Jack."

Jack stood where he was another moment, feeling the heat of her, smelling the scents of her and him mixed up together. She was right, of course. He was crazy to want her when he knew so little about her . . . about her secrets. The physical attraction between them had to be resisted. At least until a few more things got settled. "Good night, Maggie."

Jack stood looking at her for another heartbeat, then headed for the door.

"Jack."

The sadness in her voice stopped him. He glanced at her over his shoulder, repressing the urge to reach out to her. "Yes, Maggie?"

"Goodbye."

"I'm not going far. And I'll be back." He needed to finish things between them one way or another. He didn't want the memory of her, of wanting her, haunting him the rest of his life.

All he had to do was unearth the real killer. Then he'd come back and find out what secrets kept Maggie Wainwright locked in such a barren life.

*   *   *

Halfway down the stairs, Jack realized he had left Maggie alone and upset with four bottles of booze. What if she found the liquor she'd bought for him too tempting to resist?

On the other hand, it wasn't his responsibility to keep her sober. In fact, if he'd learned anything from having an alcoholic for a mother, it was that there wasn't much you could do to separate a determined alcoholic from her bottle except put her in an institution somewhere. Jack reminded himself he was better off staying out of it.

He reached the guardhouse and waited for the scrolled iron gate to open. The longer he sat there, the more agitated he became. He backed up instead of going through the gate and made a U-turn to the right—almost sliding into the empty gully where the San Antonio River would have run, except for the drought—and headed back toward the upscale condominium. He hadn't gone twenty feet before Maggie passed him headed the opposite direction in a white Mercedes coupe with a black cloth top.

She never saw him. Her eyes were riveted to the road in front of her. If he drove all the way back to the entrance, she'd be long gone before he got turned around. Jack jerked the wheel and crushed a couple hundred dollars' worth of impatiens and begonias alongside the road as he turned his truck back around.

He caught up to Maggie just as she turned

off Patterson and headed south. Jack followed her to I-35. Was she heading back downtown to the gala? Before she reached the MacArthur Freeway she headed west on I-10. The southwest side of town was mostly poor and mostly Spanish-speaking. Why would she be heading in that direction?

At least she hadn't stayed home to drink, Jack thought. That was small comfort, however, because there were plenty of bars in southwest San Antonio. Maybe she was going to see her son. Jack hoped so. If he could see the boy, see where she kept him, how she related to him, it would answer a lot of his concerns.

Maggie exited into one of the poorer neighborhoods and turned west again, deeper into Spanish-speaking San Antonio.

Jack pulled to the curb as she edged her coupe between two pickup trucks at a rowdy cantina. He started to get out of his truck, then realized Maggie was still sitting in the coupe. When a couple of drunks shoved open the wooden door and left the bar, the music was loud enough that Jack heard the twang of string guitars from a really wretched Mariachi band from where he was parked halfway down the block.

After the two men left in a rusted-out pickup, Maggie opened her car door and got out. Her sleeveless white knit top was tucked into skin-tight jeans that were tucked into bright red cowboy boots. The garish neon lights from the cantina turned her flesh green, like a piece of surreal art. This strange Texas barfly was another part of Maggie ... one he had no desire to know.

Jack started to get out of his truck, determined to stop her from going inside. Before he could act, she was back in the coupe. Stones sprayed as she backed out of the gravel parking lot and headed south again. He followed her south and west until they were in a section of San Antonio he was familiar with only because it had been singled out in San Antonio police statistics for its vicious gangs, illegal drug sales, and drive-by shootings.

Maggie pulled into the parking lot of what he thankfully realized was a Catholic church. It was old enough to be built of adobe, rather than brick or cement. After she hurried inside, he parked his truck beside her coupe, wondering whether either vehicle would be there when they came back out.

He got his Colt from beneath the truck seat, checked the rounds, and stuck it in the back of his tux trousers under his jacket, where he could get to it if he needed it. Then he headed for the door she had entered and stepped inside.

Stairs led down into a stygian gloom. Jack took his gun out and put his back against the adobe wall as he eased down toward the voices he could hear below him.

Drugs, he thought disgustedly. *She's jumped*

from alcohol to drugs. Probably needs them to deal with the guilt of killing her husband and father-in-law . . . and drowning her sons. An insidious voiced added, *And killing a bunch of kids?*

The stairs went down a long way. The place must have been a refuge from Indians once upon a time. Or maybe a wine cellar for the priests, he thought more cynically. When he got to the bottom of the stairs, Jack took a quick look around the corner, then laid his head back against the wall, closed his eyes, and slowly let out the breath he'd been holding.

"Jesus," he said. "Lord Jesus, help me."

✦ *Chapter 11* ✦

It was an AA meeting. After his mother died, Jack had sworn he'd never go to another one with anybody. Damned if Maggie hadn't tricked him into coming here! His conscience— not to mention Captain Buckelew—would never let him hear the end of it if he didn't stay and make sure she got home safely.

A man at the front of the room announced, "My name is Hector, and I'm an alcoholic."

"Hey, Hector," the crowd responded.

Jack slipped the Colt into the back of his tux trousers and eased into a metal folding chair on the aisle at the back of the room, which was filled almost to capacity. He knew there were nonsmoking AA meetings, but this wasn't one of them. A smoky haze drifted over the audience, most of whom also held Styrofoam cups of coffee.

Because of the shadowy light, the coolness of the place, and the stunted walls of dirt and straw that surrounded him, Jack had the sensation of being buried alive. He glanced over his shoulder at the long stairway that led back up to the outside world. Some of these lost souls would make it out of here. Some would not.

Jack located Maggie and watched her as the young man on a slightly elevated platform at the front of the room told the story of how he'd become an alcoholic, what had turned him around, how long he'd been sober—"two months and eleven days"—and what his life was like now—"Not too good, you know? Because my wife won't take me back, you know? Because she says I won't stay sober. And I'll hit her again." A pause and then, "I really miss my kid, you know?"

Jack hardened his heart against Hector's story. He saw himself in the victim's role, and he hadn't much sympathy for the alcoholic. Chances were, Hector *would* fall off the wagon. His wife was right to keep her distance from him. It was too bad about the kid, but based on his own experience, Hector's kid was better off without an alcoholic parent around.

That might seem heartless, but it was the way he felt.

When Jack saw Maggie head for the front of the room, he slid down to his tailbone behind the woman in front of him. He hadn't really expected Maggie to get up and talk, and he didn't want his presence to keep her from saying whatever it was she planned to say. It was obvious she knew the routine.

"Hello. My name is Maggie, and I'm an alcoholic."

"Hey, Maggie," the crowd responded.

She spoke so softly, he could barely hear her at the back of the room. He sat up and hunkered forward on his chair, listening closely.

Jack wondered why Maggie had come all the way over here to attend an AA meeting when he was sure there was a smokeless meeting held right in her own neighborhood. As Maggie began to speak, the reason she wasn't telling her story anywhere near anyone who might know her as Margaret Wainwright, attorney and daughter-in-law of the late Richard Woodson Wainwright, became painfully apparent.

Maggie seldom looked up at her fellow alcoholics. Her eyes stayed locked on her hands, which were twined and knotted in front of her. "I first started drinking when my sons drowned and my husband died all in the same week."

She cut off the sympathetic sounds from the crowd by saying, "I blame myself for their deaths. I know it doesn't make sense to think I could have caused what happened to them to happen. But I can't help thinking that if I hadn't. . . ."

She took a hitching breath, and then another. Her chin wobbled. When she looked up, her eyes were pooled with tears.

Jack waited with bated breath for the rest

of her confession. The room was absolutely silent. Had they all heard this before? Did they know what was coming? What had Maggie done? How was she responsible? Why did she accept blame for her family's deaths but not take liability for her father-in-law's demise?

Jack swore under his breath when he realized, as Maggie began speaking again, that she wasn't going to answer any of his questions. She had completely changed the subject. Jack blew out a frustrated breath as he followed her speech.

"You cannot imagine what it was like to hear that my beautiful sons, Stanley and Brian, had both drowned, and that my husband, Woody, was not expected to survive more than a few more hours," she said in a voice raw with pain. "I was beside myself, completely hysterical. I couldn't live with the guilt of knowing what I'd done. I wanted to die, to be with them."

Jack was confused. Although one of the boys had survived, Maggie was making it sound like they had both died.

She lowered her eyes again, and the lawman in him wished he could see into them to search for the truth. *What really happened, Maggie? You aren't telling us the whole story. What are you hiding?*

He was shocked by her next revelation.

"I . . . I tried to kill myself with an overdose of sedatives the hospital gave me," she said.

"My husband's uncle found me in the hospital chapel before the pills could do their work. I was kept in a psychiatric hospital for quite a while, because I made the mistake of admitting I would kill myself the instant they let me out."

Jack heard the return of the sympathetic responses from the audience that kept Maggie talking through her pain. He was intrigued—and discomfited—by what he was hearing. Maggie suicidal? Maggie hospitalized for mental instability?

"By the time the hospital released me, I realized that while I still felt remorseful, without the powerful emotions that I had felt when I first learned what I'd wrought, I no longer had the courage to kill myself."

She took a deep breath and let it out. "I hated myself for being a coward. And I blamed myself totally for what had happened to my family. I had to escape somehow, and I found that escape in a bottle."

What did Porter say that turned you around? Jack wondered. He got his answer immediately.

"Nine months later my husband's uncle sought me out. He wanted to know why I was ignoring my one remaining son in favor of a bottle of alcohol." She shook her head slightly and frowned, as though she were remembering the moment. "At first I was confused . . . because I was drunk and because what he was saying was both impossible and what I had so often dreamed of hearing.

"I told him, 'My sons are dead.' But he said, 'Brian is very much alive. He's come out of the coma, and he needs his mother.'"

Maggie's face became an image of wonder and joy. Her voice was unsteady as she finished, "That was the beginning of my struggle to stay sober. I haven't taken a drink since that day, nine years, eight months, and twenty-nine days ago."

The audience whistled and clapped and shouted enthusiastically.

Jack wanted to know who the hell had neglected to tell Maggie one of her sons was still alive. He waited to hear what had happened when she got sober and finally saw her son again. But she skipped past everything that had happened over the past nine years and focused on the present.

"My son lives in a home now, and I see him as often as I can. I have a steady job, and I'm happy. And sober."

The audience applauded again, and Maggie headed back to her seat.

Jack's mind was whirling. *Why had she thought Brian was dead in the first place? Why hadn't someone told her something sooner about her son being in a coma? Where had the child been all that time? What had made Porter Cobb come looking for her so much later? And why didn't Victoria Wainwright know where her grandson was living now?*

Jack wasn't sure how long Maggie planned to stay at the meeting, now that she'd testified, and he figured he'd better leave before he got caught. He didn't want Maggie thinking he was following her, and he'd be hard-pressed to come up with an explanation for being in this part of town. He waited until she had settled into her chair, then rose and headed for the door.

A priest stepped in front of him and said, "I hope you find the peace you seek, my son."

The words froze Jack in place, taking on a far greater meaning than he knew the priest could have intended. He'd had no peace since . . . since he'd watched the light die in a little girl's eyes.

When he could move again, he hurried past the priest and took the short, narrow stairs three at a time to reach the top and freedom. He heaved a lungful of fresh night air as soon as his feet hit the asphalt parking lot and stood waiting for the muscles in his throat to unclench so he could swallow.

The priest's offer of peace had not provided a balm for his soul. It had only reminded him of a little girl with brown eyes and pigtails he'd been trying hard to forget.

Jack's eyes burned, and his nose stung. Maggie wasn't the only one with secrets. Jack had terrible secrets of his own.

He clambered into his pickup, gunned the engine, and bumped in and out of a deep pothole as he backed out of the parking lot. He wasn't going far, just up the street where there wasn't any light, so he could watch Maggie's car to make sure it didn't get stolen, then follow her home to make sure she got there safely.

The neighborhood was surprisingly quiet, and there wasn't any traffic. Jack turned the radio dial to KASE, one of Austin's popular country music stations, but the sad wail of the violins and the even sadder tale being told in Clint Walker's nasal twang only made him feel worse.

Jack shut off the radio, but in the dark, in the silence, he had too much time to think. Too much time to remember.

Where are you, Maggie? Let's move it. Let's get out of here.

A little girl's face appeared before him. Her trusting smile was so painful to see that Jack closed his eyes to make her go away. Since she wasn't really there except in his mind, that accomplished nothing.

Jack's body tensed as the memory grabbed hold. He was in a motel room that reeked of gin. The smell of gin—his mother's drink—made his stomach knot. A nearly empty bottle of Beefeater sat on the Formica bedside table, while the woman who had drunk it sat in the center of a messed-up, sagging motel bed. She was half covered by an olive-green tufted spread, her legs curled under her, the pillows stuffed behind her. A child of four snuggled securely against her side.

The woman held a snub-nosed .38 pressed to the little girl's heart. "Tina b'longs with me," the woman sobbed drunkenly.

Her mascara-streaked eyes were unfocused from alcohol, but her agony was apparent. She had lost custody of her daughter in a hard-fought courtroom battle with her wealthy husband. Instead of turning the child over to the father, the mother had run with her. She had told the father over the phone that she would kill herself and the child if he came after them.

Because it was a kidnapping and the woman had fled through several jurisdictions, the Texas Rangers had gotten involved, and Jack had been assigned to the case. He had finally run down Lilly Mott in a seedy hotel in New Braunfels, a charming Victorian town off I-35 between San Antonio and Austin best known for its killer flash floods in the spring and its German Wurstfest, featuring sausages and beer, in the fall.

His job was simple. All he had to do was save the little girl's life and bring the mother in for psychiatric evaluation. Jack had called for backup, then, posing as the manager, talked Mrs. Mott into opening the motel room door. But nosy onlookers gave away the game before help could arrive.

Mrs. Mott had lurched away and produced a gun that she aimed at her daughter, forcing Jack to draw his weapon.

She had stumbled backward to the bed and

climbed up onto it, keeping her daughter close. "Stay away or I'll kill her and shoot myself!" she cried.

Jack had closed the door behind him to make sure she didn't throw him out and started talking as fast as he could. "Don't shoot," he said. "I'll put down my gun. Just don't shoot."

He'd laid his Colt carefully on the floor in front of his feet. He knew any minute the local SWAT team would arrive and put pressure on Mrs. Mott to give up her daughter. He was equally certain that if they did, Lilly Mott would kill the little girl.

Her despair convinced him she meant business. With nothing more to lose, it wouldn't matter to her whether she lived or died and took her daughter with her. But whatever courage had brought her this far seemed to have abandoned her. She moaned and writhed hopelessly on the sagging mattress, like a worm trapped in a bed of ants that were consuming it alive.

"Would you mind if I speak to Christina?" Jack said.

"Why you wanta do that?" Lilly said in a slurred voice.

"You have a very beautiful daughter, Mrs. Mott." The little girl had brown eyes shaped like a cat's. Her dark brown hair had a fringe of bangs and tiny pigtails held up by rubber bands with little red balls on them. "I just want to meet Christina, if that's all right."

"Okay."

Jack extended his hand toward the little girl as an excuse to move closer to the bed. Christina hid her face against her mother's breast and clutched at her mother's soiled dress. He paused within a foot of the bed. Close, but not close enough yet to try grabbing for the gun.

He let his hand drop to his side and said, "Hello, Christina. My name is Jack. That's a very pretty dress you have on."

Christina peeked out at him, then picked up the hem of her navy and white pinafore to show it to him. "My mommy got this dress for me."

Jack made eye contact with Mrs. Mott and said, "I'm sure your mommy loves you bunches and bunches."

The little girl looked up at her mother, her smile revealing the gap between her two front baby teeth. "Mommy loves me bunches and bunches."

Mrs. Mott stared down at her daughter's trusting face, her tired features strained in an agony of indecision. She looked up at Jack. In a way common to drunks, one he knew well, she spoke slowly, exaggerating each word to make herself understood.

"I—am—not—an—un—fit—mo—ther."

"Of course not," Jack agreed. "I know Christina's welfare is the most important thing in the world to you. Don't you think you should—"

"We have you surrounded, Mrs. Mott!"

Jack cursed as the amplified sound shattered the rapport he had been building with Lilly Mott.

"Stay away!" she screamed at Jack, and then to those outside, "Leave me aloooooone!"

Jack heard the child cry out sharply as her mother jabbed the nose of the gun in her side. He backed up, his hands held wide to show they were empty, and said, "Easy, Mrs. Mott. I'm not going to touch you. I'm not going to get any closer."

Her drunken words were garbled as she rattled off a stream of obscenities, but he could see the panic in her eyes. The little girl started to whimper, and Mrs. Mott put an arm around her and kissed her forehead and soothed her fears.

"It's all right, baby. Everything will be fine. Don't cry," she mumbled drunkenly.

"I'll tell them to keep their distance," Jack reassured Mrs. Mott. He shouted, "This is Texas Ranger Sergeant Jack Kittrick. Give us some peace and quiet in here to talk!"

"You've got ten minutes."

Jack swore under his breath, wondering what idiot had set a time limit on getting Mrs. Mott out of the motel, thereby increasing the pressure on the unstable woman.

She looked stricken. "Ten minutes," she sobbed. "Ten minutes. It's not enough."

"Shh. Shh, Mrs. Mott," he soothed her, feeling his heart pound and sweat dampen his armpits. "I won't let them come in here until you want them in here. You have all the time you need."

"He said ten minutes."

Jack turned his head and shouted, "Mrs. Mott needs more time. We'll let you know when we're ready to come out!" He turned back to the woman—who looked much older than she did in the recent picture her husband had provided of the three of them—and said, "Is that better, Mrs. Mott?"

Her face was puffy from the booze, and her sunken eyes had dark circles beneath them and were red-rimmed and bloodshot from crying. New tears carried clumps of mascara farther down her face. She brushed at the streaks agitatedly, blackening her fingertips and cheeks. She swiped at her runny nose with the back of her hand, smearing mucus across her face.

"I have to do it," she said, looking up at him, seeking understanding . . . and approbation.

Jack's heart clutched. "No, you don't," he said, his voice harsher than he'd intended. "Think of Christina graduating from high school, Mrs. Mott. How proud you'll be. Think of her walking down the aisle in her white wedding gown. Think of holding your first grandchild in your arms."

She looked up at him, her eyes blurred with tears, her mouth open and contorted as though she were screaming.

No sound was coming out.

"Mrs. Mott," he said, working to keep his voice calm, though he felt frantic, desperate, knowing he was running out of time. "Think about—"

"He won't let me see her," she babbled hysterically. "He says I'm an unfit mother. He says I'll hurt her. I would never hurt my child."

Jack felt the rage welling inside him, bubbling and hissing and spilling over like hot lava. He wanted to shake Lilly Mott until her teeth rattled, until she woke up and listened to herself. *I would never hurt my child.* Bullshit. She was about to *kill* her kid! Didn't that count? There were lots of ways to hurt a child besides the physical ones. What about the shame and humiliation of having a drunken mother? Didn't that count?

Jack felt the ledge he was perched on crumbling out from under him. Why had he come in here in the first place? Why hadn't he waited outside and let someone else do this? Lilly Mott was his mother come back to life, and he hated her the way he'd hated his mother. If she weren't pickled in alcohol, he could talk to her. It was the gin that had turned her so crazy. The goddamned stinking booze!

He could see Mrs. Mott was steeling herself to shoot, trying to find the nerve to end it all. He watched her finger squeezing the trigger. It was now or never.

Jack lunged for the gun.

Lilly Mott's eyes widened until the whites showed all around, and her mouth formed a surprised O.

Jack cried out in despair the same instant the gunshot resounded in the small room. The horrendous noise reverberated in his head, making his ears ring and sending shock waves through his body.

Too late! Too damned late!

His hand was clenched around hers on the .38, but he didn't bother wrenching the gun away. He stared frozen in horror at Christina as her body slumped and her eyes went blank and a trickle of blood streamed from the corner of her tiny cherub's mouth.

Noooo! Noooo! Jack screamed in his head. But the sound was real. Raw and aching, it filled the room, echoed from the walls, and carried outside to the blue sky and the green grass and the policemen waiting with guns ready.

A keening sound erupted from Lilly Mott's throat. She let the gun go and grabbed her daughter and rocked the limp, lifeless body of her child in her arms. The noise coming from her throat reminded Jack of the sounds his mother had made when she got the news his father had died. He recognized the hopeless lament. What followed after had torn his heart out and left a gaping hole in its place.

The motel door burst open, and Jack was surrounded by cops with guns in their hands.

He sat on the bed beside the grieving woman and the dead child, his body shaking so hard he couldn't move. "She killed the kid," Jack said.

A tight-faced patrolman tore Mrs. Mott away from her child and another roughly cuffed her hands behind her. Two others were tender beyond words with the little girl, who couldn't feel a thing.

A policeman tried to help Jack stand up, but when he realized Jack was in shock, ordered the nearest uniform, "Get a paramedic in here. Move your ass!"

It's my fault. My goddamned fault that kid's dead. I despised Lilly Mott because she reminded me of my mother. She must have seen the disgust in my eyes. She must have felt my loathing for her. She gave up hope because my eyes told her there wasn't any.

"Jack? Is that you?"

Jack awoke from the nightmare and found himself staring into Maggie Wainwright's curious eyes. She had pulled her coupe up beside his truck on the wrong side of the road so she could lean out the window and talk to him. A glance at the church parking lot showed it was still mostly full, but the street around them was empty. He glanced at his watch and realized thirty minutes had passed.

"I saw the truck and couldn't help looking to see if it might be yours," Maggie said. "Sometimes cars from elsewhere in town find their way to this neighborhood," she added with a smile.

Looking at her, he felt the same fierce attraction he always did—along with another feeling that always came with it, one he hadn't recognized until this moment. *Fear.*

He was getting more deeply involved with this woman—an alcoholic, like his mother—every time he saw her.

Get out while you can, Jack, a voice warned. *It's not too late.*

Maggie's brow furrowed as she stared at him. "I thought you were going home. How did you end up here?"

"I was worried about leaving you alone with all that booze. By the time I got turned around, you were leaving." He shrugged. "I decided to follow you."

"Because you thought I was headed for a bar?"

He nodded.

She pursed her lips, and he could see she was perturbed. "I suppose I ought to thank you," she said. "But I have to fight my own demons, Jack."

"I know that!" he snapped. "That doesn't make it any easier for me to stand by and watch you struggle. What if you'd ended up in a bar, Maggie?"

"I suppose we'd both have hated me in the morning," she said, with a wry twist of her mouth.

"That isn't funny."

"Did you come in and listen?" she asked.

"I heard you speak. I ended up with more questions than answers when you were done."

Several more occurred to him. *Had Maggie*

*been telling the truth about when she took her first
drink? Had she perhaps been drunk when her family needed her? Was that why she blamed herself
for what had happened to them?*

Jack took a mental step back and looked at
the woman in the car across from him. The
last thing he wanted was to want her. Maggie's fight with alcoholism would provide a
constant reminder not only of his painful
childhood but also his failure to save a child
because he had let the past color his present.
To make matters even worse, Maggie had
her own ghosts to fight and might be exor-
cising them by killing other people's children.

Jack knew he was playing with fire.

Yet he couldn't walk away. Without her, he
felt as empty inside as a gutted steer. He
would find a way to deal with her situation.
He had no choice. Because of all the women
he had ever known, only Maggie had ever
filled up the hollowness he felt inside.

If only she wasn't a murderer, anything was
possible.

"I'll follow you home," he said at last.

"It isn't necessary," she replied.

"I want to make sure you get home without—"

"Stopping for a drink?" she finished for
him. "All right, Jack, you can follow me home.
I imagine you'll be more fun at the Hollanders' picnic tomorrow if you don't spend the
night staring at the ceiling, wondering where
I am."

"I'm right behind you," he said.

Even after he made sure Maggie got home, Jack didn't sleep well. He spent the long night tossing and turning on a rumpled bed of unanswered questions.

ᴥ *Chapter 12* ᴥ

"Do you want a hamburger or a hot dog, Maggie?" Roman called out as he carried a platter of raw hamburgers and hot dogs out his kitchen door to the gas grill on the screened-in flagstone patio.

"Hamburger," Maggie called back. "And in deference to *E. coli*, char it, please." She was treading water while hanging onto the side of Roman's backyard pool. She provided a second set of watchful eyes on three-year-old Amy, who was being pushed by her mother around the shallow end of the pool in a colorful, plastic duck-shaped float.

The Easter egg hunt, with Amy wearing a pair of paper bunny ears she and Lisa had made together, had been a painful reminder to Maggie of days gone by. She had forced herself to smile and cheer on Jack and Tomas, who had followed Amy around pointing out eggs for her to find.

"Hot dogs for me and Amy," Lisa said before Roman could ask.

"One hamburger, one hot dog," Tomas volunteered from his seat on the springboard at the deep end of the pool. "Any way they come off the grill."

"A hot dog sliced down the middle with American cheese melted on it," Isabel instructed from a lounge chair near the diving board.

"Figures," Roman said with a laugh. "You like everything American."

"*Si, señor*," Isabel said with an exaggerated Spanish accent. "*Todo Americano.*"

"Jack? What about you?" Roman inquired.

"Hamburger. Rare," Jack said from his spot half in, half out of the water on the stairs at the shallow end of the pool. "I like to live dangerously," he said when Maggie opened her mouth to object.

"Be sure to put on another hamburger and hot dog for yourself, Roman," Isabel said.

"Got 'em both right here." The hot grill sizzled as the last of the meat went on. "I could use some help in the kitchen," Roman said.

"I'll be glad to help," Isabel offered, already half out of the cushioned lounge chair.

"Don't bother," Lisa said quickly. "I'll help Roman. I have some other things I need to do in the kitchen."

Maggie cringed at the obvious friction between Lisa and Isabel. Lisa had told Maggie when she arrived that things were a little better between her and Roman, but the strain on Lisa's face, and the dark looks she darted at

Isabel, left Maggie wondering just how much better things really were.

She let her gaze roam from Isabel to Roman and back again. As far as Maggie could tell, Roman only had eyes for his wife. She wasn't as sure about what Isabel felt for Roman.

Lisa's yearning look as she met Roman's gaze told Maggie her friend was hoping for a few stolen kisses in the kitchen. Lisa obviously needed someone to take over with Amy while she was gone, but Maggie noticed Isabel wasn't volunteering for that.

Maggie looked longingly at Amy, but she didn't trust herself to be responsible for the dark-haired, dark-eyed pixie in the water.

"How about if I spell you?" Jack said to Lisa as he waded toward her.

"Amy doesn't usually take to—"

"Hey there, kiddo," Jack said, smiling broadly as he slipped an arm around Amy, duck float and all. Maggie noticed the little girl was entranced by Jack's smile and didn't see her mother slipping away toward the edge of the pool.

Lisa gave Jack a thumbs-up and mouthed, "Thanks, Jack." She leaned back in the water to wet her hair, then braced her palms on the aqua tile and used her arms to push herself quietly up and out of the pool like some sleek water mammal. Lisa never took her eyes off of Roman as she reached up with both hands to squeeze the extra water out of her hair, leaving her exquisite body outlined for him.

Maggie saw the hungry look Lisa got from her husband and glanced away before she intercepted anything more embarrassing. She knew Tomas wouldn't be interested, but she made a point of watching over Amy, certain Jack's gaze would also be distracted by Lisa's stunning white-bikini-clad figure. To her surprise, Jack's attention remained totally focused on the child.

Jack moved Amy into deeper water, so he was face to face with her. "How about you and me and Donald here taking a swim together?" he said to Amy.

Amy patted the duck's head and said, "Donald."

Jack patted his own head and said, "Jack."

Amy patted his head and said, "Jack," whereupon Jack patted her head and said, "Amy."

Amy laughed, delighted with the game. She patted the duck's head again and said, "Look, Mommy. Donald."

It was only then Amy noticed her mother was gone.

Her head swiveled as she searched her surroundings. When she couldn't find her mother, Amy turned back to Jack with woeful eyes and a wobbly mouth and asked, "Where's Mommy?"

Jack turned the duck toward the patio, leaned close to Amy, and pointed to the grill. "See those hot dogs over there?"

"I like hot dogs."

"Your mom and dad are in the house getting the catsup and mustard and pickles—"

Amy wrinkled her nose. "I hate pickles."

"Me, too," Jack agreed. "But I love ice
cream."

Amy and Jack began talking about foods
they liked and didn't like, and it was obvious
that, for the moment, Amy had forgotten all
about her mother's disappearance.

Maggie couldn't believe how good Jack was
with the little girl. Amy seemed fascinated by
him, and Maggie could easily understand
why. She found Jack quite fascinating herself.

"You two look like you're having fun,"
Maggie said, unaware of the wistfulness in her
voice.

"Come on over and join us," Jack said with
a grin, splashing water in her direction with
the heel of his hand. "Amy and I could use
some company."

"Company," Amy said, splashing her hands
in the water in imitation of Jack's gesture.

"The water's too deep for me to stand up
there," Maggie protested. The last thing she
wanted to do was get any closer to Jack's practically naked body. Even from this distance,
his magnetic attraction was doing strange
things to the underwire in her swimsuit bra.
Or maybe the damned thing was just rusty . . .
like she was when it came to dealing with
male advances.

Her black suit, cut low at the top and high
in the thigh, was more than ten years old. At

the time she'd bought it, Maggie had wanted Woody to appreciate every bit of what she had up on top and down at the bottom. Right now, she'd have given anything for a swimsuit with a skirt to hide her thirty-five-year-old thighs and some sort of corrugated fabric to conceal her turgid nipples.

Jack had obliged her by scooting Amy into what, for him, was waist-deep water. "Is this better for you?"

Maggie realized she was being watched by Isabel and Tomas, and rather than "protest too much," she swam over to join Jack and Amy.

Amy immediately patted Maggie on the head and said, "Maggie."

Maggie laughed and tweaked Amy's nose. "Amy's nose."

Amy picked up on the new game, and pretty soon they were all three touching each other's noses and ears and eyes and mouths as Amy identified each part.

Maggie wasn't sure, but it seemed to her Jack's touch lingered on her mouth too long and brushed her cheek too intimately. He caressed her earlobe in a way that sent a frisson of feeling skittering down her spine.

"Cold?" he asked when she shivered.

The sun was hot, and the pool was heated. She slanted a glance at him and admitted, "As a matter of fact, it's a little too warm right now for me."

The scoundrel didn't look the least bit repentant. He bent down and grasped her chin between his thumb and forefinger and stared at her until she got lost in his steel gray eyes. When it seemed inevitable that he would kiss her, Amy grabbed his chin and said, "Whiskers."

Jack let go of Maggie as though kissing her had been the farthest thing from his mind, rubbed his thumb across Amy's chin, frowned ferociously and asked, "Where are Amy's whiskers?"

Amy giggled. "Only daddies have whiskers," she informed him.

Jack suddenly caught Maggie by the nape and rubbed his bristly cheek against hers. "No whiskers," he said sadly to Amy, shaking his head.

Amy giggled again. "No whiskers on mommies. Just daddies!"

Maggie felt Jack's thumb seductively trace her lower lip before he abruptly released her and leaned down to rub his whisker-rough cheek against Amy's baby-smooth one. Amy grabbed his ears and held on, laughing as, with appropriate grunts and groans, he tried mightily but unsuccessfully to escape her clutches.

The masculine rumble of laughter and the childish giggles brought back memories for Maggie of her twin sons at three, playing with Woody on the frozen pond behind their house. Minnesota was the Land of Ten Thousand Lakes, but it was so cold most of the year that Stanley and Brian had learned to ice skate long before they'd learned to swim. Her sons had moved on the ice like stiff-limbed Frankensteins once they were bundled up in quilted, goose-down coats, with Minnesota Timberwolves scarves wrapped several times around their necks, hats tied down over their ears, and woolen mittens tugged onto their tiny hands.

Woody, who had gone to prep school in New England and played hockey in high school, urged her onto the ice, but she was an East Texas girl and preferred dry land. She had been content to sit on a fallen log near the pond and watch. If only she had been watching when . . .

"Where are you?" Jack murmured in her ear.

Maggie awoke from her daydream—and the inevitable nightmare that would have followed—with a start and consciously willed her racing pulse to slow. She reached out to Amy with both hands, wanting to hold her, wanting to know she was safe.

"Up!" Amy said, delighted by the new game. She took both hands off the sides of the duck float and, arms reaching high overhead for Maggie, slipped right through the tube and sank like a stone.

Maggie didn't even cry out Amy's name, just dived under in search of the child. She saw Amy, her eyes and mouth open, kicking like a frog underwater. She caught the child up in her arms an instant before Jack could reach her and popped to the surface with Amy clutched tight against her breast.

Amy came up sputtering, frantically wiping water and hair from her eyes. Maggie spared a hand to do the same for herself. She took several quick, gulping breaths and waited for her wildly beating heart to stop trying to escape her chest.

"Never, never take your eyes off a child when she's in the pool!" Maggie yelled at Jack the instant he surfaced.

"I barely—"

"You weren't watching! You have to watch!" Maggie helped Amy wipe the last of the water from her nose and mouth. "She could have drowned!"

Jack shot Maggie a frustrated look. "We're standing right here. She just slipped through the duck. It was no big deal."

"What if we hadn't been here?" Maggie raged. "Amy might have—"

"Let it go, Maggie. It's all over. Nothing happened."

Amy, none the worse for her dunking, had picked up on Maggie's hysteria and began crying.

"Give her to me," Jack said, clearly exasperated.

Realizing at last that her overreaction was only making things worse, Maggie handed Amy to Jack. He calmed the little girl, then handed her to Tomas at the edge of the pool. "Amy wants to swing," Jack said to Tomas.

"Amy wants to swing," Amy agreed.

"Then Amy shall swing," Tomas said as he headed with her toward the playground at the rear of the backyard.

"Come here," Jack said, holding his arms wide open for Maggie. When she hesitated, he caught her wrist and pulled her into his embrace.

Maggie felt the warmth of him and realized she was shivering with cold . . . with fright . . . with frightful memories. "It was awful, Jack," she said, pressing her face against his chest. "It was awful."

"I'm sorry, Maggie. I'm so sorry."

She didn't say anything else, and neither did he. They simply stood in the soothing—but potentially deadly—water and let it lap around them until Maggie was calm again.

"Do you want to talk about it, Maggie?"

She shook her head and started to let go of him.

"Don't let go," he said. "My knees are like soggy noodles."

Maggie looked up at Jack and for the first time realized his features were pale, his eyes stark, like an overcast sky. "Why, you wretch! You were as scared as I was!"

"For a heartbeat, maybe. You always think you're going to be able to save them, but . . . sometimes things go wrong."

"Do *you* want to talk about it, Jack?" Maggie asked, meeting his gaze, returning his offer of solace.

He shook his head. "It's all in the past, Maggie. I can't change it . . . I just have to learn to live with it."

As she held tight to Jack, Maggie experienced a peace she hadn't felt for a long time. She wasn't the only one fighting demons. Jack understood what she'd suffered. Maybe, someday, he would tell her the rest. Maybe, someday, she would tell him, too.

"Hey," Jack said at last, looking down at her. "Are you all right?"

"I was just thinking."

"Anything you'd care to share with me?"

She focused her eyes on the glistening water. "If you listened last night, you already know most of it."

"I'm a good listener, Maggie."

Jack's invitation was more than a little tempting, but based on what he'd told her about his relationship with his mother, Jack wasn't a forbearing sort of man. He wouldn't be able to forgive what she'd done any more than she'd been able to forgive herself. He might be offering her comfort at the moment, but what he really wanted from her was down and dirty, hard and heavy, panting, sweaty sex.

If she was lucky.

Maggie found herself staring at Jack's naked chest, at the thick mat of dark hair beaded with water crystal rainbows. Woody had been blond, with only a small patch of curls in the center of his chest and a runner's lean physique. At six feet even, her husband had always seemed tall to her. Standing in Jack's shadow, Maggie was aware of his greater height, the greater breadth of his chest, his obvious strength.

If anyone had asked, she would have said such things didn't matter to her. But it seemed she was as much a creature of nature as any other animal that looked for the strongest mate, the one best able to protect her and her offspring. She found Jack's strength attractive. She laid a curious hand on his furred belly and heard him gasp.

She looked up at him, aware of his suddenly hooded eyes, his flared nostrils, the fullness of his lips. "I've always wondered what a 'washboard stomach' felt like," she murmured. Maggie brushed her fingertips across his ridged flesh. "Now I know."

Jack grasped her wrist. "What game are you playing now, Maggie?"

"The same one you were playing five minutes ago," she quipped. "What's the score?"

"So far, a big fat zero," Jack muttered. "It seems you're ready to change that. Let's get out of here—"

She laid her hand flat on his chest, a mistake as it turned out, because all she wanted to do was slide it up around his nape and pull his head down so he could kiss her. "It really is a shame I'm a murder suspect and you're . . .

who you are," she said. "Otherwise, I might be tempted to accept your offer."

"Speaking of murder—"

"Let's not and say we did," Maggie said, abruptly stepping back from him and heading toward the stairs in the shallow end of the pool.

Tomas was still pushing Amy on a swing that was part of an elaborate playground. The little girl's shrieks of laughter were disconcerting because sometimes it was hard to tell whether Amy was just excited or really frightened.

"Tomas," Maggie called, "not so high."

"She likes to go high," Tomas replied.

"It's not safe," Maggie said.

Tomas caught the swing and slowed it down. "As you wish, *mi querida*."

When Maggie turned to settle herself on the pool stairs, she found Jack already there before her. "You didn't leave me much room," she said.

"You can always sit in my lap."

Maggie shook her head. "I haven't sat in a man's lap since. . . ." *Since Woody died.* "For a long time," she finished.

"Then maybe it's time you did," Jack said, catching her as she started to sit and easing her onto his lap.

"You have bony knees," she protested with a laugh.

"They aren't the only thing that—"

She put a hand over his mouth. "You're incorrigible."

"I can't resist you, Maggie. I don't want to resist you."

"What about all my secrets?"

"You'll tell me when you're ready."

Maggie got the unspoken message. He wasn't willing to wait until she had been proved innocent. Whatever had been started between them would now be resumed . . . had already been resumed, she realized, remembering the playful touches—maybe more than that in hindsight—Jack had given her when they'd been frolicking with Amy.

Although she had carefully maintained the two inches of space between her back and Jack's front ever since she had sat down, there was nothing she could do to avoid the feel of his masculine, hair-roughened legs beneath her. Maggie felt a physical need so strong it made her ache inside. Jack seemed ready to move forward, but she wasn't so sure she was.

"I should get up, Jack. People will get the wrong idea."

"People?" Jack said. "Look around, Maggie. Roman and Lisa are in the house. Tomas is busy with Amy. And Isabel. . . ."

Maggie looked toward the lounge chair where Isabel had been sunbathing and saw she was missing. Maggie followed Jack's gaze and watched the kitchen screen door swing closed as Isabel stepped inside.

"We're all alone, Maggie. There's no one

here to stop us from doing anything we want."

"Not now, Jack," she said.

He kissed her nape as his hand closed over her breast. His touch was shattering—like a bolt of lightning streaking to her core. *Oh, God, this can't be happening. Not now. There's no privacy, no—*

"When, Maggie?" he demanded, his voice harsh with need.

"Later," she gasped.

"When?"

"Tonight."

He bit her on the nape, then kissed away the hurt, his hands making one last grasping foray across her breasts that left her shivering with need.

He let her go and said, "Okay, Maggie. Tonight."

Lisa had barely taken two steps inside the kitchen door when Roman reached for her. She shivered as the air-conditioning hit her damp skin and stepped willingly into his embrace, pressing her body against his seeking heat. His arms surrounded her, and he pulled her snugly against him, hissing as water from her suit soaked through his sleeveless T-shirt and hit his flesh.

"I'm getting you all wet," she protested with a laugh. She tried to back away, but Roman held her tight.

"I don't care," he said. "I just want to hold you."

She pressed her cheek against his. It was almost as smooth as Amy's and smelled of soap because Roman thought cologne was a waste of money. "People should smell like people," he'd said. So sometimes Roman smelled of the strong antiseptics he used at the hospital and sometimes like the soap he used in the shower and sometimes, when the musky scent of sex had permeated his skin, she could smell herself when she pressed kisses on his flesh.

Lisa had been aware of a sort of desperation in Roman's lovemaking last night. She had never been so frightened for their marriage as she was when they lay panting on the sheets afterward.

What's wrong, Roman? she'd wanted to shout. *What's happening to us?*

She and Roman used to spend hours at night in bed just talking. Last night, Roman hadn't said two words to her. The only explanation she could find for why he was coming home so late, why he no longer wanted to talk to her, why he was always so tired after a day at the hospital, was that he was spending his time and energy with some other woman. With Isabel Rojas.

Then why did he make love to you last night?

Lisa had no answer to that. Unless it was simply that she'd asked. Maybe she would start asking more often.

Lisa stood quietly in the middle of the Mex-

ican-tiled kitchen floor letting the warmth of
her husband seep into her, wondering
whether he had ever held Isabel Rojas this
way. She forced the insidious thought from
her head as her fingers trailed up Roman's
back to his nape. She felt him tremble and
marveled at the power she had to make him
quake. Could Isabel make him shiver and
shudder and cry out as she could?

Lisa's heart pounded in her chest. She knew
she should listen to the voice of reason. It told
her, *Roman would never leave you without warning in the middle of the night like your father did.
He loves you and Amy. He would never leave
Amy.*

But Lisa's mother had said her father loved
Lisa dearly, too. And her father had left one
day and never come back. Her mother had become a bitter and angry woman as they became poorer and poorer.

Lisa clutched Roman's neck tighter. If only
she could hang on to him all the time. But she
had to let go every morning so he could go to
the hospital. And nowadays she was as guilty
of coming home late as he was. Reason had
very little to do with her fears . . . or her feelings for Roman Hollander.

On the day he had come to give an evening
lecture on medical ethics at the Bates School
of Law in Houston, she had sat in the classroom, listening to the timbre of his voice and
the intelligent sense of what he had to say, and
realized long before the two hours were up

that she wanted to spend the rest of her life with him.

He might as well have been a famous movie star, he seemed so unattainable, so unapproachable. Yet she couldn't let him leave without speaking to him. She had come up to him at the lectern after class with a thought-provoking question, one that would take at least two or three cups of coffee to discuss, and invited him to a nearby coffee shop to discuss it.

"I don't know . . ." he hedged.

She had looked him in the eye and said, "I'm twenty-four, Dr. Hollander. I'll be graduating in two months, and I plan to practice health-care law. I think these issues are important to my future. I would appreciate having the benefit of your wisdom and experience."

She knew it wasn't her mind he was evaluating as he looked her up and down, and Lisa could tell he liked what he saw. She knew she looked good even in the jeans and T-shirt she was wearing. It was the first time she could ever remember being grateful for her beauty.

"All right," he agreed.

"My name's Lisa," she said, as they walked up the stairs of the tiered classroom to the door. When he didn't offer his first name in return, she prompted, "What's yours?"

She saw the struggle on his face, the wariness and the yearning. The hunger had been unmistakable in his dark eyes even then.

"Roman," he said at last. "My name's Roman."

"That's a beautiful name, Roman."

"I've always thought it was kind of . . . never mind," he said with a self-effacing smile. "I'm glad you like it."

The force of his smile had made her knees buckle. She grabbed reflexively for his arm, and he said, "Are you all right, Lisa?"

Lisa. The sound of her name on his lips had made her quiver inside. She looked for some excuse for stumbling and said, "I'm a little stiff from sitting, I suppose. The walk to the coffee shop ought to solve the problem."

"Take my arm," he said. It was a gallant gesture men her age knew nothing about.

"Thank you, Roman." She had tried to calm her rattled nerves as she slipped her arm through his and laid her hand on his coat sleeve. It was the softest wool she'd ever felt and warm from his body. She stayed as close to him as she dared for the entire walk from the law school to Carey's Coffee Connection.

They had drunk coffee until Lisa was floating, while she listened to Roman talk animatedly about medicine. He was dedicated to his work, it seemed, to the exclusion of all else. His dark eyes made her heart jump when he focused them on her, and she was mesmerized by his hands, so strong and skilled . . . and gentle. She knew they would be gentle.

It wasn't easy getting Roman to talk about

himself, but she did. "I can't believe you've never been married," she said when he admitted he was a bachelor. "You have so much to offer a woman."

A charming flush rose on his cheekbones. "I . . . I . . ." It was the first time in five hours and forty-five minutes he'd been speechless.

The blush, and the tongue-tied moment that followed it, made him seem less godlike. Those small signs of humanness made her bold enough to say, "I live near here, and this place is about to close. Would you like to come home with me, Roman, so we can continue this discussion?"

She saw his nostrils flare for the scent of her, watched his dark eyes turn nearly black with desire, saw the rigidity in his full lips. The hair lifted on her arms as he reached across the booth for her hand and held it in both of his own. She felt the pulsing beat of his heart through his skin and realized her own was racing to beat in time with it.

"Why me, Lisa?"

She hadn't expected the question but knew instinctively what he was asking, his voice harsh with confusion and sexual desire. *Why are you issuing this invitation—for which I'm grateful and honored—to make love to you? You're young and beautiful and could surely have any man you wanted. Why did you choose me?*

From things she had gotten Roman to admit, she knew he was overly conscious of the nearly twenty-year difference in their ages,

that he was aware most women didn't consider him traditionally handsome, that he was
committed to his work and had very little time
to spend dating. He had proved by staying
single long past an age when most men married that he wasn't the marrying kind. So
what, he was asking, was the attraction?

Lisa knew the answer, had known it since
Roman opened his speech in the classroom by
saying, "Life is uncertain. Everyone here
should grab for life with both hands and live
it to the fullest every day, because there are no
guarantees."

As his hands curled into fists, grabbing at a
life lived in the here and now with no thought
for tomorrow, Roman Hollander had squeezed
out the emptiness her father had left inside
her. Hope had spilled into the chasm, hope
that she could find happiness by choosing to
live each day without worrying about the future. And she owed it all to Roman. His
words, his ideas, had filled her up and made
her whole again.

But they didn't know each other well
enough for her to tell him that. She had wel-
comed the signs of his vulnerability but had
been careful to show him none of hers. "Does
it matter why?" she said at last. "I want you,
Roman. Isn't that enough?"

Despite Roman's husbandly devotion for
the past four years, Lisa hadn't been able to
shake the fear that had always shadowed her

marriage. Lately, the fear had grown to more than a shadowy specter.

"I love you, Roman," Lisa said, careful not to let him see in her eyes how much she cared, how much he meant to her. That way, it wouldn't hurt so much when he left her for another woman . . . as she feared he might someday soon. Her father had taught her nothing was certain . . . or forever. Not even love.

She felt Roman's hesitation before he replied, "I adore you, Lisa."

Adore, not *love.* He had never used the word *love,* except the day he had proposed to her. "Do you love me?" she whispered.

"More than anything," he replied.

"More than Isabel?"

She hadn't realized she had said the words aloud until he gasped and grabbed her shoulders, shoving her away from him. The blood left his face, and his eyes turned a cold obsidian.

"How could you say such a thing? Is that what's been bothering you these past three months? Isabel is my nurse, Lisa, nothing more. I don't love her."

"But you admire her."

"Of course I do! She's a damned fine nurse. But you're my wife!"

"Husbands leave their wives for other women all the time."

Before Roman could reply, the screen door slammed as Isabel stepped inside. She looked from one face to the other, and said, "Am I interrupting something?"

Lisa noticed that Roman had let go of her as soon as he saw Isabel. He wouldn't want his lover to find him holding his wife. . . .

You have to stop torturing yourself, Lisa. You have to confront Roman and tell him it's over. You have to end this now . . . before he does.

It felt like someone was squeezing her heart, and it hurt. It hurt so much. Lisa made herself walk to the refrigerator and pull open the door and reach for the bowl of cole slaw. "Would you mind taking this out to the picnic table?" She handed the bowl of slaw to Isabel, though it occurred to her how wonderful Isabel would look wearing it on her head.

Isabel looked toward Roman, as though seeking his permission. When he nodded, she said, "Sure, Lisa. Anything else?"

"No, nothing," she said with a bright smile.

"Before you go, Isabel, would you mind tasting the barbecue beans?" Roman said. "I want to make sure I've got your recipe right."

Lisa watched in disbelief as Isabel joined Roman at the oven, watched as he dipped a spoon into the casserole dish, blew on the contents to cool it, then gently, carefully, held the spoon to Isabel's mouth. Their eyes never left each other's the whole time.

It has to be tonight, Lisa decided. She couldn't bear to watch the two of them together any longer. She wanted Roman to confess the truth.

No, she decided. She didn't want to know for sure they were lovers. It might be better simply to cut her losses, to tell him she had decided to leave him, rather than wait until he left her. Because he would never let her go if he found out she was pregnant.

✎ Chapter 13 ✐

The promises Maggie had made to Jack in the pool shimmered between them at the picnic table during lunch, leaving Jack on tenterhooks. The Hollanders' picnic seemed endless. He kept expecting Maggie to change her mind.

So far, she hadn't.

She sat across from him in a pair of lightweight khaki slacks, white Polo shirt, and brown sandals—the conservative outfit she hadn't worn to the firm picnic—chatting with Tomas and Lisa about a Wainwright & Cobb associate's new baby. She seemed completely oblivious to the earth-shattering nature of the evening he had planned for them—until he caught her looking at him. Their eyes met long enough for him to see her jittery nerves . . . and the banked fires waiting to be stirred into flame.

Shortly after lunch Amy began whining and fussing, and no suggestion anyone made could keep her entertained. "She needs a nap," Lisa said. "But I hate to leave you all here without a hostess."

With that hint, Isabel pleaded work at home, Tomas said he had to change clothes and meet a friend for dinner across town, and it was easy for Jack and Maggie to excuse themselves.

"I'll give Maggie a ride," Jack told Tomas, who had brought Maggie in his car.

"Okay with you, Maggie?" Tomas said.

"I have a stop to make before I go home," Maggie told Jack.

"I'll take you wherever you need to go," Jack said, determined not to let her slip away.

"Then I'll go with Jack," Maggie told Tomas.

Jack hadn't given Maggie another chance to change her mind. They were in his pickup and on their way in a matter of minutes. When they reached Broadway and Jack started to make the turn south to Maggie's condo, she told him to go north instead.

"Where are we headed?" he asked as he made the turn.

"New Braunfels," she replied.

Jack's eyebrows headed for his hairline. "You could have mentioned that earlier."

Maggie laughed. "You seemed determined to stick with me. I didn't think it would matter."

"It doesn't."

Jack watched her smile fade as sexual tension arced between them. Maggie might have postponed the inevitable, but that only gave the pleasant tension in his groin time to build.

"What's in New Braunfels?" he asked once they had exited from Loop 410 onto I-35 heading north.

"My son, Brian."

Jack reflexively slammed on the brake, swerved around a Subaru, and when he had control of the pickup said, "You could have given me some warning, you know!"

"Would you rather not meet him?"

Jack chanced a look away from the busy traffic in her direction. "I thought he was in a coma or something."

"Well, he's not."

"Tell me about him."

"I wouldn't know where to begin."

Getting information out of her was like pulling a calf that didn't want to get born. "Why is he in a home? What's wrong with him?" Jack asked.

"He's paraparetic."

Jack heard "paraplegic" and said, "Oh, he's in a wheelchair. Isn't that fancy condo of yours rigged for the handicapped?"

"The handicapped, yes. Brian needs twenty-four-hour-a-day attention. He's para-par-e-tic."

When she said it slower, Jack heard the difference. "Para-what? What's that?"

"Paraparetic," she repeated. "Brian was in a coma for nearly nine months. It was a miracle he woke at all, but he suffered brain damage that affected him both physically and mentally. Tremors and poor muscle control of his extremities keep him in a wheelchair. He lost his memory and had to learn how to talk all over again. Mentally, he'll never get much older than the six-year-old he was when he drowned."

Jack felt his bowels clench. "I'm so sorry, Maggie." He tried to imagine what she had been going through all these years, watching her son grow into a man but remain a child.

She must have read his mind because she said, "One of my few joys is knowing Brian sees life in simple enough terms to be happy most of the time."

Jack noticed Maggie's face had paled, and her hands were knotted in her lap. "What aren't you telling me, Maggie?"

"Nothing." She tried for a smile and failed. "I'm just a little anxious."

"If you're so reluctant for me to meet your kid, why are we doing this?"

She shot him a cautious look. "I think it's time, don't you? I mean, before we get any more involved than we are."

"We aren't *involved*," Jack said more harshly than he'd intended.

"We're about to make love, aren't we?" Maggie countered. "That is what you had in mind for the evening, isn't it?"

"Sex was what I had in mind."

She shrugged and ran a hand through her hair, which she was wearing down on her shoulders. "Semantics. We'll still end up joined as intimately as two people can be. I thought you should meet my son first."

"Why?"

"I'm not sure, exactly," she said, staring out the window. "I suppose if you're going to have second thoughts about whether or not I'm a murderer—because of Brian—I'd rather you had them now."

Jack's pithy response made Maggie flinch.

"I guess that means you have a few reservations," she said.

"All right, Maggie. You want to hear what's going on in my head? Here goes. Why is your kid a forty-five-minute drive away in New Braunfels? Why not someplace a helluva lot closer to home?"

"Brian gets very good care where he is. And the surroundings are lovely and quiet."

Jack snorted.

Maggie met his glance for the two seconds he could spare from the road and said, "It's also easier to hide Brian from Victoria by keeping him out of San Antonio."

"Why the cloak-and-dagger stuff? Why can't Victoria see her grandson?"

"Uncle Porter is the one who makes the rules," Maggie said. "I just follow them."

Jack's brow furrowed. "What does Porter Cobb have to do with anything?"

Maggie picked at a loose thread on the leather seat, and it began to unravel. "Uh-oh."

Jack fought the annoyance he felt at Maggie for pulling his truck upholstery apart, knowing his irritation had nothing to do with the leather seat and everything to do with her clandestine behavior. "I'm waiting, Maggie."

She used both hands to snap the thread at its start and said, "You really should get someone to restitch these seats."

"Don't change the subject," he warned.

"It's a long story, Jack."

He gestured at the confines of the pickup cab. "I'm not going anywhere."

Maggie settled her back against the door and folded one knee on the seat between them. He wanted to reach out a hand to her but had a feeling she'd put the farthest distance she could between them for a reason. He was waiting to hear what it was.

Maggie's heart was hammering in her chest as she prepared to tell Jack what she hadn't repeated to another living soul in ten years. She had relived that awful morning in April 1987 a thousand times in her head. Every recollection was as vivid in her mind's eye as when it had happened. The memory never seemed to fade; the pain never seemed to ease. She was finally about to share the burden with someone else.

"The day my life fell apart," she began, staring at the dark road ahead of them, "the temperature was below freezing, with a wind chill cold enough to create icicles along the eaves. Woody—my husband—had to go to work in downtown Minneapolis, even though it was Saturday. I was still wearing the T-shirt and sweatpants I'd slept in when I woke up the boys and fed them a bowl of oatmeal. They wanted to go skating on the pond, but I told them they couldn't."

She turned to face Jack and explained, "The pond was still frozen over, but we'd had warm weather over the previous week that thinned the ice. I dressed the boys warmly and sent them outside to play in the backyard, then called a friend of mine to talk."

Maggie looked down at her knotted fingers. *If only I hadn't made that phone call,* she thought. *And if only pigs had wings they could fly.* There was no turning back the clock. At the time, she'd needed very much to hear a friendly voice.

"I looked out the back window several times while I was on the phone," she continued. "Every time I did, Brian and Stanley were fine. Since they didn't have their skates with them when they went outside, it never occurred to me they'd go near the pond. I had no idea. . . ."

Maggie felt tears sting her eyes. An invisible band around her chest made it nearly impossible to breathe. When she gasped a breath, it became a sob.

Jack reached out to her, but she brushed his hand away. "Don't." She wanted the comfort, but not until she was sure Jack wasn't going to change his mind about whether she deserved it.

"Are you all right?" he asked. "You don't have to do this right now."

"I want to." Maggie dabbed at her eyes with the sleeve of her Polo shirt and waited for the constriction in her chest to ease. It did, a little, and she began again. "I guess Brian must have dared Stanley to go out on the ice. Brian was always the instigator, and Stanley was always fearless." The corners of her lips quavered when she tried to smile, so she gave up and went back to playing with the remnants of the loose string on Jack's leather seat.

"Looking back, I think Brian must have started yelling for me when Stan first fell in." She shook her head, trying to remember exactly what his voice had sounded like. An annoyed screech, maybe. Just Stanley teasing Brian. "I thought they were playing, you know, like when Amy was on the swing and shrieking with laughter. So I ignored him."

"What tipped you off that something was wrong?"

"I don't know. All of a sudden I just . . . knew. When I ran to the window, the first thing I saw was Brian lying flat on the ice. He had hold of Stanley's hands, but I could see the weight of Stanley's coat and boots were pulling Stan under, and Brian was sliding in right along with him. The ice around them was cracked, breaking away."

"Jesus," Jack muttered.

Maggie had known from that first instant that it was hopeless, that she wasn't going to get there in time to save her sons. But her body had leapt into action. "I dropped the phone and ran."

Maggie suddenly realized she had unraveled so much of the string that Jack's leather seat was falling apart at the seam. She let go of the rippled black string and took a shuddering breath. "I yelled for Brian to let go."

"To let go of his brother? To let him drown?"

She nodded jerkily. "I wanted one of them to live," she said, her throat aching. "I didn't want to lose them both." She took a hitching breath. "But my son . . . my brave, loyal son shouted, 'I can't let go, Mom. Stan will go under.'"

Oh, God. It was so cold where she stood, watching her sons about to die. Her skin was gooseflesh, her lips were blue. And her heart was frozen solid.

Maggie made a soft, keening sound and felt Jack's warm, strong hand close over hers. If only someone had been there that day, someone strong enough to save her sons. But Woody had been at work.

Anger bubbled and boiled inside Maggie, anger that had been simmering for years, anger that had never been expressed because its target—Woody—was dead. *Why weren't you there, Woody? Why did you leave me alone? What happened to our marvelous fairy tale? What happened to all our dreams?*

Woody hadn't needed to go to work so early. He could have stayed at home longer with her and the boys. If Woody had been there, he could have helped rescue their sons. She wouldn't have been forced to make all the decisions herself. And if Woody hadn't been able to save Brian and Stan, he could at least have shared the guilt she had felt all these years for letting them both drown.

"Maggie? Are you all right?" Jack asked.

She swiped at her tears with the heel of her free hand. Jack held on to the other one and wouldn't let go when she tugged to free it. He was tenacious, she would give him that. Just like Brian.

"Even when I begged him, Brian wouldn't let go," she said, angry at her son, too, for being so damned noble. She had selfishly wanted him to live. It wasn't fair to blame her son for loving his brother enough to cling to him past life. But she did.

"I stood watching Brian being pulled under the ice, screaming for him to let go of Stanley. But he held on until Stan's weight finally pulled him under, too."

"Jesus. You must have felt so helpless."

How did he know? she wondered. It was exactly what she'd felt.

"I'm sure you did everything you could," he said quietly.

"I've told myself that a million times," Maggie said with a shake of her head. "But in those few precious seconds when something might have been done . . . I did nothing."

She turned to Jack and saw her pain re-

flected in his eyes. "It all happened so fast.
Stanley sank like a stone and dragged Brian
right in under the ice behind him. And they
were just . . . gone."

She tried again to pull free of Jack's hold,
but he said, "Let me help you, Maggie."

She stopped struggling, but her heart was
pounding. She ached for her lost sons. "It's too
late, Jack."

She had stood paralyzed while her sons
were drowning. Shame as fresh and raw as
what she'd felt that day washed over her as
blood rushed from her chest to her neck and
up across her cheeks leaving them awash with
a guilty flush.

"What did you do after they went under?"
Jack asked when she didn't continue.

*I screamed. I begged God to save my sons. But
God wasn't listening.*

"I spread myself out on the ice as wide as I
could and inched myself toward the hole
where they'd gone under. It took forever to get
there, because the ice kept cracking."

She remembered how she had shivered with
cold and fear until she'd thought she would
shake the ice apart. How the damned unfor-
giving ice had crackled around her, threatening to break apart and tumble her into the cold
black depths of the pond. How the sharp ice
crystals had scraped her bare hands and arms,
drawing blood as she clawed her way across
it on her belly.

"One of the strings on the hood of Brian's

jacket had caught on the ice, but my hands were so stiff and numb, it was hard to grab hold of it." Her shoulder muscles had knotted with excruciating pain as she used the thin cord to pull her son back from a watery grave.

Jack felt his insides clutch. He was there with Maggie, standing in the frigid wind with gooseflesh on his bare arms, his heart in his throat. He tried to imagine the presence of mind it had taken for her to lie down rather than to try walking onto the ice. The courage it had taken to slide out onto the brittle surface, knowing that if she fell through the ice, she would likely drown as well. He looked at her with awed respect. How many other women would have managed to do as much?

"I finally dragged Brian out of the water," Maggie said, "but the surface began to break away around us. I was afraid both of us would go under if I didn't get us out of there."

It was her excuse, Jack realized, for why she hadn't stayed to hunt for Stanley. "You couldn't save them both, Maggie."

"Why not?" she demanded. "I should have done more. *Something!*"

"What else could you have done?" he argued. "It wouldn't have helped Brian if you'd drowned yourself."

"I wish I had!" she cried. "Oh, God, I wish I had."

He squeezed her hand so hard he feared he would break her bones, but it took that much pressure to get her attention. When she finally looked at him, he said, "I'm glad you didn't die, Maggie. I'm glad you're here with me now."

Jack stared down at the fragile female hand clasped in his own. Maggie hadn't died with her sons, but she had stopped living. It was apparent in her barren apartment, in the lack of so much as a pet to keep her company. And she had stopped feeling because, as he knew now, feeling was too painful.

Jack wanted to comfort her. Wanted to keep her company. Wanted to make her feel everything again . . . with him.

When Maggie began talking, he realized the story wasn't over yet. She held on tight to his hand and continued, "Brian was so cold, he wasn't even shivering. He wasn't breathing, either."

Jack lifted her hand as he brushed his knuckles gently, reassuringly across her cheek. "Go on, Maggie."

"I carried Brian to the house, but I have no idea how. The police said with all the water that had soaked into his clothes, he must have weighed close to a hundred pounds. I grabbed the phone to dial 911, but my girlfriend must have realized something was wrong and had already called. I could hear them at the door.

"One paramedic went to work on Brian while I hurried the other out back to show him where to look for Stanley. Then I raced inside and called my husband."

She leaned her head against the seat and sighed. "I wonder sometimes if things would have been different if I'd taken the time to calm down before I called Woody. Once I got Brian out of the water, I kind of lost it.

"I was blubbering so much on the phone with Woody, it's a wonder he could understand what I was saying. He wanted to come home, but I told him to go directly to the hospital to be with Brian, while I waited for the dive team that was going to search for Stanley."

Jack heard in her voice the fact she hadn't expected to find Stanley alive.

"It took two men thirty minutes to find him," she said quietly. "His Timberwolves scarf had caught on a rotten log at the bottom of the pond."

"I'm sorry, Maggie." Jack pulled her hand onto his thigh and held it there.

Jack swerved onto the New Braunfels exit off I-35, grateful to be out of the worst of the traffic and onto the small-town streets shaded by live oak and pecan trees. "Where to now?" he asked.

"Not far," Maggie said, giving directions. "Only another five minutes."

Jack hoped that was enough time for her to finish her story. He wanted it all said, so she could let it go and answer the rest of his questions, like why Victoria Wainwright was not allowed to visit her grandson. And why Porter Cobb was now calling the shots.

"When I got to the hospital, I was surprised that Woody hadn't gotten there before me. Of course, none of the efforts to resuscitate Stanley had worked. When I asked about Brian, nobody could tell me anything, because there had been a terrible car accident and everyone was working on the victim."

Jack felt a chill run down his spine. "It was Woody, wasn't it?"

He watched Maggie swallow painfully before simply nodding. Her blue eyes were as bleak as he'd ever seen them.

"An eyewitness said Woody was going too fast to make the turn onto the hospital road. When he finally braked, he caught an icy patch and skidded right into a tree. He was thrown through the windshield."

Jack saw why Victoria might blame Maggie for her son's death, since Maggie had called Woody out onto the road. But she wasn't responsible for Woody's reckless driving.

"I'd only been in the emergency room a matter of moments when they wheeled Woody out of a treatment room on his way to surgery," Maggie said. "His face. . . ."

She moaned, and Jack said, "Don't, Maggie. No more."

"His face was . . . unrecognizable," she grated out. "I guess I went a little crazy then."

Who wouldn't have? Jack thought. "Maggie," he said in the softest voice he had ever used with her. "It wasn't your fault. You didn't kill your family, they—"

Her head whipped around to face him as she snatched her hand out of his. "You don't know everything, Jack. You don't know everything!"

"What more is there?" he demanded as he pulled into the parking lot of the Shady Oaks Nursing Home and abruptly cut the engine. He grabbed her by the shoulders, turning her toward him. "So you weren't watching your kids every minute. What parent does? It was all a series of tragic *accidents*, Maggie! Victoria's wrong to blame you—"

"I wished them all dead!" she cried. "Don't you see? I wished them dead, and then they were!"

"What?"

Before he could stop her, she shoved the truck door open, and ran.

Jack caught up to her among the moss-laden live oaks for which the nursing home had been named. He snagged her around the waist with one hand and pulled her to him, grabbing a handful of her hair and angling her face toward him. "Maggie. Maggie, talk to me! Explain."

"Don't you see," she said, staring at him through tear-drenched eyes. "It *is* my fault. All of it. I wished them dead, and God answered my prayers."

She dropped her forehead against his chest, her body sagging in defeat. He let his hand slide through her hair and tightened his arms around her, holding her upright.

"Oh, Jack, I didn't mean it. I never meant it! If I could take it all back. . . ."

"Maggie, Maggie . . ." He could see the anguish on her face, but he had no idea how to comfort her. "What did you do that was so wrong you've needed to pay for it with ten years of your life?"

Tears brimmed in her eyes and one spilled over. "I made an awful wish, and it came true," she said sadly.

"An *awful* wish?"

"I wished I hadn't married Woody, because nothing turned out as I had dreamed it would. I wished I didn't have my twin sons, because they had kept me from going back to law school. I felt trapped in my marriage, and I wished I could start all over again without Woody and the twins."

She looked up at Jack and said, "Don't you see? I wished them gone . . . and then they were."

This was the terrible secret that had kept her life barren, Jack realized. This was the reason she had cut herself off from men, from any chance of another involvement that might lead to another husband and family. Maggie had wished one family away, so she didn't deserve another.

Jack thrust his hands into the golden hair on either side of Maggie's face and forced her to look up at him. "You're not to blame for any of it, Maggie. Do you hear me? You're not to blame."

"I wished them gone!"

"That's not what caused them to go," he said fiercely. "It was fate, or karma, or just their time to leave." He didn't know what he could say to make her believe him. Deep inside he knew that wishing someone dead didn't kill them. Otherwise, his mother would have died long before she had. And wishing someone alive didn't keep them that way, either. Otherwise, a gap-toothed little girl would be finishing kindergarten in June.

"Let it go, Maggie." Jack pressed reassuring kisses on her forehead, on her cheeks, and finally on her mouth. Her lips remained stiff and unyielding, so he kept on kissing her. Small, soft kisses that begged her to trust him. "We all do second-guessing about the things we wish we'd done differently," he said.

"But my wish was granted!" Maggie said. "It's my fault, Jack. I didn't wish them dead, but I wished them gone. It's the same thing, isn't it?"

"No, Maggie. No, it's not." Jack held her close and rocked her.

Who hadn't played that mental "what if" game at one time or another? It could have been him in her shoes. How many times had he wished his father were alive and his mother had died instead? Yet when she was finally gone, he'd been desolated. How much worse, Jack thought, to have your wish granted the instant you made it . . . and with such devastating consequences.

Jack kissed Maggie, pressing his lips to hers insistently, feeling the last of her resistance give way as she finally surrendered. He let his tongue slip into her mouth, offering comfort . . . and something more.

"It's time to let yourself love again, Maggie," he murmured.

She leaned back and searched his face. "That's a strange thing for you to say, Jack. If I did let myself love you, would you be willing to love me back?"

Jack's heart picked up a beat as his "fight-or-flight" instinct kicked in. He let her go and took a step back. "How did we get on this subject?"

Maggie dared glance at him. "You're the one who suggested I start loving someone. I just wondered if you meant you."

He tugged his hat back down, so it shadowed his eyes. "I'll have to think about that."

"All right, Jack. You do that. Here's a little something to help you think."

She lifted up on her tiptoes, put a hand around his nape, and drew his head down so her lips could meet his. She kissed him like she meant it, with her mouth and her tongue and her whole body pressing into his. Jack grabbed her and held on tight as she rubbed herself against him. He was breathing hard, busy yanking her shirt out of her trousers, when Maggie caught his wrists. "Not here," she said breathlessly, reminding him where they were.

She backed up abruptly, but he saw from her flushed cheeks and her lambent eyes that she wasn't in much better shape than he was.

"I have a present for Brian in my bag in the truck," she said as she backed away from him.

Jack followed after her. "I still have some unanswered questions, Maggie."

"Ask them, and I'll see if I've got answers." She opened the truck door, reached into the bag that held her swimming clothes wrapped in a towel, and pulled out a purple-and-white stuffed rabbit wearing a yellow bow around its neck.

She held it up to Jack, hopped it toward him in mid-air, and said, "What do you think?"

"It's a stuffed rabbit."

She grinned. "Your perception amazes me."

"It's cute," he conceded. And a warning to him, he realized, in case he hadn't already gotten the message, of the personal baggage that came along with Maggie. She was still dealing with a lot of pain and anger, and she felt a tremendous burden of guilt over what had happened to her husband and sons.

His gut instinct told him none of that had turned her into a killer. But he'd been wrong before. And who else besides Maggie would be grieving every year on the anniversary of all those deaths in Minnesota?

Victoria.

Jack felt like he'd been hit between the eyes with a sledgehammer. Why hadn't he thought of Victoria as a suspect before? She had as much motive as Maggie, and opportunity, at least as far as the San Antonio murder was concerned. As for whether she'd been in the vicinity of Dallas and Houston when the other deaths had occurred . . . He'd have to do some checking.

"How much does Victoria know about the story you've just told me?" Jack asked, as they headed to the entrance to Shady Oaks.

"When I first saw her at the hospital in Minnesota, in the chapel, I blurted out everything. You can imagine her reaction."

Jack could. It wasn't a pretty sight.

"Victoria told me she'd never forgive me for the deaths of her grandsons, for Woody's accident, or for the stroke Richard suffered on the flight to Minnesota. I had no idea how really distraught she was that day, how angry and vindictive, until nine months later."

Jack pushed an errant curl behind Maggie's ear. "What happened nine months later?"

"That was when I learned Uncle Porter had sent Victoria to the chapel that day in April to tell me Brian had been resuscitated, and that the doctors held out some hope he would recover. Instead, when I asked her what word there was of Brian, she told me he was dead— that I'd killed him as surely as I'd killed the rest of my family."

"It's hard to believe anyone could be so cruel," Jack muttered.

Maggie smiled bitterly. "After Victoria's announcement, I went crazy. When I was admitted to the mental ward at the hospital, Victoria took charge of Brian and had him moved to Texas, arguing with Uncle Porter that I would be in no shape to care for him anytime soon. No one ever told me my son was alive. They all assumed I knew it."

Jack was astounded by what he was hearing. "But the funeral—"

"I was in the hospital when my family was buried. I never went to the cemetery later, for reasons that should be obvious."

"You mean no one ever contacted you to tell you Brian was still alive?"

Maggie shook her head.

"What about the medical bills?"

"Uncle Porter took care of everything. And I refused to see anyone. It wasn't until Brian woke up and began recuperating that Uncle Porter came to Minnesota to see if I could be retrieved from among the damned. He was incredulous, as you can imagine, when he learned that Victoria had told me Brian was dead. And absolutely *furious* with Victoria."

"How did you feel when you learned your son was alive?"

Maggie made a small sound in her throat, a cry of pain that Jack felt in his gut.

"I was so drunk at the time . . . I thought I was hallucinating everything." She looked at Jack with an expression of wonder in her eyes that she must have worn that long ago day. "When I realized Brian was really alive, my stomach churned and . . . and I threw up," she admitted ruefully.

"Uncle Porter promised me that if I quit drinking, he'd take care of all Brian's medical bills, pay my way through law school, and help me get a job so I could take care of my son on my own. I had a second chance . . . if I could only get sober and stay that way."

Jack looked at Maggie now, at her clear, beautiful eyes and tender mouth, at her lithe, graceful body, and tried to imagine her as the sodden, vomiting drunk she had described. It was impossible.

The image that came to mind instead was his mother. She'd had a chance to sober up, too, for the sake of her child. Captain Buckelew had offered to keep Jack while Jean Kittrick went to a treatment center in San Antonio. His mother had refused. *Not at all like Maggie*, Jack thought. When Maggie's chance had come, she'd grabbed at it with both hands.

They might both have been drunks, but the similarity ended there, Jack realized. Maggie had some inner source of strength his mother had lacked. More love for her child? Or more guilt, maybe? It didn't really matter why or how she had found her way to sobriety. Jack was just very glad she had.

"How did Victoria react when you finally retrieved your son?" Jack asked.

Maggie's eyes narrowed. "When I showed up wanting my son back, she threatened to abscond with Brian and hide him where I couldn't find him. Uncle Porter was having none of that. In fact, he's the one who suggested I put Brian somewhere safe, somewhere Victoria wouldn't be able to get to him. I owe Uncle Porter a great deal," Maggie said. And he'd extracted his pound of flesh in payment.

"It's hard to believe that in ten years Victoria's never been able to locate Brian," Jack said. "It seems to me it would be easy for her to hire someone to follow you and—"

"If she wanted badly enough to know where he is, she could find him," Maggie agreed. "In fact, she did find him about a year after I came back to Texas."

"What happened?"

Maggie paused at the steps to the nursing home with her back to him. Jack could see she was trying hard not to cry. "Maggie?"

She turned and met his gaze, her beautiful eyes floating in tears. "Victoria was repelled by the sight of him. She wanted to know if Brian's limbs were always going to tremble like that and if he'd always be so uncoordinated and whether he was always going to be in a wheelchair. When she found out the limitations of his recovery . . . when she realized Brian would never be . . . perfect . . . again, she turned her back on him and walked away."

Jack felt enraged for Maggie's sake and for Brian's. "If she doesn't want to be near him, why the continued secrecy?"

"Uncle Porter insisted upon it," Maggie said. "He said that until Victoria was willing to accept her grandson as he was, she didn't deserve to see him. And since I haven't yet repaid Uncle Porter everything I owe him, he still makes all those decisions.

"But as you've seen, Victoria never misses a chance to throw it in my face that she isn't 'allowed' to visit her grandchild. Not that she would, even if she could!"

The door to the Shady Oaks Nursing Home opened and Victoria Wainwright stepped out. "Hello, Margaret. Luckily for my grandson, someone remembered to visit him on Easter Sunday."

᧥ *Chapter 14* ᧥

"What are you doing here, Victoria?" Maggie demanded, stepping in front of the older woman to keep her from moving any farther down the wooden stairs. Maggie was aware of Jack standing behind her, knew he was there if she needed him, but was glad he didn't interfere. Victoria was her problem.

"I told you, I was visiting my grandson." Victoria reached up with white-gloved hands to adjust a spectacular Easter bonnet—decorated with exquisite ribbons and sleek feathers—that matched a suit in robin's-egg blue. She looked cool, comfortable, and composed, despite the awkward situation and the afternoon heat. "What on earth have you got in your hand?" Victoria asked, pointing to the stuffed rabbit Maggie held by its cottontail.

"It's a gift for Brian," Maggie said, twisting her wrist so Victoria could see what she held.

"He's a little old for a purple rabbit, don't you think?"

Maggie stared Victoria down. They both

knew Brian's biological age had no correlation to his mental age. Maggie started to ask how Victoria had talked the nurses into letting her see Brian, then realized the nursing staff had changed several times in the years since she had last mentioned that her mother-in-law was not allowed to see Brian unless Maggie was there. Victoria hadn't shown any interest in Brian for so long, Maggie hadn't anticipated this visit. It was alarming—frightening—to think Victoria could have walked in and kidnapped Brian today without her being any the wiser.

"Is there some reason you're standing in my way?" Victoria asked pointedly.

"How is Brian?" Maggie asked.

"Unfortunately, the same," Victoria said.

The slight, distasteful twist of Victoria's lips hit Maggie like a dentist's drill on an open nerve. She bit back a mouthful of expletives, counted to five—she couldn't make it to ten—and said, "Don't come back, Victoria. You aren't welcome here."

"I go where I like, when I like," Victoria replied, undaunted.

"Brian won't be here," Maggie said, feeling the threat without a word being spoken.

The smug smile on Victoria's lips made Maggie's blood run cold. "You can't hide him from me, Margaret. I'll find him. Why bother upsetting the boy by moving him?"

Victoria's words suggested consideration for Brian, but Maggie knew better than to think

Victoria had Brian's best interests at heart. So why didn't she want him moved? "Why did you decide to visit Brian after all this time?" Maggie asked.

Victoria let down her guard for no more than an instant, but Maggie felt a visceral reaction to the brief expression of anguish she saw in Victoria's eyes.

"Thanks to you, he's all I have left," Victoria said.

Maggie suffered the accusatory blow without being crushed by it. Victoria hadn't said anything Maggie hadn't heard before. Or believed herself. "Does Uncle Porter know you're here?"

"Porter is foolishly sentimental when it comes to that boy," Victoria said, irritation plain in her voice. "He seems to think I would upset Brian if I saw him, which is ridiculous. I've certainly spent enough time with children who aren't entirely themselves to know how to entertain one."

"How did you entertain Brian?" Maggie asked.

Victoria looked down her nose a long way at Maggie—quite a trick, with a nose as short and sophisticated as Victoria's—and said, "I read *Peter Rabbit* to him, of course. Now, if you'll both excuse me, I have a dinner engagement with Porter."

Victoria didn't wait for Maggie to move, she simply started down the stairs and expected Maggie to give way. Maggie hesitated only an instant before she backed up against the decorative gingerbread railing that framed the wooden porch steps and let Victoria pass. Victoria never looked back, yet Maggie couldn't take her eyes off the woman.

"She's amazing," Maggie murmured.

"Yes, amazing," Jack agreed. "Shall we go inside?"

Maggie turned to Jack, aware of him for the first time since she'd begun talking to Victoria.

"I thought you might like to check on Brian," Jack suggested.

Maggie's stomach clenched. She turned and sprinted up the stairs, struggled with the old-fashioned brass doorknob, and finally shoved her way inside. The Victorian home had been built with high ceilings to accommodate the Texas heat, and a breeze through the open windows carried out the medicinal scents and antiseptic cleaners, leaving the nursing home smelling less like what it was.

She arrived at Brian's bedroom door breathing hard and stopped to calm herself so she didn't upset her son—assuming Victoria hadn't already sent him into hysterics. Brian didn't do well with disruptions in his routine.

Maggie put a restraining palm on Jack's chest and said, "Give me a minute with Brian before you come in. I'd like to make sure he's all right, and if he is, tell him about you before he meets you." She handed the rabbit to him. "Hold this for me?"

"Sure." Jack stuck the stuffed rabbit in the

crook of one arm and leaned back against the wall. "Call me when you want me. Or if you need me," he added, reaching out to squeeze her hand.

Maggie felt a tickle at the back of her throat, like she was going to cry. She cleared her throat and made herself let go of his hand.

As she entered her son's room, she was disappointed to see that Brian was in bed instead of sitting in his wheelchair. Maybe the nurses had decided he needed a rest after Victoria's visit. Speaking of nurses, where were they? Maggie didn't recall seeing anyone at the front desk, and several nurses usually showed up in the hall with other patients during her visits.

Suddenly anxious, she crossed quickly but quietly to Brian's bedside. On the table next to his bed sat an expensive, gold-trimmed, hardbound copy of *Peter Rabbit*. Brian was lying still, his head turned toward the window. At first Maggie thought he was asleep. She took another step and saw the tears on his cheeks.

"Brian?"

His head lolled slowly in her direction. "Mommy?" He seemed surprised to see her, before joy made his young face radiant. "Mommy, Mommy, Mommy! You came, you came, you came!"

"Is everything all right, Maggie?" Jack called from the doorway.

"Yes," Maggie choked out. The metal bedrail rattled down, and she settled on the twin hospital bed beside Brian, hauling him upright into her arms. He wasn't as big as a normal sixteen-year-old, but he was still sizable. He did his best to put his arms around her, but they didn't obey the commands his brain sent to them. She helped him by wrapping his arms around her shoulders.

"I'm here, Brian. I told you I would come. What made you think I wouldn't?"

"She said you wouldn't come. She said I had to get into bed. Then she read me a story."

Damn you, Victoria! Rage filled Maggie's head and heart and made her squeeze her son too tightly.

"I can't breathe, Mommy," Brian said.

Maggie loosened her grip and realized her hands were trembling almost as much as Brian's. Her voice ragged as she suppressed the murderous urge to strangle her mother-in-law, Maggie said, "I'm here, Brian. And I've brought someone else to see you."

Brian clutched her as tightly as he could. "Stay here, Mommy. Don't go away."

The tickle in Maggie's throat returned with a vengeance. Brian had obviously been confused by Victoria's visit, because he feared she was going to leave him with another stranger. She pressed her cheek against her son's and felt the adolescent fuzz that preceded whiskers. "I'm not going anywhere, Brian."

For a moment she contemplated excluding Jack from the visit. Before she could make that choice, he showed up at her side.

"I couldn't help overhearing," he said in

apology for disobeying her request to stay by the door. "Hello, Brian. I'm Jack."

Brian stared at Jack with wide-eyed, open curiosity. "Jack?"

"Jack's a friend of mine," Maggie said. "He's brought you a present."

Jack made a face at her, but held out the purple rabbit. "Here you go, Brian."

"For me?" Brian said wistfully, hopefully.

"Sure," Jack said as he settled on the bed beside Maggie. Maggie saw the moment he realized her son didn't have the coordination to accept the rabbit, because Jack tucked the stuffed animal between Maggie and Brian and said, "He wants a hug, too."

Maggie had never felt so grateful to anyone in her life.

At that moment one of the regular nurses appeared in the doorway. "Maggie! We didn't expect you today. We've been having an Easter party in the Rec Room . . ."

"I'm here, after all," Maggie interrupted. She would make sure the nurses knew before she left not to let Victoria in again. "I'd like to take Brian for a walk outside, if that's not a problem."

"You know it isn't any trouble at all," the nurse chided, eyeing Jack, seeking an introduction that Maggie reluctantly provided. "This is a friend of mine, Jack Kittrick."

"It's good to see Maggie with a male friend," the nurse said with a smile as she pushed the wheelchair close to the bed. "We all think she deserves the best."

Maggie flushed to the roots of her hair. "Jack's not—"

When the nurse reached for Brian to pick him up, Jack said, "I can lift him. All right, Brian?"

Brian looked down at the rabbit he had managed to grasp in both hands and back up at Jack with a smile. "Okay, Jack."

Maggie was surprised on two counts. First, that Jack had offered to help Brian into his chair. And second, that Brian had agreed to let him do it.

A transfer that would have been awkward if handled by either Maggie or the nurse alone, Jack did with ease. He simply picked Brian up and settled him comfortably in the wheelchair. "All right, sport?" Jack asked.

"I'm Brian," Brian said.

"I was speaking to the rabbit," Jack said. "His name's Sport."

Brian seemed to like the idea. "Yeah. Sport's all right."

Maggie wasn't sure what she had been expecting from Jack, but his nonchalant attitude toward Brian's disability was somewhat disconcerting, even though she felt relieved.

"You seem to know your way around a wheelchair," she ventured.

"My mother spent the last year of her life in one," Jack said. "She came to live with me the last few months, so I could help take care of her. She brought her cat along. It lives in the tree in my backyard."

That explained the wheelchair ramp she'd found at Jack's back door, Maggie thought. And the bowl of food on his back porch. "Your cat lives in a tree?" she queried.

"It likes to jump on unsuspecting persons," Jack explained. "Gets a real kick out of hearing them scream."

Maggie laughed and shuddered at the same time. Thank God she hadn't ventured outside to investigate the first night she'd gone to Jack's house. But she wished, just once, that Victoria would come visit . . . and meet Jack's cat.

They had just wheeled Brian down the ramp that bordered the front stairs of Shady Oaks when a 1958 Cadillac skidded to a halt in front of them, and a man in sweat-stained, raggedy-looking clothes stepped out. A second look revealed the two-toned orange and white car was still half-covered with car wax.

"Uncle Porter!" Maggie exclaimed. "What are you doing here?"

"I was waxing one of my cars under a tree in the backyard, when I had a sudden urge to come visit Brian."

In response to Maggie's stunned expression he said, "Don't believe that one? All right, when I took a break to go inside for a glass of iced tea, I checked my phone messages and saw there was one from Victoria. She said she was coming to visit Brian—here at Shady

Oaks—before we had dinner tonight."

Maggie heard both the warning and the dread in his voice. "She was here," Maggie said. "She made Brian cry. She told him I wasn't coming."

Porter gave Brian a visual once over and said, "Is he okay?"

"Brian's fine," Maggie said, threading her fingers through her son's fine, wheat-blond hair. "She only read to him from a book."

Jack had been watching the eye contact and body language between Maggie and Porter Cobb from the instant the elderly man stepped out of the half-waxed Caddy. Cobb was wearing an old fishing hat replete with trout lures, a pair of baggy khaki shorts, a faded, pond-scum-green shirt, and Docksiders with mismatched socks that came halfway up his hairy calves.

Jack was certain nobody ever saw Porter Cobb looking like this. Which meant some dire emergency—Cobb had said it was the call from Victoria Wainwright—had brought him here. What was it Cobb feared? Jack wondered. What was it he really thought Victoria Wainwright would do if she was left alone with her grandson?

Jack watched as Porter crossed to Brian, put a hand on the boy's shoulder, and said, "Hello, Brian. How are you today?"

It was clear to Jack that the boy knew and liked his great-uncle. "I'm fine, Uncle Porter," Brian replied, smiling broadly. "See what Jack brought me?" He held out the purple rabbit.

For the first time Cobb focused on Jack, and Jack watched the old man's soft hazel eyes turn hard as agates.

"What is the law doing here?" Cobb said.

"Jack came with me," Maggie interceded, shooting a quick glance in Jack's direction. "We got here as Victoria was leaving."

Jack stared at Maggie, who had the grace to lower her eyes. So she hadn't kept his secret from everybody; she had told Cobb. *Why Cobb?* Jack wondered. But the answer was obvious. Maggie felt a great obligation toward the man . . . and Cobb was clearly running the show.

"Are you sure Brian's all right?" Cobb asked Maggie, touching the chair-bound boy again.

"Brian's fine," Maggie reassured him.

Jack frowned. Maggie had expressed her concerns about Victoria's interaction with Brian in terms of his grandmother kidnapping him. Porter Cobb seemed more concerned about Brian's well-being, as though he feared Victoria might do the boy some physical harm.

"Jack and I were going for a walk with Brian," Maggie said. "Would you like to come, Uncle Porter?"

Jack watched Cobb's dawning realization of how he was dressed, the fact that his car was half-covered in paste wax, and the fact he'd revealed a great deal more of his personal family business to a stranger—a Texas Ranger, no less—than he'd intended.

"I need to get home," Cobb said to Maggie. "I just wanted to make sure Victoria hadn't—"

Jack watched Cobb cut himself off before he revealed too much. Only, it was too late for that.

"Brian is fine, Uncle Porter. I'd appreciate it if you'd speak with Victoria about—"

"Say no more," Cobb said. "It's done."

Jack watched the byplay between Cobb and Maggie and felt something click inside. He had a gut feeling that Victoria Wainwright had done a lot more back in Minnesota than simply lie to her daughter-in-law and steal away with her grandson. Jack was convinced Porter Cobb knew the whole of it. But considering the fact Victoria was his sister, Jack doubted Cobb would ever tell what he knew. Still, Jack wondered just how much the old man was keeping from Maggie.

"Goodbye, Mr. Kittrick," Porter said.

"I'd keep a close an eye on my sister if I were you," Jack said quietly.

"I do," Cobb said as he slid behind the wheel of the boatlike Caddy. "I do."

"Let's walk," Maggie said. She pushed Brian's chair ahead of her along a winding asphalt path.

The trail they took was covered by a latticed arbor so overgrown with heavily scented wisteria and bougainvillea and mandevillea that it reminded Jack of the perfume aisle at a mall department store. Bees whisked among the lavender and fuschia and pink flowers, while patches of diamond-patterned sunlight heated Maggie's flesh until Jack could see a faint sheen of sweat on her skin. When he leaned close, his nostrils flared for the scent of her, and it was sweeter than any flower.

Jack would have been happy to lay her down in that shaded bower and make love to her. But there was the small matter of a little boy—well, not so little anymore, a woman who could not be trusted with him, a brother who kept her secrets, and Maggie . . . who knew a great deal and hadn't told him all of it. Yet.

Maggie had waited all afternoon for Jack to ask her about Uncle Porter's peculiar visit to the nursing home, but he hadn't uttered a word. He had entertained Brian until her son had actually been reluctant to let Jack go when they left.

She had kissed Brian on the forehead, a signal that her visit was over, and reluctantly left him to the care of his nurses. If she tossed out the brief contretemps with Victoria, it had been one of the nicest afternoons Maggie could remember having with her son. Having Jack with them had made all the difference.

She and Jack had already been waved through the gate at 200 Patterson, and they would be arriving at the portico any moment. She wondered if Jack still wanted to come up-

stairs and make love to her. She wondered if
he still considered her a possible serial killer.
She wondered—

"I'm coming up, Maggie," he said as he
stopped his pickup at the etched glass doors.

He was telling her, not asking for permission, Maggie realized. She shot him a sideways glance. She had been aware of a
simmering undercurrent between them all afternoon. Even so, Jack didn't look like a man
in the mood for love. But it had been ten years.
She might be a little out of practice recogniz-
ing the signs.

"All right, Jack."

Maggie felt nervous, edgy, excited. She had
wanted Jack to pass scrutiny with Brian before
she allowed him any further into her life, and
he had done so with flying colors. She wasn't
so sure she had done as good a job convincing
Jack she knew nothing about the murders of
all those children. The entire incident with Victoria must have looked particularly havey-
cavey.

Yet Jack hadn't asked any questions. He
hadn't said much of anything on the ride back
to San Antonio from New Braunfels except,
"Your kid's all right." And much later, "I like
the smell of wisteria . . . the way the blossoms
look like a bunch of grapes hanging from the
stem. I'd like to plant some in my backyard
someday."

He'd seemed lost in a world of his own. It
wasn't until they arrived at her condominium

that he had begun showing signs of life. First the statement he was coming up, and then his hand on her back urging her toward the elevator—very much like a policeman escorting a prisoner to the interrogation room.

Maybe Jack wasn't in the mood for love, after all.

Maggie found out how wrong she was when the elevator doors opened onto the tenth floor. He quickly backed her up against her door. In the same instant he plunged the key into the lock, he plunged his tongue into her mouth. The piercing stab of his tongue was matched by the thrust of his hips against hers, leaving no doubt about his state of sexual readiness.

Jack barely got her front door open, shoved her inside, and slammed it behind them before he yanked her shirt out of her trousers and pulled it up over her head.

"Jack—"

His hands cupped her breasts through her cotton bra, and Maggie thought she would swoon as his thumbs and forefingers turned her nipples into small knots of pleasure. *Dear God. It feels so good. I can't believe how good it feels.*

She grabbed Jack around the waist to have something solid to hang onto as her knees buckled. She latched her mouth onto the first flesh she could find, which happened to be Jack's neck, and suckled hard. She heard him groan and reached for his mouth with hers.

"Maggie," he rasped. "I want you. I need you."

She didn't say what she was feeling. She couldn't have described it if she'd tried. It was all too confusing. The want and need were mixed up with guilt and shame. But desire—raw animal lust—stood head and shoulders above everything else.

It had been too long, Maggie realized. She had denied herself for so many years that she had forgotten what it was she had given up. Jack's basic, animalistic drive to put himself inside her fitted her needs exactly.

He broke the zipper on her slacks getting them off and left her underwear hanging off her right ankle as he stripped her naked. He barely managed to get himself unzipped and his jeans flayed wide before he shoved her against the wall and thrust himself inside her.

It hurt.

The cry of pain was out before she could stop it, and she felt Jack's shudder as he realized what he'd done. But he was already seated to the hilt by then, and the pain, she knew, would pass.

"It's all right, Jack," she whispered against his throat, her hands knocking his hat off and tangling in his hair. "It's been a long time. I'm all right."

"Maggie."

She heard regret in his voice and an agony

of need. "Please, Jack," she whispered. "Don't stop."

She felt the taut muscles in his shoulders and hips and buttocks as she ran her hands over him, urging him back to the frantic love-making she had craved so much, testing the restraint he was forcing on himself, wanting him to lose control. And at last driving him over the edge.

"Come on, Maggie," he urged, as he drove into her. "Don't leave me now."

Maggie wasn't thinking anymore. She wasn't even there with him. She was on some selfish plane of her own, searching for the feelings she knew were out there somewhere. Feeling the ripples of ecstasy slide through her. Feeling the heat and hardness of Jack inside her, unbelievably aware of the exquisite way their flesh met and separated as he became a part of her and withdrew.

She would have settled for less if he'd let her. But she heard his guttural voice in her ear, urging her to take what he offered her, urging her to come with him, urging her *to feel, to feel, to feel.*

The shattering cry of joy came from deep within her, a grating, gravelly, animal sound that could as easily have been of pain as pleasure, because it rode the border between the two.

Maggie held herself perfectly still while the resonating shudders rolled through her, leaving her totally enervated, then collapsed against Jack's chest, panting for breath, clinging like a limpet to the last thing standing between her and the ground.

∂ *Chapter 15* ∂

At 5 A.M. on Monday morning, the stairwell of seventeen-story San Antonio General felt as deep, dark, and deadly as a mine shaft. The full concrete stairwell lighting didn't come on until six, and Jack felt the hairs stand up on his neck as he traversed the menacing shadows. He paused at the fifth-floor stairwell door, wondering whether stealth was really necessary.

Evil undeniably lurked somewhere inside. Someone was killing children. Quickly, painlessly, but definitely leaving them dead.

The echo of a voice and footsteps far above him gave Jack the impetus to move inside to the fifth floor hallway. He crept down the hall, feeling a little silly. There wasn't anyone to hide from. Amazingly, all the worker bees in the huge hospital, which buzzed like a productive hive during the day, seemed to have disappeared.

Jack stopped at a linen closet down the hall from the pediatric ICU. A sign done in Magic

Marker that was stuck to the door with two ragged strips of masking tape said "Linens moved to 5th Flr. West." Jack tried the knob and found it locked. He knocked.

Plainclothes San Antonio Police Detective Philip Fuentes opened the door looking rumpled in an open-collared blue cotton shirt, pulled-down tie, Western-belted navy blue trousers, and scuffed black cowboy boots. He had looked the same way—except in brown—the previous Friday afternoon, when Jack had met with him at the police department and discussed what surveillance the San Antonio police were able to provide at the hospital. Jack figured the haggard-looking detective worked a second job, maybe as a security man somewhere, because the bags under his eyes looked more like steamer trunks.

"Good morning," Fuentes whispered.

"Why are you whispering?" Jack said in a regular voice. "There isn't anyone—"

Detective Fuentes grabbed him by his bolo-tie, hauled him inside, and eased the door closed behind him. "Nurse Cole went to the john. Be out any minute," he said quietly.

"Oh," Jack said, feeling even more foolish for not being cautious.

"It's a little tight in here," Fuentes said with tremendous understatement as he backed his way farther inside the narrow rectangular space. The odor of some strong detergent permeated the place.

Besides a great many linens on wire racks,

the tiny, hospital-green space also contained a metal folding table jam-packed with video surveillance equipment to monitor the pediatric ICU. A phone that flashed instead of ringing connected Fuentes to the outside world and to Jack, who was wearing a beeper so he could roam the hospital.

Monitoring had gone on-line at midnight so the ICU was covered on the inclusive calendar days of the previous murders. Jack knew the graveyard shift must have been boring and perhaps seemed a waste of time, since none of the previous murders had occurred during the early morning hours. But he wasn't taking any chances. He planned to spend a lot of time at the hospital over the next week.

"How's it going?" Jack asked, studying the monitors. Three scanning video cameras had been set up at various angles in the ceiling of the pediatric ICU to be certain every bed could be seen.

Fuentes slumped into the metal folding chair closest to the wall, gesturing Jack into the one by the door. "I was hoping you'd show up with coffee," he said in a whiskey-rough voice.

Jack reached inside the Levi's jacket he had buttoned at the waist and pulled out a thermos of coffee and a bag of Krispy Kremes. "I figured you'd be hungry, too. These are all yours. I ate mine on the way over."

Fuentes grinned. "You Texas Rangers aren't half—"

"Who's that?" Jack asked as a nurse appeared on the center screen at the bedside of a sleeping, blond-headed child.

Fuentes glanced up and said, "Nurse Cole. She's on the same hours as me. Pretty good at what she does, from what I can tell," he said through a mouthful of jelly doughnut. "Does regular checks, administers medication as called for. Gentle with the kids."

"How do you know she's doing what she's supposed to be doing?" Jack asked.

Fuentes held up a clipboard. "Have a list here of all the prescribed meds and which bed gets them when. She's the only nurse on duty in the ICU and visiting hours don't start till nine, so anyone else is a suspicious person."

Jack grimaced. The surveillance seemed too little, and he was very much afraid that if they weren't able to identify the killer when he—or she—came into the ICU, their efforts would be too late to save the next victim. But he didn't know what else to do.

They could sit in the ICU and guard the kids for the next seven days, but that would tip off the murderer, who could easily go somewhere else. Dr. Hollander had medical privileges in more than a few hospitals in the city. Isabel likely had friends who were nurses all over town. And Maggie . . . Maggie represented every hospital in MEDCO's system.

It's not Maggie, Jack thought. *No way could I feel what I feel when I'm with her, if she was the evil I'm trying to destroy.* Jack wiped his sweaty palms on his jeans. But after what she'd revealed to him last night in bed, he wasn't willing to bet on anything.

While Fuentes ate doughnuts and drank coffee, Jack went over the events of the past evening in his head. It should have been a matter of reliving a glorious evening in the sack with a beautiful woman. But nothing about his relationship with Maggie had been the least bit typical.

Jack had never lost control with a woman like he had with her last night. He'd acted like some beast in rut. Maggie had told him she hadn't been with a man in ten years, and he'd believed her. Yet once he had her in his arms, his animal instincts had taken over, and he wasn't sure anything could have stopped him. Thank God she'd been willing. Thank God he hadn't hurt her.

She had reassured him the second time they'd made love—this time in her queen-sized bed—that she was fine. In fact, she'd been so fine he'd found himself slowing down to enjoy touching her and tasting her. She had met every touch as though she had never been touched before . . . as though it were all happening to her for the very first time. And maybe it was.

Afterward, he had put his arms around her and held her close. Not that she'd demanded it, or anything like that. He had wanted to do it, which surprised him. They had fit together as precisely as pieces of a jigsaw puzzle, and

Jack hadn't been about to deny himself the enjoyment of her soft, feminine warmth.

Things got a little tense when he started asking her the questions he should have asked before he'd gotten distracted by her rosy nipples and her bony shoulders and other interesting sites.

Lying in the darkness beside Maggie, he'd murmured, "Why is Porter so afraid to let Victoria be alone with her grandson?"

Her whole body had gone rigid in his arms, and he'd almost wished he hadn't asked. Except he needed to know. He was a Ranger, and someone was killing kids. So he'd repeated the question. "Why is he so afraid, Maggie?"

"I don't know," she answered.

He had tightened his arms around her until his sweat and hers were so mixed up they smelled like the same person. "That's not the right answer, Maggie," he whispered in her ear.

"It's the only one I have for you, Jack. If you want a better one, you'll have to ask Porter Cobb yourself."

"Do you think Victoria would ever try to hurt Brian?" he asked.

"I think Uncle Porter believes she would."

"Is she capable of murder, Maggie?"

"I don't know," Maggie said agitatedly. "I just don't know!"

He hadn't asked her any more questions, because he'd wanted to believe her. Maybe she didn't know any more than what she'd told him. It was possible she was totally ignorant of whatever it was Victoria Wainwright had done to make her brother so leery of leaving her alone with her grandson.

Jack had held Maggie until she fell asleep, but he'd been awake long afterward, because he wanted to savor the experience in case it never happened again. And because he was worried about Brian Wainwright.

Over the past twenty-four hours, Jack had come to the conclusion that Victoria Wainwright could very well be the serial killer he was seeking. He knew the idea of society doyen Victoria Wainwright committing cold-blooded murder was farfetched. For that matter, none of his suspects seemed like the kind of person who'd kill a kid. But one of them was doing it.

And while Jack had made provisions to watch and protect the children in the hospital's ICU, if Victoria was the murderer, Brian Wainwright was very much at risk during the coming week. What Jack needed to ease his mind—or to justify surveillance on Brian—was a way to tie Victoria to the killings at the other hospitals.

He had left Mazggie alone in bed, covering her with a sheet so she wouldn't catch a chill—and so he wouldn't be tempted to make love to her again—and gone to call Harley Buckelew.

"It's the damned middle of the night, Jack. This better be good."

"I think Victoria Wainwright is the one killing kids." Jack heard silence on the other end of the line. "Did you hear me?"

"I heard you. I'm trying to decide whether I should've let you take that thirty days' leave, after all."

"Listen to me for a minute, Captain. Then if you're not convinced, I'll take that leave, and you can bring someone else in here to take over."

Jack outlined everything he knew about Victoria Wainwright and finished, "I need you to have someone follow up on whether Victoria was on the scene at the time of the murders in Dallas and Houston. Maybe she went there for some charity function or to visit Maggie. What I need is some proof she was around when the first five kids died."

"I guess you aren't crazy," Harley said. "Get some sleep, Jack. You're going to need it."

"What about surveillance on Brian Wainwright?" Jack asked. "Can we get that authorized?"

"I don't know, Jack. I'll work on it."

"I need it yesterday, Harley."

It wasn't until he'd spoken the urgent words that Jack realized he'd called the captain by his first name. He knew Harley had realized the same thing, because he said, "Is everything all right, Jack?"

"I've met Maggie's kid, Harley," Jack said,

accepting the captain's invitation to talk.

"And you're in love with his mother?" Harley probed.

Jack felt his heartbeat quicken at the question but merely answered, "I wouldn't want to face her if anything happened to her son."

"I'll get the surveillance okayed, Jack. Don't worry."

"Thanks, Captain."

Jack had gone back to bed, aware of how right it felt to ease himself around Maggie's slim body, to spoon her buttocks against his groin, and to wrap his arms around her and cup her breasts in his hands. He had fallen asleep holding her in his embrace.

It was the third time they'd made love, before he'd left her that morning, that had caused Jack to wonder what was wrong with him. He'd never been the least bit sexually insatiable, yet he couldn't seem to get enough of Maggie. He loved kissing her, loved the sounds she made when he put his mouth on her, loved the way her whole body writhed toward him as he seated himself deep inside her.

Jesus. He'd made noises himself he'd never heard come out of his mouth. What the hell was it about Maggie Wainwright that made him trumpet like a bull elephant when he came inside her? It was downright embarrassing. But it had also been the most intoxicating, fulfilling night of sex he'd ever had.

"I got somebody in the ICU don't belong

there," Fuentes said abruptly. "She's got a needle, and she's headed for the kid in bed three."

Jack was out of the linen closet and running before Fuentes had stopped speaking. He shoved open the swinging ICU door and said, "Stop right there! Don't make another move."

Isabel Rojas turned, jaw agape, needle poised in her hand, as Jack aimed his Colt .45 at her heart.

"What's in the needle, Isabel?" Jack demanded in a hard voice.

"KCl."

"What is that, exactly?"

"Potassium chloride."

The ICU door suddenly banged open behind Jack, and Nurse Cole yelled, "Izzy, come quick!"

Jack whirled and barely kept himself from squeezing the trigger.

Nurse Cole saw the gun, gasped, and backed up until she'd flattened herself against the wall, staring at the gun in Jack's hand.

"What's wrong, Frannie?" Isabel said in a calm voice.

"Dr. Hollander needs you in the ER. STAT!" Nurse Cole said, without taking her eyes off Jack's gun.

"Miss Rojas isn't going anywhere," Jack said.

"What's going on, Izzy?" Nurse Cole asked, visibly shaking.

"Damned if I know," Isabel said, staring

with disgust at the gun Jack had aimed at her. "What's the emergency, Frannie?"

"It's the doctor's little girl, Amy. She drowned!"

Lisa languidly stretched her arms high over her head in the king-size bed, arching her entire body from her toes to her fingertips, stretching like a cat that is supremely comfortable in its surroundings. She let her gaze stray to the middle of the bed, where her husband lay sprawled, soundly sleeping. The feeling of total relaxation dissipated.

The sensation of well-being was an illusion. Like her happy marriage. Like the fantastic sex of the night before. It could all disappear in a puff of smoke, like the pacing tiger in a magician's trick at the circus.

Lisa turned on her side and braced her cheek on her palm. This was when she liked Roman best, when his hair was mussed from sleep and beard stubbled his jaw and he smelled faintly of the musky scent of sex. And when his dark, piercing eyes were closed and not demanding answers she couldn't give.

She reached out to caress Roman's shoulder but didn't actually touch his flesh, because that would have awakened him. The long months of avoiding her appeared to be over. He had made love to her again last night.

Liza frowned. She hadn't been thinking much about it at the time—she had been overwhelmed by sensation—but Roman had made

love *to* her, not *with* her. He had aroused her
with his mouth and hands and brought her to
orgasm again and again without ever putting
himself inside her. Now that she thought
about it, he had never even taken off his
clothes until he had left her to go shower.

But he had kept her from asking about Isabel Rojas. And another morning had dawned
with her fearing the worst, yet loath to confront her husband. When Roman woke up, she
was going to have to ask him the question she
should have asked last night.

Are you having an affair with Isabel Rojas?

Eight little words. How hard could it be?

*It's Monday morning. You both have to get
dressed and go to work. Wouldn't it be smarter to
wait until tonight?*

But Monday mornings were no different
than any other time for Roman. He always had
rounds, or surgery scheduled, or meetings he
couldn't miss. And after all, how long could it
take to say eight words? Or to receive a one-
word answer?

Yes. Or no.

Lisa made a growling sound of frustration
in her throat and watched Roman frown in his
sleep as though he'd heard her. She would
make sure Amy was taken care of first and
confront her husband at breakfast, she decided. She couldn't go on any longer like this.
She had to know the truth. One way or the
other.

"Mommy," a small voice whispered from
beside the bed. "Are you awake?"

Lisa eased out from under the covers, grabbing Roman's thick maroon terry cloth robe from the foot of the bed and slipping it on over the pink silk negligee she had donned after he had pleasured her the previous night.

She lifted Amy into her arms and carried her out of the room, closing the door with a quiet *click* behind her. Roman got too little sleep as it was. And this morning, she wasn't at all anxious for it to be disturbed.

She headed downstairs with Amy, keeping her voice low as she padded barefoot down the lushly carpeted stairs. "What would you like for breakfast this morning, sweetheart?"

"Cocoa Krispies," Amy said.

"All right, I'll—" Lisa opened the cupboard and realized they were out of Cocoa Krispies. Connie usually did the shopping, and with her gone, the chore had fallen through the cracks. "How about Fruity Pebbles?" Lisa asked.

"Nooo," Amy moaned. "I want Cocoa Krispies!"

Lisa briefly debated putting on some clothes and heading out to the H.E.B. for the box of cereal, but a glance at her Seiko confirmed it was 6:05. They were already running a little late this morning, and she had a confrontation with Roman to fit into their tight schedule.

"I don't have Cocoa Krispies," Lisa said firmly.

Amy's eyes filled with giant tears, as though she'd just been told that after fourteen years of practice she wasn't going to make the

Olympic gymnastic team. Lisa marveled at how her daughter managed the impressive waterworks. But she wasn't strong enough to resist that sort of emotional blackmail.

She rubbed a soothing finger over Amy's pouting lower lip and said, "How about if I make something really special instead, like French toast?"

Amy blinked once, and her whole visage changed from tragedy to ebullience. "French toast!" she cried, as though she'd just won the gold.

Her daughter's engaging grin was reward enough for the race Lisa knew she was in to prepare French toast from scratch. It wasn't all that difficult, just time-consuming. She opened the refrigerator and reached for the eggs and milk.

"I want Donald," Amy said.

Lisa turned and saw Amy's nose and mouth were pressed against the sliding glass door that led to the pool area, creating a smudge in the center of the glass. The plastic duck floated in the center of the pool. "Donald's happy where he is," she replied.

"I want Donald!" Amy insisted.

"You can play with Donald another time," Lisa replied impatiently. "I don't have time right now to get him for you." Another glance at her watch showed it was 6:11. "Go wake up, Daddy," she said, her arms loaded with spices as she shepherded the little girl out of the kitchen and toward the stairs. "Ask him to help you get dressed. Tell him we're having French toast for breakfast."

Lisa knew French toast was not only Amy's favorite breakfast, but Roman's, too.

Why do you care about pleasing him? The marriage is all but over.

Lisa fought to ignore the raspy voice that haunted her, battered her, as she searched for the electric skillet, slamming cupboards right and left. Where had Connie put it the last time she'd used it? Lisa found it in the cupboard above the stove, set it on the counter, and jammed in the plug. This was insane. She didn't have time to be making breakfast, even if Roman would love having it.

Why cater to him? Any day now he's going to leave you for another woman.

It was the voice of her mother, warning her that no man could be trusted. Warning her of the danger of falling in love and giving her heart to a man. Warning her to plan well ahead to take care of herself, so she wouldn't be left destitute—as her mother had been—when her husband walked out on her.

"Lisa!" Roman called down the stairs.

"What?" she called back up from the kitchen, whipping the eggs and milk together in a glass bowl. There was some reason her mother had told her she wasn't supposed to use aluminum, but Lisa couldn't remember what it was.

"Come get Amy while I take a shower!" Roman shouted.

"I'm making breakfast, Roman. You dress her and then send her down to me before you take your shower," Lisa shouted back at him as she dumped in vanilla and sugar and cinnamon and nutmeg. The nutmeg was what made her French toast so special.

"I don't have time for that!" he protested. "I've got surgery scheduled at seven."

Lisa glanced at her watch. 6:23. "It'll only take you three minutes to dress her, Roman. I'm busy, too." She dumped a tablespoon of butter into the skillet and heard it sizzle. That meant the pan was too hot, but she needed the French toast to cook in a hurry. "I've got a pretrial negotiation all the way across town at seven-thirty," she shouted back to Roman. She grabbed a loaf of bread and tore it open, dipped four successive slices in the milk-and-egg mixture with her fingers, and laid them in the skillet to cook.

Roman appeared in the kitchen doorway bare-chested and barefoot, a towel wrapped around his waist, with Amy thrown over his shoulder in a fireman's carry. The sight of him made her insides clench with desire.

The romantic bubble quickly burst as he set Amy down—still in her pajamas—and snapped, "Why don't you quit that damned job! We don't need the money. I can take care of you."

"My job is as important to me as yours is to you!" Lisa retorted, anger flaring at his offer, kindled by her fear of abandonment. "Why don't you quit?"

Roman punched his glasses high up on his nose with a forefinger. "You're talking nonsense."

"It's no more ridiculous than me quitting my job! I'll need my job if you ever leave me."

"Leave you? Who said anything about anybody leaving?"

Lisa crossed her arms defensively over her chest. "I've seen it coming, Roman."

Roman snorted. "Then you can see a damned sight better than I can!"

"You never say you love me," she accused.

He stood stymied for an instant.

"I love you, Mommy."

Lisa stared down at Amy, who stood knee-high between the two of them, eyes pooled with tears, chin trembling. "Oh, my God, Amy." She lifted Amy into her arms and pulled her close. "I know you do, sweetheart."

Lisa stared at Roman accusingly.

"We shouldn't be having this argument in front of Amy," he said through clenched jaws.

"Then take her upstairs and dress her," Lisa said, holding her out to Roman, aware she was as much in the wrong as he was, but unable to let go of her anger. "You could have finished dressing her in the time you've spent complaining to me."

Roman took Amy, set her down, and said, "Go play in your room, Amy. Mommy and Daddy have to talk."

"Are you fighting?" Amy said, clinging to his leg.

"We're working out some problems," Roman said, picking her up and hugging her quickly. He set her on her feet again and said, "Go upstairs now and play in your room."

"I'm hungry."

"You can get that bacon biscuit you like on the way to day care," Roman said placatingly.

"I want French toast," Amy whined.

"No French toast today," Roman said, his patience obviously waning. "Go upstairs, Amy, before I. . . ." His threats were meaningless, and Amy obviously knew it, because she stayed right where she was. He was clearly at the end of his rope and looked to Lisa for help.

Roman indulged Amy often enough that she was a little spoiled, Lisa conceded. She was almost as bad as he was, but someone had to be firm. Between them, it was Lisa who usually ended up denying their daughter what she wanted. "Go upstairs, Amy," she said. "Daddy will come and get you soon."

"I can't take her, Lisa. I can't be late," Roman protested angrily. "I'm never late!"

"Then you will be this time!" she retorted.

Amy had paused in the doorway, and Lisa snarled, "Get upstairs!"

Amy scrambled up the stairs, howling at the top of her lungs.

"Now look what you've done!" Roman said.

"Me? You're the one who couldn't be bothered to dress your daughter."

"You're going to have to take care of Amy this morning," Roman insisted. "I've got to meet Isabel—"

"Didn't you get enough sex last night? If you need another fuck this morning, it's your own damned fault. I was willing, Roman. You never asked!"

Roman's face bleached as white as the powdered sugar Lisa had pulled from the cupboard to dust on the French toast when it was done. "What is that supposed to mean? If you're insinuating—"

"Are you having an affair with Isabel?"

Once the words were out, Lisa wished them back. There was no going back now, no pretending nothing was wrong.

The shock, the hurt, the disbelief on Roman's face should have told her everything she needed to know. But she heard her mother's voice saying, *"He lied to me for years. He swore there was no one else. Until one day I came home and found he'd taken everything and left."*

"What have I ever done to make you doubt my love?" Roman said.

Lisa swallowed over the lump of pain in her throat. "You're never home anymore, Roman. We never talk. And you never say the words, Roman. You never say the words."

"I do . . ." He stared at her, his eyes liquid, his mouth working, but no sound coming out.

"I've got to get dressed," Lisa said, "or I'm going to be late." She brushed past Roman, afraid he might try to stop her, and raced up the stairs.

"Lisa, we have to talk," he said, following after her, taking the stairs two at a time. He caught up to her in the bedroom, grabbed her arm, and hauled her around to face him. "I'm at the hospital so much because my patients need me."

He was angry now, but so was she. "I need you, too!"

"You have me. All of me. Don't you know that?" Roman cried.

"I don't know anything!" she said. "Except that the woman you spend all your days with looks at you with eyes that eat you alive. You've been acting so strangely. I don't even know if you want a wife anymore."

"I do, Lisa. I . . . I . . ."

She watched him struggle to say the words. Struggle and fail. "Am I so unlovable, Roman?" she grated past the knot in her throat.

He was silent too long.

The sudden shrill of the smoke alarm sent them both clambering back downstairs. Clouds of choking smoke rose from the blackened and charred remains of the French toast. Lisa covered her mouth and nose as she pulled the plug on the electric skillet, while Roman crossed to open the sliding glass doors to let in some fresh air.

"When did you open this?" he said as he

pushed it wide. And then, "No. *No!*"

Roman's agonized cry made Lisa's blood run cold. She turned in time to see him slam open the sliding glass door and race outside.

"Roman? What's wrong?" She crossed to the open doorway and stepped through to see what had panicked him.

Amy was floating facedown in the pool.

⸙ *Chapter 16* ⸒

"Shoot me or put it away, Kittrick," Isabel said. "The doctor needs me in the ER, and that's where I'm going."

Isabel handed the potassium-filled needle to Nurse Cole and gestured to the blond-headed girl in bed three. "This is for Patty. The doctor said we'd do additional surgery if she wasn't any better this morning, and her potassium level is low. Under the circumstances, Hollander probably won't do the surgery. See who's backing him up."

Jack realized he was seeing exactly why Roman Hollander valued Isabel Rojas so much. He had never seen anyone, male or female, react so calmly and capably in a crisis.

"Hold up there a minute," he said, when Nurse Cole started to follow Isabel's orders. What Isabel had said sounded perfectly rational, and Jack doubted whether a murderer would have handed over the murder weapon to a substitute and instructed her to go on with the dirty deed. But he had no way of knowing for sure. Maybe that was exactly how Hollander and Rojas were killing kids without getting caught.

"Put the needle down, Nurse Cole," he ordered.

Facing a Colt .45, Frannie Cole did exactly as she was told. The needle landed on the table beside bed three.

"Wait right here and don't move a finger—unless one of the kids needs you," Jack said. "A detective will be here in about thirty seconds to brief you on what's going on. Meanwhile, don't say anything to anyone about any of this, do you understand?"

Nurse Cole nodded vigorously.

Jack slipped the Colt .45 into the front of his jeans, where it was hidden by his Levi's jacket, and gestured Isabel out the door. "Shall we go, Ms. Rojas?"

She marched out ahead of him briskly enough that he figured she probably did wind sprints to stay in shape. Jack was grateful the elevator arrived the first time she punched it, because he had a feeling that otherwise she'd have taken the stairs.

"I'm waiting to hear what this is all about," Isabel said when the elevator door closed, leaving them alone together.

Jack wasn't sure what to say. If Isabel was a murderer, she was about the coolest killer he'd ever seen. Because his heart had been in his throat with fear, he'd gone off half-cocked and blown his cover bigtime. He met Isabel's forthright stare and said, "I'm a Texas Ranger, Isabel."

"I didn't figure you were Batman."

Jack laughed and said, "Don't make me laugh, Isabel. This is serious."

"As a heart attack," Isabel agreed. "What did you think I was going to do to that kid?"

"Kill her," Jack said.

Isabel's eyes goggled. "No shit?"

Jack felt the urge to laugh again and stifled it. If Isabel Rojas was a murderer, he'd eat his new Resistol. "I'm here to find out—"

The elevator doors opened with a chime, and Isabel brushed past him and went whizzing down the hall to the ER. Jack was grateful he'd gotten himself a hospital ID that gave him access everywhere, because a couple of orderlies were serious about keeping unauthorized folks out.

The ER was nowhere near as quiet as the rest of the hospital. Here was the center of the hive, where watchful worker bees guarded the heart of the place and never slept. People and machines were crowded into too small a space, and the cries of the wounded and their families filled the air with an anguished cacophony. Jack stayed close to Isabel, figuring she knew where she was going.

He was unprepared for the sight of three-year-old Amy Hollander lying in the center of a metal hospital gurney, IVs taped grotesquely to the right side of her neck and her wrist, her tiny body hooked up to monstrous machines that beeped and blipped and hissed and hummed.

Roman Hollander stood beside his daughter wearing a white doctor's coat open over his bare chest. Jack wondered if Hollander was dressed at all and stepped close enough to see the doctor was wearing a pair of zipped but unbuttoned black jeans and mismatched tennis shoes.

Jack was amazed to see Lisa Hollander in the ER, considering the goons at the door, but even more astonished to note that she was standing on the opposite side of the gurney from her husband, glowering at him, instead of at his side, being comforted by and comforting him.

Jack backed up along the wall, close enough to listen to the questions Isabel was asking— *Cardiac monitor? Pulse oximeter? Arterial line? Foley catheter?*—and to hear the answers she was getting—all affirmative—but not close enough to intrude on the family's anger and grief.

"What's the prognosis?" Isabel asked Roman.

Trust a nurse to get to the point, Jack thought.

Hollander seemed to be in some kind of trance, and it was the ER physician who answered, "She's slipped into a coma. We're keeping her on a respirator—"

"And I want her off," Hollander said authoritatively.

"Don't any of you touch her!" Lisa said, dark eyes alert, guarding her daughter like a lioness with her cub. "I won't let you do this, Roman. I've read every word you've ever written, and I don't care what Amy's like when she wakes up, so long as she does wake up!"

"A breathing apparatus is only prolonging the inevitable, Lisa. I've seen cases like this too many times—"

"This isn't a case," she hissed, leaning across the gurney to confront him. "This is your daughter. How can you not want to do everything you can to save her?"

"Don't you understand? There's nothing I *can* do to save her!" He shoved both hands through his short-cropped hair. "There's not a goddamned thing I can do for her!"

Jack understood, all right. The almighty Dr. Hollander, who had the precise skill and knowledge to save other people's children, did not have the precise skill and knowledge to save his own. Whether Amy Hollander came out of the coma hale and hearty depended on how long her brain had gone without oxygen before she was discovered and resuscitated. Five minutes was about the limit before brain cells started to die.

"How long was she underwater?" Isabel asked, apparently having followed the same line of reasoning as Jack.

"I don't know!" Hollander said. "Lisa and I . . . I don't know!"

"It couldn't have been more than five minutes!" Lisa insisted. "It couldn't! I was watching the time all morning! The smoke alarm went off so quick—"

"Smoke alarm?" Isabel said.

Jack saw the byplay between Hollander and his wife before the doctor said, "It was nothing. Some French toast got burned."

"How did Amy get outside to the pool without either of you noticing?" Isabel asked, looking from one of them to the other.

"We . . ." Hollander stopped and stared at his wife, his mouth grim. "We were upstairs, and we thought she was, too."

"She wanted to play with Donald, and I told her no. I never thought . . . I never thought. . . ."

Jack's heart went out to her. *Why doesn't Hollander hold his wife? What's wrong him? Can't he see how much pain she's in?*

But the two of them seemed very far apart.

"I knew Amy was smart," Hollander said, brushing tenderly at the dark, still-damp curls on his daughter's forehead. "But the security lock on the sliding glass door . . . It's so complicated. . . ."

It was gut-wrenching to watch Hollander battle to control his quivering chin. Jack looked away as the doctor's features crumpled.

Lisa took a step toward her husband, but stopped when Isabel reached him first.

Jack had never seen a more tortured look

than the one on Lisa Hollander's face as her husband wrapped his arms around Isabel Rojas, pressed his face tight against her shoulder, and sobbed.

Maggie had slept like the dead. It was no wonder after the night she had spent with Jack. She had woken feeling wonderful—until she glanced at her watch and saw that if she didn't get a move on, she would be late for the Monday morning bioethics committee meeting . . . again.

As she inched out of bed, she realized she was sore in places she had forgotten she had. There were bruises on her inner thighs, her arms, and—she knew from a midnight visit to the bathroom—a hickey high enough on her throat that she was going to have to do some creative dressing. She didn't remember getting any of the marks, only the joy and the passion and the pleasure of the night just past.

When the phone rang, her heart leaped, because she was certain it was Jack. He had told her in the early morning hours—after he had made love to her for the third time—that he would have to leave before she woke up. But he had promised to call her. She picked up the phone expecting to hear his voice.

Instead, Victoria Wainwright said, "You'd better get to the hospital on time this morning. The committee has an important matter to consider."

"What is it?" Maggie asked, more irritated than interested.

"Amy Hollander drowned. Dr. Hollander wants to take her off the respirator, but his wife is refusing."

Maggie's legs buckled, and she ended up on her knees beside the bed. "Oh, my God."

"Don't be late, Margaret. You know how Dr. Hollander likes to start on time."

The phone clicked in Maggie's ear.

"Nooooo," Maggie moaned. "Nooooo." She dropped the phone into the cradle and lowered her face into her hands. *This can't be happening.* She knew exactly what Lisa and Roman were feeling right now—the guilt and the anguish.

The phone rang again, and Maggie hesitated before she answered it. *Please, not more bad news.*

"Maggie? Are you there?"

"Lisa? Where are you?"

"You've got to come to the hospital *now*, Maggie. Roman's threatening to take Amy off the ventilator. He's petitioning the bioethics committee this morning to get their consent. I need you to argue on my behalf at the meeting, Maggie. I need you to be on my side."

"Lisa. . . ." It was a clear conflict of interest for Maggie to speak on Lisa's behalf when she legally represented the hospital—who represented Roman Hollander. But there was no reason why she couldn't speak up as a friend and a concerned party. "I'm on my way," she reassured Lisa. "Don't let them do anything without me."

"Hurry, Maggie. Hurry!"

Lisa's plea played constantly in Maggie's head as she toweled off after a quick shower, grabbed a power suit from her closet—she was going to need it this morning—dragged a brush through her hair, and drove like a wild woman through rush-hour traffic to the hospital. She didn't bother with the elevator, just hiked up her skirt and took the stairs to the second floor two at a time. As she pushed open the stairwell door a voice said, "You're late."

Maggie whirled to find Jack Kittrick leaning against the wall, his arms and legs crossed.

"I've been waiting for you," he said as he straightened up. "Amy Hollander drowned."

"I know."

When Jack opened his arms, Maggie walked into them and held him tight around the waist, pressing her nose against his throat. "I know what Lisa's feeling, Jack. It hurts."

"I know," he said. "I feel it, too."

She leaned back and looked up at him.

"I saw Amy in the ER," he said. "They had so damned many tubes in her. . . ."

Maggie searched Jack's face and saw the dark shadows beneath his eyes. "You must be tired."

"Given the choice of sleeping or spending the night the way I did, I'd rather be tired," he said with a tender smile. He caressed the bruise on her throat and said, "Did I do that?"

Maggie groaned. "I was going to cover that with a scarf."

He leaned over and kissed the spot, then pulled up the collar of her blouse and said, "There. All gone. You're ready to go to work, counselor. Here's a little something for luck."

Jack kissed her on the lips so gently that Maggie scarcely felt the touch. Yet the kiss moved her more than all the passionate embraces he had given her the previous night.

"Thank you, Jack," she said. "I needed that." As the two of them walked down the hall toward the conference room she said, "Roman wants to disconnect the ventilator."

"I know. Can he do that?"

"Medically, he can recommend removal. Legally, if Lisa wants it on and he wants it off, it's a problem. Ethically, he shouldn't be treating his own family. But he has enough friends on the committee to get them to recommend what he wants. After that, Lisa's going to have a fight on her hands."

"Where do you stand?" Jack asked.

Maggie looked him in the eye and said, "I'm on Amy's side."

The tension in the conference room was palpable. Instead of sitting in her usual seat, Maggie took the empty seat Lisa had saved for her near the head of the conference table. Jack took the only seat left—Maggie's place at the foot of the table.

The secretary finished reading the minutes

of the previous meeting, and Roman called for additions or corrections. The minutes were approved as read, and the tension went up a notch as Roman began reciting the facts of Amy's case.

"We don't know how long she was underwater—" Roman said.

"Not for very long!" Lisa interjected.

Maggie gripped Lisa's wrist to silence her, and Roman continued without looking in his wife's direction.

"—before efforts to resuscitate were begun. The child began to breathe on her own, but stopped breathing on the way to the hospital and was put on a respirator when she arrived. The three-year-old victim is in a coma, and only time will tell whether—"

Lisa leapt up and said, "She's not 'a victim,' she's our daughter!"

"Sit down, Lisa," Roman said.

"Roman, you can't do this," Lisa pleaded. "You have to save Amy. You have to!"

The committee remained silent as the two adversaries confronted each other across the conference table.

"Don't you see, Lisa?" Roman said in a voice racked with grief. "I can't save her. That's what this meeting is all about."

Maggie stood up beside Lisa, put an arm around her shoulder, and murmured, "Sit down, Lisa. Let me ask the questions that need to be asked."

"But—"

"Trust me, please."

Maggie watched Lisa sink into her chair, then turned to Roman and said, "What about Amy's brain wave activity?"

Roman rearranged a folder of papers in front of him as though looking for the results of the brain scan, then said, "There are some irregularities."

"But she's not brain dead, is that correct?" Maggie asked.

"Yes, that's correct. But—"

"Then I don't understand why you're recommending removal of life-support systems," Maggie said. "There's no legal basis for it."

The conference table suddenly buzzed like bees around a particularly succulent flower.

"I don't believe life support will do any good," Roman said, rising, as though being seated while she was standing gave her too much power in the argument.

"Is that your medical opinion, or your opinion as the father of a child who's been the victim of a tragedy?" Maggie challenged.

"I've seen cases like this before," Roman said ominously.

"And?" Maggie prodded.

"Sometimes the victim's condition deteriorates so slowly, it takes months for the child to die."

"And other times?"

Roman made a face as though to dismiss those statistics.

"What happens in the cases where the victim's condition doesn't deteriorate?" Maggie insisted.

"The child can recover completely, or recover with various levels of damage to her physical or mental capabilities . . . everything from a slight speech impediment or a limp to paraparesis," Roman said.

Maggie felt Victoria's eyes on her at the mention of "paraparesis," but refused to look at her mother-in-law. They both knew the physical and mental devastation that could occur. Maggie believed a life like Brian's was worth living—that any life was worth living—to the very fullest of the individual's abilities. Brian's unfettered joy in life had helped Maggie to find the joy in her own.

To Maggie's astonishment, Victoria said, "Tell us about paraparesis, doctor."

Victoria knew full well what paraparesis was—her own grandson was paraparetic. She could only be asking the question to sway the committee to vote against keeping Amy Hollander on a respirator.

"If a drowning victim suffers global brain damage, paraparesis may result. It can include speech and memory problems, poor muscular control, tremors—"

"The quality of life Amy will enjoy—if she survives—is not the issue we are here to discuss, Dr. Hollander," Maggie interjected.

"Why not?" Victoria said. "It's the duty of this committee to be the moral voice of this community. Why can't Dr. Hollander make an ethical decision to remove his daughter from a respirator based on the kind of life she'll lead in the future?"

Maggie met Victoria's pale blue eyes across the conference table and said, "Because the ethical issue is moot so long as the child has a medical chance of survival." Maggie turned to Roman and said, "Will the respirator help keep Amy alive, doctor?"

"I don't think—"

"Yes or no, Dr. Hollander. Will a respirator extend your daughter's life?"

"Yes."

"Then legally, she's entitled to that support." Maggie met Roman's obsidian eyes for long enough to see the concession there before she sat down.

The committee decided, by a vote of 11 to 9, that it was inappropriate to disconnect Amy Hollander from the respirator at this time.

As soon as the vote was announced, Lisa rose and left without excusing herself. Maggie wanted to go after her, but the meeting wasn't over, and she wasn't sure what other shenanigans Victoria might instigate if she wasn't there to keep an eye on her.

Roman appeared distracted for the remainder of the meeting, and Maggie suspected he was at the end of his rope by the time the meeting was adjourned. As the committee, including Victoria, filed out of the room, Maggie took the few steps to reach the frazzled doctor, wanting to offer what comfort she could.

"Roman, I'm so sorry about what's happened to Amy. I know what you must be feeling right now."

"How the hell would you know that, Maggie? You've never even had a child of your own. How would you know what it feels like to lose one to drowning?"

Maggie's jaw dropped at the virulence of Roman's attack and the unfairness of it. This was the price she paid for all the secrets she had kept. If Roman had known the truth, he might have been able to accept what comfort she had to offer. Instead, Maggie found herself facing a man whose impotence—when he was used to exercising almost godlike powers of healing—must have been particularly galling.

"Excuse me for butting in, Dr. Hollander, but Maggie knows what it feels like because she has a son who's paraparetic as a result of drowning."

Maggie's heart skipped a beat. She turned to stare at Jack, whose steel-gray eyes were focused on Hollander.

"Her sympathy was well-intentioned," Jack said. "She knows exactly what you're going through, and she knows what it might be like for you if Amy doesn't fully recover. I think you owe her an apology, doctor."

"Maggie, I . . . I don't know what to say."

Maggie tore her gaze from Jack's face and turned to Roman. "It's my fault, Roman. I should have told you about my son Brian a long time ago."

"Does Lisa know?"

"No. No one knows except my family."

Roman shot Jack a quizzical look, as though to ask how he had become privy to the information, then asked, "Why keep such a secret, Maggie?"

"Because, as I suspect you're doing right now, I blamed myself for what happened."

The small sound Roman made was evidence that Maggie had guessed right. "From what you've said, it wasn't anybody's fault Amy drowned. It was just a tragic accident. It'll help if you can keep that in mind."

"I'll try," Roman said. "Now, if you'll excuse me, I want to check on my daughter."

Maggie watched Roman till he was gone, then turned to face Jack and asked, "Why did you tell him about Brian?"

"Why not?" Jack said.

"It wasn't your decision to make, Jack."

"You've carried the burden by yourself long enough, don't you think, Maggie? Why not let some of us who care about you share it?"

Jack cupped Maggie's nape with one large hand and drew her toward him. Maggie waited for some urge to resist to rise up and rescue her from Jack's comforting hug. But in the cold, cold place deep down inside of her, within the thick block of ice that was her heart, a warm spring thaw was going on.

"I'd be happy standing right here for the rest of my life," Maggie murmured.

Abruptly, Jack shoved her away from him,

fumbled to get a beeper out of his jeans pocket, and looked at the number. "Gotta go."

"I didn't hear a beep," Maggie said. He didn't answer, because he was already gone from the room.

Maggie stared after him, her brow furrowed. Then it dawned on her what she'd said: *I could stand right here the rest of my life.* She knew why Jack had beat such a hasty retreat. He didn't want to get involved. He wasn't interested in commitment. "The rest of my life" was pretty serious stuff.

Maggie had to remember the rules. After all, she had set them herself. She could get close, but not too close. She could like Jack, she just couldn't love him.

"Oh, hell," Maggie said. It was already too late for that.

♊ *Chapter 17* ♋

When the beeper vibrated in Jack's pocket, his first thought was, *Another victim!* A glance at the phone number on the beeper revealed he was needed by whoever was monitoring the ICU, but there was no emergency.

His second thought was, *I wish I didn't have to let go of Maggie.* He had a lot better idea now why she'd posted all those No Trespassing signs to keep men—him—away. But her attitude had obviously undergone a recent change.

His third thought was, *Just about every murder suspect I have just left the conference room headed for the ICU. Maybe the situation on the fifth floor is more dangerous than the cop on duty realizes.*

All three thoughts together took less than a second, so Jack's "Gotta go" came in tandem with his examination of the beeper. He realized on his way out the door that Maggie had no idea what had sent him flying, but he obeyed the instincts that told him, *Go now, explain later.*

He bolted out the door of the conference room and raced up three flights of stairs, unwilling to take a chance on the elevator. The heart that was already pounding in his chest from holding Maggie began tripping double-time, and Jack's gut squeezed tight with fear.

He headed straight for the linen room, where Detective Fuentes had been replaced by another detective whose name Jack couldn't recall. "Why'd you beep me?" he said the instant he came through the door.

"There are too many people in the room for me to watch all of them at once. I figured better safe than sorry."

Jack saw the problem immediately. Lisa was sitting on one side of Amy's bed—bed eight, in the farthest corner of the room—while Dr. Hollander talked with Isabel on the other side. The replacement for Nurse Cole was attending to the little girl in bed three—Patty, Jack remembered—while Victoria sat in a chair next to Patty, wearing a peach-colored hospital volunteer's jacket and reading the unconscious child a book.

It was hard for Jack to do nothing but watch, because the way people were moving around, it was difficult to see their hands at all times. He wanted to stand unobtrusively in a corner of the ICU. But in that case, the murderer would hardly be likely to show himself. Or herself. Jack sat down beside the detective—Joe Harkness, he remembered—and began to watch. And wait. And think about Maggie.

So far, Jack hadn't let himself fall in love with Maggie Wainwright. At least not the sappy "She can do no wrong/Isn't she perfect?" kind of love. He saw Maggie with eyes that were all too clear. And she was far from perfect.

She was outspoken and opinionated. She was consistently late for meetings. She had a caesarian scar on her abdomen. And of course, she was an alcoholic. Jack could easily have fallen in love with her despite her flaws. . . . despite all her flaws but one.

He would have to be a fool to let himself fall in love with an alcoholic. Especially when he knew the downside and the dangers of the disease.

Jack Kittrick was no fool.

So as much as he wanted to love Maggie, Jack wasn't going to let it happen. He knew he ought to tell Maggie how he felt. Especially after what he could see was happening. It wasn't fair to let her fall in love with him, when he had no intention of loving her back.

Roman was speaking with Isabel, rearranging his surgical schedule, but his eyes were on his wife on the other side of Amy's bed. She was holding Amy's tiny hand, the back of which contained an IV held in place with an X of surgical tape. He could see Lisa's lips moving, so he knew she was talking to their daughter, but from where he stood, he couldn't make out what she was saying. What was she telling Amy?

He knew what he would say. *Fight hard. Get well. Mommy and Daddy love you.*

Roman wanted so much to sit beside his wife and hold his daughter's hand. But after what had happened at the committee meeting, he wasn't sure what Lisa would do if he put his hand on her shoulder to comfort her.

He had tried to make his wife understand why he was against life-support measures. He wanted Amy to live every bit as much as Lisa did. But he had seen too much, he knew too much . . . and he was too much afraid to take a chance.

Now it looked like he was not only going to lose his daughter, he was also going to lose his wife. It wasn't only that they had disagreed on what to do about Amy's medical condition. Lisa's attack at home early this morning had caught him totally by surprise. She had hidden her doubts and fears about their relationship from him every bit as effectively as he had hidden his doubts and fears from her.

He knew Lisa deserved more time, more attention, more of everything. Even now, when she needed to know it the most, he was unable to show her how much he loved her.

What she suspected—an affair with his nurse—was so far from reality. . . . He wanted desperately to pull her out of that chair and into his arms. But the thought of her bristling like a porcupine or retreating like a turtle kept him where he was.

Roman made himself look at his surgical nurse and see her as his wife did. Even at forty-one Isabel was pretty, he realized. More than pretty. And when he looked into her eyes—really looked—Roman perceived what he'd been too selfishly blind to see. Isabel Rojas was in love with him.

What a fool he'd been!

Roman knew now why Lisa had turned her back on him three months ago. She must have seen Isabel looking at him with love in her eyes and assumed their long-ago affair was on again—or had never ended. The quickest, easiest way to assuage Lisa's concern was to ask Isabel to transfer to another surgical team. It would be a sacrifice—he would lose both a good friend and a good nurse—but Roman was willing to do anything necessary to convince Lisa he valued her love above anything else in his life.

Even that might not bring them back together if Amy died.

Roman couldn't breathe when he thought of Amy dying. His mind went blank and the world got dark when he tried to imagine a life without her and Lisa in it.

"Dr. Hollander?"

Roman gave his attention to Isabel. "Where were we?"

"You wanted me to see if Dr. Morgenstern

can cover the surgery on Patty Watson. Anything else?"

"That's all for now. I think I'll stay here a while longer."

"I'm so sorry about Amy," Isabel said.

"I know. Isabel . . ."

"Something else you need?"

"We have to talk later about . . . about some things."

She gave him a quizzical look. "All right. Call me when you're free."

He waited for Isabel to leave before approaching his wife. His stomach churned when he saw her visibly stiffen as he crossed around the foot of the bed. He didn't think waiting was going to make things better, so he forced himself to say, "Lisa, we need to talk."

She turned and stared up at him, her heart in her eyes. "She has to live, Roman," she said fiercely. "I won't let her die."

Because there was no chair, Roman crouched down beside his wife. He reached for her hand and was grateful that she let him clasp it in his own. "Lisa, I . . . we. . . ."

She sighed, a sound so woeful and defeated that Roman wanted to scoop her up in his arms and promise her right then and there that everything would be all right. But he couldn't make that promise.

"We have to talk," he managed to say.

"I can't talk about . . . anything . . . right now," she said. "Later."

"Tonight?"

She turned toward Amy and reached out a hand to caress the one small spot on their daughter's cheek that was not covered by surgical tape holding the respirator tube in place. "If she dies—"

"The first twenty-four hours are critical. She may not . . ." He couldn't finish.

"I'll see you at home," she said. "Tonight."

The morning seemed endless to Lisa, who never left Amy's side. The respirator pumped and hissed, pumped and hissed, as it forced air in and out of Amy's lungs. Sometimes Lisa thought Amy's eyelashes fluttered. Sometimes she thought Amy's fingers twitched. But it was her own wishful thinking.

Wake up, baby. Mommy's here. Mommy and Daddy love you.

But did Daddy love Mommy?

"Mrs. Hollander?"

Lisa looked up to find Victoria Wainwright standing beside her with a children's book tucked under her arm. She fought back the spurt of resentment she felt toward the woman for arguing against keeping Amy hooked to the ventilator and forced politeness into her voice. "Hello, Mrs. Wainwright."

"Hello. How is Amy?"

It was an insensitive question, because the answer was obvious. "The same," Lisa replied. As she rose, her muscles protested the long inactivity. She put a hand to the small of her back to counter the ache there as she glanced at her Seiko. 1:33 P.M. She'd missed lunch. And breakfast. No wonder she felt so empty inside.

"I'd be glad to sit and read to Amy for a while to give you a break," Mrs. Wainwright offered.

Lisa's first inclination was to refuse. But her stomach growled, and she realized she had to eat something soon. "Thank you. I'd appreciate that."

"Don't worry, Mrs. Hollander. I'll watch over her for you. I'm a grandmother myself, did you know? I have a grandson, Brian. Maggie's son."

Lisa couldn't believe what she was hearing. "Maggie has a son?"

"I know she'd want me to tell you about him. You see, he drowned, too, ten years ago. Unfortunately, he suffers from paraparesis. You do remember what that is, don't you, Mrs. Hollander?"

"Yes," Lisa breathed.

Mrs. Wainwright brushed aside a lock of Amy's hair and said, "It would be awful if that happened to Amy. That's why I argued against a respirator, you know. It's so tragic when they don't recover completely."

"Mrs. Wainwright—"

"Go have something to eat, Mrs. Hollander. Amy will be perfectly safe with me. I'll read *Peter Rabbit* to her while you're gone."

Lisa watched as Victoria Wainwright settled herself in the uncomfortable plastic chair beside Amy's bed and opened a gold-trimmed hardbound book. Lisa wanted to yank the other woman out of the way and sit back down herself. But she didn't see how she could accomplish that without making a scene, and she had already made quite enough scenes for one day.

On the way downstairs to the cafeteria, Lisa realized that if she ate, she would only end up with indigestion. Her stomach was one giant knot from anger. At the unfairness of it all. At Roman for arguing against the ventilator. At Maggie for keeping such a secret. At herself for shouting at Amy. At God. . . . If she didn't vent some of that anger, she was going to explode.

Maggie was the target she chose.

Lisa headed down Travis Street toward the Milam Building, aware of how warm the sun felt on her shoulders, how blue the sky was, what a beautiful spring day it was. *Amy should be enjoying this,* she thought.

She took the elevator to the top floor, greeted Trudy with a quick, false smile, and hurried past before the receptionist could offer sympathy Lisa couldn't handle right now. She hurried down the hall to Maggie's corner office, closed the door behind her, and said, "I thought we were friends. Why didn't you tell me you had a son who drowned? Why did I have to find out about it from Mrs. Wainwright?"

She saw the shocked look on Maggie's face,

the oh-so-familiar pain, and burst into tears. "Maggie, help me. I don't know what to do."

Maggie had been dreading—yet expecting—the truth to come out for so many years that it was almost a relief to have it happen. And though she felt sorry for Lisa's obvious distress, she was grateful for the respite from answering Lisa's questions. She wrapped her arms around Lisa and offered what comfort she could.

It was a while before Lisa's tears were spent. When they were, Maggie settled Lisa in one of the black leather chairs in front of her desk and seated herself in the other. "I guess I owe you an explanation."

Lisa blotted her eyes with a Kleenex. "You don't have to tell me anything," Lisa said in a voice hoarse from crying.

"I think maybe it's time," Maggie said, hearing the hurt behind Lisa's anger. "Especially with what's happened to Amy."

"Amy's not going to end up like your son."

"Maybe not," Maggie said. And then more softly, "But you have to face the possibility she may."

"No."

"I never expected my sons to drown, either. But—"

"*Sons?* Plural?"

Maggie nodded. "I had two sons who drowned. Twins. Stanley died, but Brian survived and lives in a very fine nursing home in New Braunfels."

"And you can give me the address in case I need it?" Lisa snapped.

Maggie felt stung, as though she'd been expecting a kiss and gotten slapped. "If you want it, I have it," she managed in a steady voice.

Lisa leapt from the chair and began pacing like a caged animal. "I'm sorry, Maggie. I don't know where that came from."

The pain, Maggie thought. She knew about the pain.

"God help me. What will I do if the same thing happens to Amy that happened to Brian?"

"Survive. We women are very good at it, I've discovered."

"I can't bear it, Maggie. I can't bear thinking about it."

"Then think about something else just as important."

"What else could be more important right now than Amy?"

"Your marriage to Roman."

Lisa stared at her, dumbstruck.

"You have to support each other during this terrible time. And you mustn't blame yourselves." Maggie had suffered on that rack for too many years.

Lisa stared at her knotted fingers and said, "Roman and I may separate for reasons that have nothing to do with Amy."

Maggie crossed and put an arm around Amy's shoulder. "Can you be happy living without Roman?"

"I don't think I can be happy living with him," Lisa admitted in a small voice. "At least, not the way things are right now."

"Don't give up without a fight," Maggie urged. "You owe it to yourself—and to Amy— to try and resolve your differences with Roman. Tell him what you're feeling. Tell him what you need from him. It's not too late for you."

Maybe if she had talked with Woody sooner, he would have rearranged his priorities and put her and the boys first. Maybe he would have been home that Saturday morning. Maybe her life would have been entirely different as a result.

"I accused Roman of having an affair with Isabel," Lisa blurted.

"What did he say?"

"He never had a chance to answer. The smoke alarm went off and..." Lisa sniffed and wiped her nose with the Kleenex. "He wants to talk about it tonight."

"Then I suggest you keep the appointment," Maggie said.

Lisa's stomach growled loudly. "I need to eat something. And I need to get back to Amy."

"I'll walk you back to the hospital. You can get a sandwich at the shop downstairs on the way."

"It's a deal," Lisa said.

On their way out, Maggie told the receptionist, "I'll be at San Antonio General with Mrs. Hollander, if anybody's looking for me."

As the elevator doors closed behind them, Lisa said, "How about taking some of your own advice, Maggie?"

"What do you mean?"

"Are you going to let Jack Kittrick get away?"

Maggie laughed self-consciously. "You make it sound like he's a steer I've got hogtied for branding. I don't have any ropes on Mr. Kittrick. He goes where he pleases."

"You should talk to him, Maggie. Tell him how you feel."

"I don't know how I feel," Maggie said irritably.

"You're in love with him," Lisa said.

Maggie stared at her friend. The elevator doors opened with a *ding*, and they headed for the sandwich shop. "That's a pretty big assumption to make."

They entered the sandwich shop, and Lisa told the server, "Tuna salad on whole wheat and a Diet Coke." Then she turned to Maggie and said, "I've seen the way Jack looks at you."

"That's lust."

"You aren't the type of woman men lust after," Lisa said matter-of-factly.

Maggie laughed rather than feeling insulted. "Oh? What type am I?"

"Wholesome. The one-man-one-woman-till-death-do-us-part type," Lisa said, accepting a brown paper bag and handing over her money.

"Well, phooey," Maggie said as they headed out the door of the Milam Building onto Travis Street.

"What's the matter?" Lisa asked.

"I think Jack's the love-'em-and-leave-'em type."

Lisa laughed, and Maggie joined her.

"How could you make me laugh at a time like this?" Lisa said, grabbing her ribs. "When Amy may be—" Her voice broke, and her eyes filled with tears.

Maggie put an arm around Lisa's waist and kept on walking. "Come on. Take one step at a time. That's the way you get through the tough times. Think you can do it?"

"What other choice do I have?"

"You can give up," Maggie said. "You can stop living. You can hide in a bottle, or the closet, or your job. I've tried them all, and believe me, none of them works worth a damn."

Lisa laughed again, then sobered. "All right, Maggie. I'll take one step at a time. Any other suggestions?"

"Pray."

Maggie walked Lisa all the way to the nurse's desk at the ICU. No one seemed to be on duty. Lisa glanced through the porthole window into the ICU. "I guess Mrs. Wainwright had to leave."

"She was here?" Maggie asked.

Lisa crossed and picked up the copy of *Peter Rabbit* on the ICU nurses' reception counter and said, "She promised to read to Amy while I went to get something to eat. I guess she forgot her book."

Maggie took the expensively bound copy of Beatrix Potter's *Tales of Peter Rabbit* from Lisa and felt a chill run down her spine. How had Victoria gotten this book from Shady Oaks? The nurses there had strict instructions not to allow her on the premises.

Maybe it's a duplicate copy.

Maggie opened the book to the flyleaf and read, "To my grandson, Brian. May the angels keep you always."

Something clicked in Maggie's head, like a light switch going on, and she winced in the blinding glare.

"Oh, my God."

The ICU nurse came out of a door down the hall and headed for the desk. "Can I help you?" she said.

Maggie grabbed her by the arm and said, "How is Amy Hollander doing?"

"Vital signs haven't changed," the nurse said.

"When was the last time you checked?" Maggie demanded.

"Two minutes ago, okay?"

Maggie released the nurse and straightened out her uniform where she had wrinkled the sleeve. "Sorry. I was afraid something might have happened to her. Guess I overreacted a little."

"We get a lot of that around here."

"Is it all right for me to sit with my daughter?" Lisa asked.

"Sure," the nurse said, ushering them beyond the swinging ICU doors.

As Maggie watched Lisa settle in the uncomfortable plastic chair beside her daughter, she realized there was something she had to tell Jack. Something she had thought a lot about since he had come into her life, asking questions and digging up the past. Something that had prompted her to make some phone calls to the hospital in Minnesota where Woody and Stanley had died. Something Jack needed to know. A matter of life and death.

But there was someone else she needed to speak with first.

✎ Chapter 18 ✑

Maggie discovered Uncle Porter was out of town on Monday afternoon, so she made an appointment to see him bright and early Tuesday. When Maggie checked with his secretary Tuesday morning, he had rescheduled the meeting for late Tuesday afternoon. Maggie had no choice but to wait.

She checked on Amy's condition several times during the day by phone from her office, but it remained unchanged. She was trusting Jack to watch over Amy and make sure nothing happened to her. Maggie didn't call Jack because she wanted to speak with Uncle Porter before she disclosed her suspicions to him. But she noticed Jack hadn't called her, either.

Maggie told herself it was foolish to wait by the phone, hoping to hear from him. So she carried on as though Jack Kittrick's face was not constantly appearing before her, roguishly smiling, eyes filled with teasing laughter.

She realized she had truly made herself

crazy, when she battled her secretary late in the afternoon to answer the phone, hoping it was Jack. She was chagrined when her secretary won and said, "Mr. Porter says he can't see you until tomorrow."

In a day filled with waiting for things that didn't happen, that was the final frustrating straw.

Maggie marched around to the managing partner's office, ignored the protests of Uncle Porter's secretary, and moments later was standing in front of Porter Cobb.

"You've been putting me off," she said.

"I've been busy."

"I'm afraid this can't wait, Porter." For the first time, the familial address she had always accorded him was missing.

"What is it you've come to discuss?"

"Victoria. And what happened in Minneapolis." Maggie was watching for a guilty reaction, but she didn't get one. Porter was one cool customer.

When he reached for a cigar from a box on the desk, Maggie put her forefinger on the humidor. "No cigar. They aren't good for you. And they stink."

Porter harrumphed, but conceded the issue without further protest. Maggie knew he wasn't done posturing when he leaned back and put his booted heels on the antique desk alongside the rowel marks from Sheriff Tommy Cobb's spurs and the seven notches etched in the oak for the seven outlaws brought in by Texas Ranger "Big John" Cobb.

"I'm not intimidated by that desk, Porter," Maggie said firmly.

"What about the man sitting behind it?" he asked.

Maggie settled herself on the corner of the desk bearing the personally carved initials of Colonel William Travis, who had died at the Alamo. "I want to be sure I can hear you, and you can see me."

"This sounds important."

"It's a matter of life and death."

He cocked a brow. "That sounds a bit beyond my legal expertise."

"Don't play dumb with me," Maggie said. "I've seen you argue before the Texas Supreme Court. And in this case, you're the person with all the answers."

"Very well. Get on with it, girl."

Maggie ignored the diminutive address. Or rather, let it slide. It was impossible to ignore the way Porter Cobb was looking down his nose at her. She recognized the gesture because she had seen Victoria do it. She realized suddenly that they had both probably learned it from one of their parents.

She countered his condescending glance with an equally withering one of her own.

"Very well done, my dear," Porter said with a chuckle. "You're learning, I see."

"I picked up everything I know about trial tactics from you," she said.

"Who's on trial, if I may ask?"

"You are."

Maggie saw the slightest lift in the heels of Porter's ostrich cowboy boots before he relaxed back into the swivel chair.

"Very well," he said. "Ask your questions, counselor."

Maggie opened her mouth, and her throat suddenly closed. She wanted to know the truth, but she was also afraid to know it. She managed to say three words.

"Victoria killed Woody."

It hadn't been phrased as a question, yet only the flicker of an eye gave away Porter's discomfort and dismay. Anyone who didn't know him as well as Maggie did would never have seen it. She swallowed over the thickness in her throat and said, "Well?"

"That is a deep, dark subject, my dear."

"Don't you think you've buried the truth long enough?"

Porter's sigh eddied in the room before it settled in the silence between them. "How did you figure it out?"

"The clues were always there."

"I could never have proved she killed Woody. Or Richard, either."

Maggie gasped. "She killed her own husband?"

The expression of pain on Porter's face was answer enough for Maggie. She had come here with questions and suppositions. She hadn't

realized Porter would provide such honest—
and monstrous—answers.

"I didn't think any purpose would be
served by telling anyone the truth," he said.
"Or as much of it as I could figure out from
hints Victoria gave me. I've kept a close
watch on her to make sure it never happened again."

"But it has happened again," Maggie said.
"More than once."

Porter's boots came off the desk and landed
with two distinctive thumps on the Persian
carpet. "The hell you say."

Maggie stood, laid both palms on the infa-
mous desk, and stared Porter in the eye. "Six
children are dead. And I believe Victoria killed
them."

"Children?"

"Every one under ten years old," Maggie
said, her voice strident with anger. "Some of
them babies. Six children dead. And if Victoria
isn't stopped, it will be seven, or eight, or God
knows how many!"

Porter was on his feet, taking back the position of authority. Maggie straightened up,
matching him move for move, her legs spread
wide, her fisted hands on her hips.

He shook his head. "Damn it, girl. I suppose
it's that Texas Ranger making accusations
against her."

"They're not just accusations. The Texas
Rangers have proof from autopsies done on

victims who were murdered by an overdose of potassium chloride."

"There's no proof Victoria committed the murders," Porter blustered, "or she would have been arrested by now."

"Kittrick said there were only three people with a common bond to all the victims—Roman Hollander, his nurse, and me. We know there was one more, don't we? Victoria inevitably found a reason to visit me—to persecute me—on the anniversary of Woody's death every year. She came to Dallas, and she came to Houston. And she's been working as a volunteer in pediatrics at San Antonio General for as long as I've been counsel there."

"I swear I never had an inkling of what you're accusing her of doing."

"You believed she had killed twice. You were careful to keep Brian safe. Yet you never suspected she would kill again?" Maggie asked incredulously.

An eyelash flickered again, and Maggie saw the truth.

He knew! He knew—or had at least suspected— all along.

"How could you stand by and do nothing to stop her?" Maggie said bitterly.

"She's my sister."

"Nine years ago I blessed your soul every night before I went to sleep for coming to rescue me from the depths of despair. But you never did it for me, did you? You did it for her. To give her someone to hate besides herself."

"She couldn't bear being near Brian the way he was. That's why I came to find you."

"Because you *knew* she would kill him," Maggie spat. "Like she killed all those other kids!"

"There's no *proof!*" Porter said, pounding the desk with his fist. "Kittrick can't do a thing to her without proof!"

"You could," Maggie said.

"What?"

"You could have Victoria committed. You could get her the care she needs."

He sank into the swivel chair, his fingers rubbing at his temples. "Victoria would never stand for it."

"You have the power to arrange it. Before she kills again."

Sweat beaded the old man's forehead and gathered above his upper lip. Almost the instant the signs of nervousness appeared, he withdrew a pristine handkerchief from his pocket and dabbed his age-mottled skin dry. "I'm sorry, Margaret. I can't help you."

"You mean you won't."

"You don't seem to understand—"

"No. You don't understand. If you won't take care of the problem, I will."

"What is it you intend to do?"

"Tell Jack Kittrick everything I know, for a start."

"What good will that do? It doesn't give

you the proof you need. And believe me, if Kittrick tries to arrest Victoria without sufficient—"

"She's a murderer. She should be put away where she can't hurt anyone else."

"She's the only family I have left."

Maggie turned and headed for the door.

"Where are you going?" Porter called after her.

"To find Jack Kittrick," Maggie said.

"Please, don't do that, Margaret."

Maggie turned and stopped like a wind-up toy that quits in midmotion when she saw the huge gun in Porter's hand. She could hear the slow, steady thud of her heart and wondered why it wasn't moving any faster. Where was her "fight-or-flight" instinct when she needed it? "Are you planning to use that gun on me?"

"This isn't just a gun. It's an 1851 Navy Colt revolver." He examined it and said, "Quite a relic, actually. Belonged to some ancestor or another—I forget which one."

Maggie shook her head. "I don't believe you'd shoot—even if that gun was loaded, which I doubt. You're not Victoria. You aren't crazy. And you're not a killer."

"Are you suggesting Victoria is crazy?"

"Do you really believe she's not?"

"I could send her out of the country," he said.

"She wouldn't go, and you know it. Texas is the only home Victoria knows. She's like a predator with her territory marked. She'd never give it up. Put the gun down and help me find her before she kills again."

"It isn't loaded," Porter said with a heavy sigh as he opened a side desk drawer and slid the gun back inside.

"I knew that," Maggie said. Sure she had. That's why her heart—which had finally kicked into high gear—was galloping in her chest. *Whoa, Nellie. Take it easy. We've got a long way to go yet today.*

From her office she called the number Jack had given her for his beeper and waited impatiently for him to call her back. When the phone rang, she grabbed it.

"Hi, there, sweetheart."

Maggie was taken aback by the greeting. She hadn't been called sweetheart for a long time, especially not in such a husky voice. And by someone who had apparently waited for her to call first. Damn him.

She made herself focus on business, when what she really wanted to do was tell Jack she loved him and wanted to spend her life with him. "I have things to tell you. When can we get together, and where?"

"Are you all right?" he asked.

She took a deep breath and said, "I have another suspect for you, Jack."

"Victoria Wainwright?"

"How did you know?" Maggie asked.

"All the murders have occurred the same

week of the year everyone died in Minneapolis. If you weren't the killer, it had to be her. I've been waiting for Victoria to make a move in the ICU."

"You're waiting for her to kill again?" she asked, frowning.

"I don't intend to let her go through with it."

"Isn't there some way to keep her away from the children altogether?"

"Not without tipping my hand, Maggie. Trust me, I have the situation covered."

"I'm coming over to help," she said.

"Someone will be taking over for me at six. Meet me at the doorway to the second floor stairwell at six-oh-five," he said.

"Why there?"

"Just do it, Maggie." He hesitated and added, "Please."

"All right, Jack." Maggie hung up and headed on foot the few blocks down Travis Street to the hospital. She had barely shoved open the second-floor stairwell door when someone grabbed her wrist and pulled her through the door. She yelped with surprise and resisted for an instant before she heard Jack say, "I've missed you. Come here and let me hold you."

Then she was in his arms, being hugged tight and liking it a great deal more than she knew she should . . . at least, until she and Jack had done some more talking.

Ask him why he didn't call, a voice said.

Maggie ignored it and said, "Did you have

someplace in mind where we can talk privately?"

Jack dragged her down the hall to a room with a hospital bed where the ER physician on call could come to sleep when things weren't busy.

"Are you allowed to be in here?" Maggie asked.

"It's been appropriated for police use," Jack said, ushering her inside. He closed the door, leaned back against it, and pulled her between his splayed legs.

"Jack," she murmured as he kissed her throat beneath her ear. "What if a doctor shows up?"

"He'll have to wait his turn."

Maggie chuckled. "You Texas Rangers are incorrigible."

He lifted his head and looked into her eyes. "I hope that means I'm going to get lucky."

"Aren't you supposed to be guarding children?"

"I'm on my dinner break. We have a half hour."

"Shouldn't we do some talking?"

"We can talk later," Jack said. "First things first."

He eased his tongue deep into her mouth, and she returned the favor. Jack's need built quickly, and Maggie's matched it. She felt a new freedom to enjoy life, liberated by the knowledge she wasn't responsible for Woody's death or her father-in-law's demise.

The years of self-denial and self-flagellation were finally over, ended by the knowledge of Victoria's part in the tragedy.

"Maggie, I want to be inside you," Jack said urgently as his hand slipped inside her blouse and cupped her breast.

"No more than I want you inside me," Maggie replied.

Jack made an appreciative sound in his throat. "I like the way you think, counselor."

They never made it to the metal-railed hospital bed. Jack turned her so her back was to the door, stripped down her pantyhose, hiked up her skirt, and put himself inside her. It didn't take more than a couple of thrusts before her body convulsed and he climaxed, each of them muffling their cries against the other's shoulder.

"Damn, damn damn," he muttered, when he lifted his head.

"What's wrong?"

"I didn't use any protection."

Maggie stared at Jack. He'd been careful to use a condom each time they'd made love before, because she'd told him she wasn't on any kind of birth control. She'd been glad of his thoughtfulness, because the last thing she wanted was an unplanned pregnancy.

"How could we have done something so stupid?" he said. "It's a little late to ask, but is this the right time of the month for you to get pregnant?"

Maggie couldn't believe she was having this

conversation half naked pressed up against a
door in the hospital with a man she'd known
for barely more than a week. "My period is
due in a few days," she said, still half dazed
from Jack's lovemaking.

"Thank God for that," he said with a relieved sigh. "Now, where were we?" he said,
nuzzling her neck.

Maggie wasn't sure whether to howl with
indignation or with laughter. "Wait a minute."
She made the referee's sign for a time out.

Jack rearranged his jeans. It wasn't fair that
he could be dressed and dignified so quickly
while she was reduced to reaching down to
her ankles for her pantyhose. She left off her
shoes and padded stocking-footed over to the
bed. When she started to climb up onto it, Jack
caught her at the waist and sat her on the
edge.

He eased her skirt up and stepped between
her legs, laying his hands on her thighs. She
put her arms around his neck and said, "We
need to talk, Jack."

"About what?"

"Victoria, for one thing. And us, for another."

"Us?" He nudged her hair away with his
nose and kissed her throat. She let him do it
because it felt so good, but she knew she had
to make him stop or they'd be making love
again and nothing she wanted to discuss with
him would get discussed.

"You were right, Jack."

"That's good to know," he said with a smile she could feel against her flesh. "Right about what?"

"About women and commitment."

He kissed her lips. "Hmm. What about women and commitment?"

"I don't want to have an affair anymore, Jack. I'm interested in something more permanent."

He withdrew his hands from her thighs, reached up to remove her hands from around his neck, and took a step back. "Would you like to run that by me again? I thought you didn't want to get involved."

"I'm changing the rules, Jack. I want it all."

"You know how I feel, Maggie," he said, his features suddenly stony.

"I see." She crossed her arms over her breasts, feeling nakedly exposed to him, though she was completely dressed.

She slipped off the bed past him, found her shoes, and slipped them on.

"I guess I'd better tell you what I came to say," Maggie said. Before he beat the obviously hasty retreat he had in mind. "I think Victoria may have killed Woody. Porter thinks she might be responsible for her husband's death as well."

Jack came right up behind her. "Say that again."

She straightened her skirt and turned to find herself face to face with Jack. "It seems I'm not responsible for Woody's death, after all. I checked the hospital records in Minnesota. He was recovering before he died suddenly of heart failure."

"Jesus." Jack forked a hand through his hair. "I never suspected that."

"I feel like this giant millstone has been lifted off my shoulders, and I can do more than trudge through the next fifty years of my life," Maggie said. "I can run and dance and play. I want to play, Jack," she said, reaching up to brush at his long sideburns.

He grabbed her hand. "If all you wanted to do was play, I'd be your man, Maggie. But you want more. I don't."

He let go of her and took a step toward the door. He was leaving, and Maggie knew he wouldn't be back. "Do you have to go right now?" She took the step forward necessary to kiss him on the mouth, her lips clinging.

"We have to stop, Maggie," Jack said. But his mouth was hungry on hers. "If you keep kissing me, I'm going to lay you out on that bed, and we'll both be sorry later."

"I'm not ready to let you go, Jack."

Jack suddenly went rigid.

"Jack? What's wrong?"

"Stay here!" He was out the door and headed for the stairwell in a matter of seconds.

Maggie ran after him. "What is it?" she demanded, catching up to him on the third floor stairwell and taking the stairs two at a time with him.

"I thought I told you to wait for me in the doctor's lounge."

"I'm not too good at taking orders. Tell me why we're running up the stairs like a couple of bats out of hell."

"I got a beep—a vibrating buzz—from the detective watching the ICU." Jack grabbed the fifth floor stairwell door and yanked it open. "One of the murder suspects is in there with the kids."

As Roman closed the front door behind him, he called out, "Lisa? Are you home?"

"I'm upstairs, Roman."

He took the stairs slowly, wanting to post-pone their confrontation as long as he could. When he looked up, he saw Lisa waiting for him at the top of the stairs.

She was dressed in a pale blue negligee that once upon a time he would have had off of her in nothing flat. He settled on the stairs right where he was and dropped his head in his hands.

"Roman?"

He heard Lisa pad quickly down the stairs. He could smell her flowery perfume as she settled on the carpeted stair beside him. He took her hands in his, praying that what he had to say would make a difference.

"I spoke to Isabel today and asked her to transfer to another surgical team," he said.

"If you think that's best . . ." she murmured.

He gripped her hands more tightly, willing

her to believe him. "I never realized Isabel was in love with me, Lisa. If I had, I'd have done something about the situation a lot sooner. I'm not in love with her. I never was. I haven't looked at her—or any other woman—since the first time I laid eyes on you."

He took a deep breath and continued, "I didn't spend all those late nights at the hospital to be with her. I stayed away from home because I wanted you so much, I was nearly crazy. And you didn't seem to want me."

"I see," she said quietly, her eyes focused on her bare feet.

He caught her quivering chin and lifted it, so he could see into her eyes. "What is it you see?"

"I've treated you abominably, yet you're willing to give up the best surgical nurse on staff for my sake," she said in a small voice.

"I would do anything for you, Lisa. Haven't you realized that by now?" Roman heard the quiet desperation in his voice and reached for more self-control. It was difficult when he felt like any second the fragile shell of his marriage would fracture and fall to pieces around him.

"I'm making the change for Isabel's sake too," he admitted. "Because I like her—don't stiffen up like that," he pleaded. "I didn't say I love her. I said I *like* her, and I think she'll be happier if we're not in each other's company so much."

"And you think working with you in the future will make her unhappy?" she asked.

Roman nodded. "Because she wants something from me that I can never give her."

"What's that?"

"My heart, Lisa. It already belongs to you."

She took a sobbing breath and said, "I've got something to tell you, too, Roman."

He was afraid to ask, but he needed to know. "I'm listening."

"Three months ago, I saw you with Isabel at the hospital. You were both laughing and . . . It was so obvious she loved you!"

"Why didn't you say something at the time?"

"I was afraid."

"Of what?"

"That you would leave me."

"What?" He was appalled to think the idea had even crossed her mind. "Why would you think something like that?"

She took a shuddery breath and said, "Because my father left my mother for another woman. She always warned me to be careful not to give my heart to a man. She told me to be sure I had a good job and could support myself if he ever found someone else—"

He pulled her into his arms. "God, Lisa. I'd never leave you." He understood so much that he had never understood before. Why she was so insistent on keeping her job. Why she was afraid to meet his eyes when she said "I love you."

"I'm not your father, Lisa. And you're not your mother. We aren't going to make the same mistakes they did."

"We aren't?" she said hopefully.

"We're going to talk to each other about our problems, rather than let them simmer between us. We're going to carve out time from our careers to spend with each other. And we're going to trust our love to get us over any difficult spots."

He watched her eyes well with tears and reached down to kiss away the teardrops as they fell. "Don't cry, darling. Please don't cry."

"I'm just so happy, Roman. You see, there's another reason why I've been so very tired lately." She smiled shyly and said, "I'm pregnant."

Roman's eyes shot to his wife's belly. He met her gaze and found the joyful confirmation there. Slowly, reverently, he reached out to touch.

She put her hand on his and leaned over to press her lips against his.

Roman felt a dozen things, among them wonder and awe and relief and fear. He lifted Lisa onto his lap, and she put her arms around his neck and laid her head on his shoulder. "When I think how close I came to losing you. . . ."

"We didn't plan—"

"I love the idea of having another child. Amy has been . . ."

Roman's vision blurred. He pulled Lisa close, seeking comfort and receiving it.

"She'll be all right, Roman," Lisa whispered in his ear. "Believe it."

"I love you, Lisa."

She looked into his eyes and said, "I love you, too."

❧ Chapter 19 ❧

"What are you doing here at this hour, Mrs. Wainwright?"

Victoria made a startled sound in her throat. "Oh, hello, Ms. Rojas. You frightened me." She knew Hollander's surgical nurse only slightly but was irked that the woman had shown up at so inopportune a time. The hospital was all but deserted at this hour. It would have taken only a moment to do what she had come to do. Ah, well. It shouldn't take long to get rid of her.

Victoria was sitting on the bed beside Amy in the ICU, instead of on the uncomfortable plastic chair that had been provided for visitors. She held up the copy of Beatrix Potter's *Tales of Peter Rabbit* and tugged at the volunteer's jacket she wore over her suit. "I came to read to Amy."

She felt the needle shift in her jacket pocket. She had already filled it with potassium chloride from the drug room. If Hollander's nurse would leave she could help this child—and her parents—find peace.

Isabel frowned. "I thought you only volunteered on Mondays and Wednesdays."

"That's true, but Amy is a special case. I didn't think anyone would mind if I paid her some special attention."

"I'm sure Amy will appreciate it." Isabel brushed her fingers against Amy's cheek. "She looks so peaceful, doesn't she? As though she were just sleeping."

"Yes, she does," Victoria agreed, glancing at the child. She frowned and said, "Should her eyelashes be fluttering like that?"

When Isabel put her fingertips on Amy's face to lift her eyelid, the child fought her touch. *"Dios mio,"* Isabel whispered.

"What's wrong?"

Amy's head rolled as she fought the ventilator tube in her sleep, and Isabel said, "Easy, baby. Easy."

"What's going on?" Victoria asked, slipping off the mattress onto her feet.

"She's waking up. She's coming out of the coma!"

Victoria stared in horror at the child. This couldn't be happening. She had hoped to spare Amy's parents the painful experience of being unrecognized by their daughter, of seeing her limbs fly about, of seeing her looking dazed and lost.

"Don't fight it, baby," Isabel crooned as Amy continued to battle the respirator tube. She turned to Victoria and said, "I'm going to make a call to Dr. Hollander. Will you keep an eye on Amy for me and call the ICU nurse if she gets any more agitated?"

"Of course," Victoria said, smiling. "I'd be glad to."

"If Amy wakes up, explain to her where she is. Try to keep her from panicking," Isabel said on her way out the swinging doors.

Victoria sat back down on the bed beside the child, who remained restless. "It's all right, dear," she murmured. "It will all be over soon."

She reached a hand into her pocket, searching for the capped needle, but before she could take it out, Amy's eyes fluttered open. The child slowly turned her head and looked directly into Victoria's eyes. She looked confused, but not frightened.

Victoria hesitated. None of the others had been awake. Certainly not Richard or Woodson. Or any of the nine children. Amy would make ten. One each year since Woodson's death. Ten families saved the anguish she had suffered, knowing her son would never be perfect again.

It was better to let children be remembered as they were. She was especially aware of the favor she was doing these families since Porter had forced her to allow Brian to live. Her brother had actually threatened to go to the police if she harmed her grandson! Victoria's insides trembled and quivered—like Brian's limbs—whenever she spent any time at all with her grandson. Was there ever such an *im-*

perfect child? Who could love such a creature? He was better off dead than unloved and un-wanted.

Victoria frowned as Amy lifted a forefinger from where her hand lay flat on the bed and pointed. Victoria followed the little girl's finger to the book under her arm and held out the cover for the child to see. "You like *Peter Rabbit?*" Victoria said.

Unmistakably, behind the Xs of tape that held the respirator in place, the little girl smiled.

Victoria wasn't sure what to do. The child showed no signs of paraparesis—she had no telltale tremors and could control her finger enough to point without difficulty. Her memory apparently hadn't suffered if she could re-member *Peter Rabbit.* Victoria gripped the needle in her pocket. She had to make a de-cision quickly. Isabel would be back soon.

"Victoria. Don't."

Victoria turned and confronted the intruder. Jack Kittrick. And who else right behind him but Margaret! "I'm afraid I don't understand, Mr. Kittrick. Don't what?" she said with feigned innocence. One look at his face told her he wasn't fooled. Who was he, really? Not an insurance investigator, she'd wager. No wonder she'd seen him as a predator. One rec-ognized another of the same species.

How had he come to suspect her? How much did he really know? Victoria held out the book to him. "I was planning to read to

Amy. She says she likes *Peter Rabbit*."

"She can't talk, Victoria," Maggie said flatly. "She's in a coma."

Victoria shot her a superior smile. "Not anymore."

"What?"

"See for yourself," Victoria said, standing back and gesturing to the child.

She watched them rush to Amy's bedside like avenging angels ready to do battle if the child had been harmed. Amy recognized the two of them with widened eyes, smiled, and pointed with a single forefinger at them.

"Oh, Amy, you're awake. And smiling!" Maggie said, laughing and crying. "Jack, she's smiling!"

"I see that," Jack said.

Margaret's eyes were wet with tears, and she was grinning like a fool, Victoria noticed. Kittrick's eyes glistened with emotion as well. Victoria felt her own eyes begin to prickle. Her nose began to burn. *If only it could have been like this with Woodson. If only it could have been like this with Brian.*

The pain leapt up to grab at her like a ravening beast, tearing at her throat, sealing it closed so she couldn't speak, could barely breathe. Victoria took a faltering step back.

"Are you all right, Victoria?"

Victoria looked into her daughter-in-law's concerned eyes and saw ten years of torment reflected back at her. Her own torment. It was time to end it once and for all. It was fine to help others, but it was time to help herself. She would never be free of the pain until she was free of the final source of that pain.

Brian had to die.

"I'm fine, Margaret," she said in a very calm voice. It was easy to be calm, now that she had made up her mind what to do. "I guess there's no need for me to stay and keep Amy company. I suspect it's going to be very busy around here once word gets out that she's woken up."

At that moment, the ICU doors banged open and Dr. Hollander came striding in, his wife by his side, his arm curved protectively around her waist. "How's Amy? Is she all right?"

Victoria stepped aside and let the doctor and his wife pass by. They were followed immediately by Isabel and the ICU nurse. It was easy, in all the commotion, to ease through the swinging doors and disappear from the room.

Maggie stepped aside to make room for Lisa and Roman. "Amy's awake, Lisa, and she seems to recognize us."

Maggie saw Roman's hands shake as he reached down to examine his daughter with an exquisitely tender touch.

Amy squirmed on the bed and struggled against the tube in her mouth.

"She wants the tube out, Roman," Lisa said agitatedly. "Can't you take it out?"

"Just a moment," he said, his voice choked

with emotion. "Let me make sure—"

Maggie saw Roman was trying to remove the surgical tape without causing his daughter any pain. He was fumbling so badly, Isabel took over and said, "That's nurse's work."

Quickly and efficiently, she removed the tape and instructed Amy what to do as she removed the tube from her throat. "There, that's better, isn't it?" Isabel said with a reassuring smile.

Amy opened her mouth to speak, but nodded instead.

"Her throat's sore," Isabel explained to anyone who might need an explanation.

"Can I hold her?" Lisa asked Roman.

"Why don't you sit on the bed beside her?" he instructed. When Lisa had trouble getting onto the high hospital bed, Roman lifted her from behind, helped her get settled, then picked Amy up and laid her in Lisa's arms.

Amy didn't say anything, just curled up against her mother, made a satisfied sound, and lay still. Roman put his arm around his wife and child, and Lisa exchanged a look with her husband that made Maggie's heart ache with envy. Whatever had been wrong between them obviously had been mended.

Lisa brushed at Amy's bangs, apparently unable to take her eyes off the child that had been miraculously restored to her and asked, "Does this mean she's going to be all right, Roman? That she's going to recover completely?"

Roman nodded, and Maggie realized he was too overcome with emotion to speak.

"She's going to be fine, Mrs. Hollander," Isabel said for him. "If you don't need me anymore, Dr. Hollander, I'll leave you two alone."

"That's all, Isabel. Thank you."

Maggie heard the finality in the words and watched the glance being exchanged between the doctor and his nurse. So that, too, had been resolved, she thought. She felt a pang of sorrow, and sympathy, for Isabel's plight. One couldn't choose whom one loved. Isabel had fallen in love with a man who didn't love her back. Was that what she had done? Maggie wondered. Please God, let that not be the case.

Isabel was almost to the door when Lisa said, "Isabel, wait."

Isabel paused and turned to look back.

"Thank you for calling us tonight. And for helping with Amy."

"You're welcome," Isabel said. "I'm so glad everything turned out all right." Maggie watched Isabel give Roman one last regretful, almost wistful, look before she turned and left the room.

Maggie felt Jack's arm slide around her waist, and she let him lead her away.

"I think the Hollanders could use some privacy," he said. "And I want to check on Victoria."

Maggie shot Jack a surprised look. "Check on Victoria? If she's not in the ICU, the children are safe."

"Brian's not."

Maggie's heart did a shift sideways and began beating an off-kilter tattoo. "In all these years she's never harmed Brian. What makes you think she'd try something now."

"She knows I'm onto her."

"How is that possible?"

Jack shrugged. "Intuition. I could feel it when she looked at me."

"Why didn't you stop her from leaving?" Maggie demanded. "What if she gets to Brian before we can stop her?"

"I've got somebody watching Brian," Jack said as he pushed the elevator call button.

"What?"

"I've had somebody watching Brian since I first realized Victoria might be the one killing kids. But I think it might not be a bad idea to move him, Maggie."

"Why don't you just arrest her, and get it over with!" Maggie cried.

"You know why," Jack said quietly.

The elevator arrived with a chime. They got on, and Jack pushed the button for the ground floor. Maggie remained silent, because the elevator was full of people, but the instant they headed down the hall for the parking garage she said, "Porter knows about her, too, Jack."

"That makes him an accessory," Jack said.

Maggie snorted. "Try proving that. They're going to get away with it, Jack. Both of them. There's nothing anyone can do to stop them."

"Victoria isn't going to kill another kid, Maggie."

"Who's going to stop her?" Maggie demanded.

"I am."

Jack had known the instant he walked into the ICU and saw Victoria poised over Amy's tiny body that she was the killer he'd been seeking. Her pale blue eyes had defied him to stop her. If she'd made her move then, as Mrs. Mott had, he'd have been helpless to prevent another death. And they'd both known it.

But Victoria was different from Mrs. Mott. More patient. More shrewd. More dangerous.

If he'd had probable cause, he'd have searched Victoria. He was willing to bet he'd have found a syringe on her, too. But Jack knew enough about unlawful search and seizure to know that even if he'd found a syringe, the evidence would've been thrown out in court. What reason did he have to suspect Victoria Wainwright of being a serial killer? Coincidence? Supposition? Intuition?

It wasn't enough.

And yet Jack had seen the challenge in her eyes. *Catch me if you can.* How the hell was he going to do that? He had plenty of eyes on the ICU, but Jack knew she wouldn't go back there again. Not when she knew he knew. She didn't even have to know exactly who he was to realize he was a threat to her. And he knew that he'd been made.

Victoria would have to wait a year to kill again . . . or kill at another hospital. In which case she would undoubtedly succeed. The only chance he had of catching her was if she went after her grandson, in which case Jack intended to be waiting for her.

Jack knew that was what she would do . . . because of the challenge. And because Brian could be identified as a source of her pain—if pain was the reason she killed.

He made a stop before they left the hospital to phone the policeman who'd been assigned to guard Brian Wainwright.

"Been quiet as a mouse around here," the cop said. "Not a creature stirring, et cetera."

"Victoria Wainwright left San Antonio General about ten minutes ago," Jack said. "Keep an eye peeled for her. I expect to be at Shady Oaks myself shortly."

"What's going on, Jack?" Maggie said as she followed him out to the garage and got into his pickup.

He gunned the engine and heard rubber screech on cement as he exited the parking garage. "I think Victoria's planning to kill Brian."

"Tonight?"

He nodded.

"Why haven't you called the police?" Maggie said, her voice frantic.

He turned to look at her. "I just checked in with the policeman who's guarding Brian."

"I mean call *lots* of police. Surround the place."

"Then she won't come at all."

"I don't care if you catch her, Jack. I want Brian to be safe."

"Don't you see, Maggie? Brian will never be safe until Victoria is caught in the act. It's the only way of proving she's the killer."

Jack watched Maggie stare out the window at the dark countryside along I-35, her jaw clamped tight. He reached for her hand, but she pulled it away, crossed her arms, and stuck her hands under her armpits. "You have to trust me to know what I'm doing, Maggie."

"You let that other little girl get killed."

Jack focused hard on the road in front of him, speeding up to pass a semi on the dark road, then slowing down again. "Sometimes the good guys don't win, Maggie. But we keep trying."

"All right, Jack. If you say this is the only way to catch Victoria, I'll believe you. And I'll put Brian's life in your hands. Because I love you, and I trust you not to let anything happen to him."

He met her gaze in the green light from the dash. "Aw, Maggie. That's a hell of a load to lay on me."

"You can handle it, Jack. I've got faith in you."

She was in love with him, and it felt good hearing her say it. *Why can't you love her, Jack? Why can't you just let go of the past and love her?*

Because the hurt little boy inside was running the show, while the grown man was standing by letting him do it. It was a question of which choice was less painful—being alone all his life, or being with someone who broke his heart every day.

Maggie won't break your heart, a voice said. *You can trust her with your life.*

Jack wished there were a crystal ball he could look into that would tell him the future, because he was tempted, so tempted, to love her. He just didn't want to make the same mistake twice.

He wasn't going to make the same mistake with Victoria that he'd made with Lilly Mott. If it came to a choice, he'd save the kid first. Then, if Victoria was still alive, he'd let a judge decide her fate.

꧁ *Chapter 20* ꧂

It helped, Victoria thought, *to be clever. And to think ahead.*

She had known Jack Kittrick would set someone to watch for her, and she hadn't been mistaken. She had disguised herself as an old woman, the grandmother she was, and walked right up to the front door of Shady Oaks. The stoop-shouldered, gray-headed lady wearing a K-Mart jersey dress that came to mid-calf with an oversized gray cardigan sweater, crepe-soled black shoes tied in double knots, and nylons that bagged at the ankle, was not the least bit threatening.

The policeman at the front door had been quite thorough, however, asking for her identification. Victoria had acted nervous and anxious and pitiful, pleading the lack of I.D. because she'd only intended to visit her granddaughter and didn't know it would be needed. The wonderful thing was, she had been visiting a little girl in this disguise for nearly a month posing as the child's grandmother.

She had first met the girl in the pediatrics ward at San Antonio General and had followed her here. It was how she had accidentally found Brian. She had come up with the disguise so there would be no questions about Victoria Wainwright's involvement when the little girl mysteriously died.

One of the nurses identified her for the policeman. "That's Mrs. Hartwell. She wouldn't hurt a fly."

And she was inside.

Of course, she had to visit Susan Hartwell before she could do what she had come to do. Maybe this would be a good time to ease the path of Susan's mother, whose marriage, Victoria had learned, was in jeopardy because of the child.

So far Victoria hadn't been able to bring herself to end Susan Hartwell's life. It was the girl herself who forbid it. The seven-year-old child's dark eyes always latched onto hers the instant she entered the room and never let go.

"Well, Susan, I've returned," Victoria said, settling into the wooden ladderback chair next to her bed.

"I'm glad," the child said. "Did you bring a book to read to me?"

"Actually, I have a copy of *Peter Rabbit*." Victoria reached into the brown shopping bag the policeman had searched so thoroughly and pulled out the book. She eased out the syringe she had slipped between the binding and the pages of the book and hid it in her palm before handing the book to Susan. "Why don't you look at the pictures for a while? I have someone else I'd like to visit."

"All right," Susan said. "Promise you'll come back?"

"I don't make promises," Victoria said.

Susan grinned. "I know. Because then you don't have to break them."

Victoria smiled back. The child was positively delightful. She really didn't belong in a home like this. It was too bad about the AIDS. But her father was afraid of her, and her mother feared for the other children in the household. Susan really didn't deserve to die all alone. Victoria was glad she would be there for her at the end.

She paused at the doorway before heading down the hall to Brian's room. She wondered why a police officer wasn't stationed at Brian's door but realized it was probably a matter of not enough police to go around, and it made the most sense to screen visitors before they got into the house. Victoria eased into Brian's room and closed the door after her.

Brian was sleeping. A small light beside the bed remained on so that a night nurse could check on him. Victoria glanced at her Piaget. Stupid policeman. He hadn't even noticed she was wearing it. She should have taken it off, but she didn't have a substitute. 9:34. The nurse would be by to check on Brian at 10 P.M. She had time.

Maggie had put a comfortable rocking chair

in the room, and Victoria settled into it and began to rock. It was comforting to hear the creak of wood and the rustle of the live oaks outside the open window and the sound of Brian breathing through his open mouth.

She closed her eyes and rocked. Soon the pain would be gone. For Brian. And for her. She would be able to stop killing. Except maybe for Susan. She would have to see how things went with Susan. When the little girl got worse, it might be necessary to ease her pain. The shot was quick and almost painless.

Victoria felt certain that anyone with a care for the child would do the same thing. It was just that nobody seemed to care much for Susan. Except her.

"Victoria."

Victoria opened her eyes slowly. She had been almost in a trance, and it was a shock to open her eyes and find Maggie standing in the doorway.

"I see you managed to sneak inside, after all," Maggie said.

"It wasn't difficult. Where's Kittrick?"

"He stayed on the front porch to talk with the policeman—who said no one had been by here tonight except an old lady who came to visit her granddaughter."

Victoria smiled. "That was me." She took the syringe out of her pocket and heard Maggie hiss in a breath as she uncapped it.

"Don't do it, Victoria," Maggie said.

"It's the only way, don't you see? The only way any of us will ever have any peace."

Maggie didn't see how she could reach Victoria before she killed Brian. She only knew she had to try. The whole distance of the room stood between her and the other woman, while Victoria was less than three feet from Brian's bed. Maggie had to keep Victoria talking, distract her, so that she could get closer.

"You've been very stupid, Victoria," Maggie said.

Victoria sat up straight in the rocker and gave her full attention to Maggie. "I don't see how."

"You've been found out. You're going to go to jail for the rest of your life."

Victoria laughed. "Oh, my dear girl, you are almost as delightful as Susan."

"Who's Susan?"

"A little girl dying of AIDS who lives down the hall. I've been visiting her."

Maggie felt a chill go down her spine. "Are you planning to kill her, too?"

"Perhaps. If it becomes necessary."

"Are you listening to yourself? Do you hear what you're saying?" Maggie asked. "You're talking about taking a human life."

"An imperfect life," Victoria corrected. "I've only ended imperfect lives."

"There's no such thing as a perfect life," Maggie snapped. "We're all flawed. Porter's weak willed. I'm an alcoholic. Jack's haunted by ghosts. And you're a murderer." She was halfway across the room, yet Victoria hadn't seemed to notice. "There's no such thing as perfection where humans are concerned."

"Do you really think so?" Victoria said, her brow furrowing. "That explains a great deal, I suppose. Like why I never felt loved by Richard. If love can be achieved only through perfection—and there is no perfection—then there can be no love."

Maggie tried to understand what Victoria was saying, but it made no sense. "The only kind of love I know about is given without conditions of any kind."

Victoria snorted. It was the most unladylike sound Maggie had ever heard her make.

"Are you saying you love Brian even the way he is? Or that Jack can love an alcoholic?"

"Of course I do," Maggie said. "And of course he can."

"I don't believe you," Victoria said.

"Call him in here and ask him," Maggie said.

Victoria made a moué. "You really must think I'm stupid to invite him in here. What is he, anyway, FBI?"

"Texas Ranger," Maggie said.

"Once the deed is done, there's no way to prove I did it," Victoria said.

"I'll know. I'll tell."

"I'll say you did it," Victoria countered. "And Porter will back me up. Who'll believe you?" she said triumphantly.

Maggie had been watching and waiting for Victoria to make her move, and when she did, Maggie launched herself the short distance that remained between them, grabbing Victoria's wrist to deflect the needle from its goal. Victoria struggled mightily to reach Brian's arm. Maggie was able to keep her at bay, but she wasn't sure how long she could hold on.

"Don't try to stop me, Margaret. This is the way it has to be," Victoria said.

"I'm not going to let you kill Brian," Maggie cried. She managed to turn the needle away from Brian, but it was now aimed at her own forearm.

"So you love your son, Maggie. Enough to die in his place?" Victoria said.

"Let go, Victoria, or I'll scream for help," Maggie said.

"Go ahead and scream," Victoria said, shoving the syringe toward Maggie's wrist. "Help will come too late."

Jack felt jumpy and wasn't sure why. According to the cop on duty, nobody had been by to visit tonight except an old woman.

"She was dressed like a bag lady but had on this really terrific diamond watch. Eccentric, I guess," the young policeman said.

"A diamond watch? On a bag lady? And you didn't think that was strange?"

The young man stood up straighter. "I guess I thought—"

"Call for backup," he shouted as he sped

away. "Then come find me." Jack was already through the front door and on his way down the hall when he heard Maggie's scream. He shoved his way through Brian's door, his gun drawn, and found Maggie and Victoria locked in a deadly contest. Victoria clearly had the upper hand. All it would take was a quick jab and Maggie would be dead.

Jack's heart leapt to his throat. There was nothing like the threat of losing someone forever to put things into quick and accurate perspective. He loved Maggie Wainwright. He wanted to spend the rest of his life with her. Which meant he'd better make sure she lived through the next few minutes. But in case she didn't, there was something he wanted said.

"I love you, Maggie."

"A fine time you picked to tell me, Jack," Maggie said.

"I've decided I can live with your imperfections."

"All of them?" Maggie said.

"Every one."

"This is all very touching, Margaret. It's really too bad Mr. Kittrick didn't say something sooner, when it might have made a difference." Victoria turned to Jack and said, "Put down your gun, or I'll kill her."

"Not this time, Victoria."

"What is that supposed to mean?"

"It means that if you don't let go of that needle I'm going to shoot to kill."

"Maggie will be dead before I hit the

ground," Victoria promised, holding the needle pressed against Maggie's skin. "Did I tell you I tried this first with a cat? Didn't even get half the syringe pumped in before the animal was dead. Heart stops instantly. There's nothing you can do to stop it or reverse it. Think about that, Jack."

Jack was thinking, and he didn't like his choices. He wasn't going to stand by and watch Maggie die. He had to come up with some way to break this stalemate, and fast. Some way that didn't give him the wrong result.

"Mommy?"

Jack lunged the instant Victoria and Maggie looked at Brian. He braced his left hand to shove Maggie's wrist away from danger and brought his right hand, with the gun in it, down hard on Victoria's wrist.

The syringe clattered to the floor.

Victoria stared at him with stunned eyes. Before she could move, he kicked the syringe into the corner.

"It's over, Victoria." He waited for her to make some false move, but she faced defeat with quiet dignity.

Jack met Maggie's gaze where she sat on the bed, her arms surrounding Brian protectively. "Are you all right?" he asked.

"I'm fine."

At that moment, the cop who'd been guarding the front door showed up and took in the situation at a glance.

"Cuff her," Jack said. "And get her out of here."

Once Victoria was gone, Jack turned his attention back to Maggie. "Is Brian okay?"

She nodded and said, "We're both okay."

But Jack could see she was trembling. He crossed and sat down beside Maggie, enfolding her and her son in his embrace. "I meant what I said, Maggie. I love you."

She leaned her head against his shoulder, swallowed hard, and said, "I love you, too."

Jack hugged them both tighter, unable to speak past the painful lump in his throat.

๑ *Chapter 21* ๛

Jack hadn't seen Maggie for almost a week. It had taken that long to process all the paperwork. He had been surprised this morning to read in the *San Antonio Express* that Porter Cobb had retired from the firm of Wainwright & Cobb and would be spending his time at a ranch in West Texas near the hospital where his sister had been committed. Jack wondered how Cobb's departure affected Maggie's position at the firm. It was one more thing to discuss with her when he finally saw her.

"All right, son, what's the problem?"

Jack glanced up from his desk at Ranger headquarters and met Harley Buckelew's shrewd gaze. "Problem?"

"Don't play dumb with me. I want to know why you're still hanging around here when I know there's a young lady in San Antonio who must be wondering where you are."

"I haven't quite finished the paperwork—"

Harley scooped up the papers in front of Jack and said, "I can take care of this. Git."

His bluff called, Jack stared at Harley, his heart pounding. "I told her I loved her," he said.

Harley smiled. "Well. It's about damn time you found yourself a good woman and settled down."

"She's an alcoholic, Harley."

Harley frowned. "Still drinking?"

"No. She's been sober for nearly ten years."

Harley snorted. "A man doesn't get guarantees with any woman, Jack. But it sounds to me like maybe she's got her problem licked. So why haven't you proposed to the lady?"

"I've been busy—"

Harley dropped the papers back on the desk and pointed a finger out the door. "Git, boy! And don't come back until you're ready to invite me to a wedding."

Jack grinned, grabbed his Resistol from the hatrack by the door, and left the building with a bounce in his step. He made record time getting from Austin to San Antonio. He stopped by his house to pick up a present for Maggie, made a phone call to confirm she'd left work for the day, then headed for 200 Patterson. But Maggie wasn't there.

Where are you, Maggie?

Because he was in the neighborhood, Jack took a chance and drove to Roman Hollander's home in Alamo Heights. Sure enough, Maggie's coupe was parked in the brick driveway. He pulled up behind her car and sat there for a minute, trying to decide whether what he had to say could wait until some other time.

But now that he'd made up his mind, Jack didn't want to wait. He wanted to claim Maggie for his own, and he wanted to hear her say she'd be willing to spend the rest of her life with him. He rang the Hollanders' doorbell, but when he got no response, went around to the back gate.

"Hey! Anybody home?"

"Jack!" Maggie cried. She came running to open the wooden gate. She had taken off her suit jacket and unbuttoned the top buttons of her blouse. She looked more carefree than he'd ever imagined she could.

"What are you doing here?" she asked with a smile that told him he was welcome.

Jack realized he should have held out his arms. He had a feeling Maggie would have run right into them. But he hadn't and she didn't, so they stood staring at each other saying nothing.

Jack felt a tug on his pants and looked down to find Amy with a handful of his jeans. "Hey, there, squirt," he said, bending down on one knee beside her. "You look good as new."

Amy grinned, an enchanting three-year-old smile guaranteed to steal one's heart. Jack gave his up without a struggle. "You look pretty as a princess," he said to the little girl.

She turned in a circle, holding her dress out to the sides and said, "Pretty as a princess."

When Jack looked up, he found Roman and

Lisa Hollander standing arm in arm nearby. He stood and said, "Amy looks great. How is she?"

"Sassy as ever," Roman said, scooping Amy up in one arm.

"It's good to see you, Jack," Lisa said. "Will you join us for supper?"

Jack looked at Maggie and said, "I need to talk with Maggie first."

"Sure," Roman said. "We'll go get the fire started."

Jack couldn't resist touching Maggie. He adjusted the collar of her blouse and said, "Busy day?"

She gave him a fleeting smile. "I got named managing partner of the firm."

"Congratulations." Jack hadn't considered that. Maybe now she'd be too busy for him . . . for them. "That'll probably keep you pretty busy—"

"Not too busy for us, Jack," she interrupted.

He met her gaze and saw both hope and fear. He realized she was waiting for him to reaffirm his feelings, the ones he'd spoken of a week past. It was harder than he'd thought to say the words because a gigantic lump had lodged in his throat. He forced them out anyway. "I love you, Maggie."

The smile came slowly, but when her lips were finally fully curved, she looked radiant.

"I don't want to live any more of my life without you, Maggie," he said.

"I feel the same way."

He gave her a quick, hard kiss. "Good. I've got something for you."

Jack felt anxious all of a sudden. From the look on Maggie's face she was expecting him to give her some traditional sign of commitment, like a ring. But Jack had known exactly what he wanted to give Maggie for a long time, and it wasn't made of cold metal or glittering stone.

He reached inside his buttoned-up Levi's jacket and pulled out a bundle of calico fur. "Here," he said.

"What on earth?"

He saw the confusion on her face, and then the delight as she realized what he'd given her.

"It's a kitten! Oh, Jack. It's a kitten!" Tears sprang to her eyes as she rubbed the kitten's fur against her cheek. "You don't know how much I've wanted a cat!"

Jack smiled. The four fake cats had sort of given it away.

"She's adorable," Maggie said. "Where did you find her?"

"My mom's cat had a litter. Tinkerbell was hiding them in the garage."

Maggie laughed. "You call a cat that leaps onto people from a tree *Tinkerbell?*"

"I didn't name her," Jack said. "By the way, there are five more where that one came from," he said, stroking the kitten's nose. "I wasn't sure what color you'd like."

"Oh, Jack, she's perfect."

"What are you going to name her?" he said.

She looked up at him, and Jack watched her face as she realized the significance of the gift. The significance of naming the kitten. The significance of keeping it. She would have to start living again. No more hiding from life. She would have to open the door and let him in, along with the cat.

Give us a chance, Jack prayed.

The kitten began purring, and Maggie laughed, a throaty, pleased sound. She looked up at him, her heart in her eyes, and Jack felt his insides tumble. He reached for her and drew her protectively into his embrace. She held the kitten close with one hand, while she curled the other around his neck and drew his face down for her kiss.

"I love you, Jack," she said. "So very much."

The warmth of her kiss seeped inside him and filled the empty spaces. Jack took Maggie's face between his hands and looked into her eyes as he said, "Will you marry me, Maggie?"

"I made so many mistakes the first time, I'm not sure how I'll do the second time around," she said in a shaky voice.

"We'll work it all out," he said. "I don't need someone perfect. I need you. Say yes, Maggie."

The kitten meowed.

Maggie laughed and said, "Yes, Jack."

"I want kids, Maggie. A houseful of them."

She took a shuddering breath and let it out. "That's such a big step, Jack."

"I'll be there with you, Maggie. We'll make it together."

He saw the moment she began to believe in happily ever after. The look on her face was peaceful, accepting, happy. "All right, Jack," she said with a wobbly smile.

He pulled her close and kissed her hard.

"Maybe the Hollanders wouldn't mind if we excused ourselves," Maggie suggested when she came up for air. "After all, we have a hungry kitten here who needs her mother."

"I like the way your mind works, counselor."

Maggie smiled. "I'm going to remind you of that, Jack, the first time we have an argument."

Jack kissed her again. They would argue. And they would disagree. And they would have problems. All couples did. Life was never perfect. There was no perfect. But he would love her anyway. As she would love him. After all, they belonged together. Two imperfect halves that made one absolutely ideal whole.

He tugged his hat down and said, "Come on, Maggie. Let's go home."

℘ Author's Note ℘

Dear Readers,

If you enjoyed *Heartbeat* and *I Promise*, you might like to try some of my Hawk's Way contemporary novels, including *Hawk's Way: The Virgin Groom*, which is in bookstores now.

My novella entitled "A Hawk's Way Christmas" will be in a hardcover gift collection with bestselling author Diana Palmer titled *Lone Star Christmas*. It should be available in bookstores by mid-October, in plenty of time to make a delightful holiday stocking stuffer.

My next historical romance novel, a sequel to *Captive* and *After the Kiss* called *The Bodyguard*, tells the story of an English duke tricked into marriage by a spirited Scottish lass. It's a March release and will be available in bookstores in mid-February 1998.

I love hearing from you. If you would like to be on my mailing list, please send a postcard to me at P.O. Box 8531, Pembroke Pines, Florida 33084. If you send a letter with comments or questions and would like a reply, please enclose a self-addressed, stamped envelope.

Happy trails,

Joan Johnston

September 1997

America Loves Lindsey!

The Timeless Romances
of #1 Bestselling Author

KEEPER OF THE HEART	77493-3/$6.99 US/$8.99 Can
THE MAGIC OF YOU	75629-3/$6.99 US/$8.99 Can
ANGEL	75628-5/$6.99 US/$8.99 Can
PRISONER OF MY DESIRE	75627-7/$6.99 US/$8.99 Can
ONCE A PRINCESS	75625-0/$6.99 US/$8.99 Can
WARRIOR'S WOMAN	75301-4/$6.99 US/$8.99 Can
MAN OF MY DREAMS	75626-9/$6.99 US/$8.99 Can
SURRENDER MY LOVE	76256-0/$6.50 US/$7.50 Can
YOU BELONG TO ME	76258-7/$6.99 US/$8.99 Can
UNTIL FOREVER	76259-5/$6.50 US/$8.50 Can
LOVE ME FOREVER	72570-3/$6.99 US/$8.99 Can

And in Hardcover
SAY YOU LOVE ME